MALAMOR TRILOGY

Book 1
TO THE END
OF THE WORLD

José Ignacio Valenzuela

Translated by
Aurora Lauzardo and David Gasser

de
le
tre
a ◉

For Cecilia and José Miguel, who gave me the gift of life and the story of *Little Green Riding Hood*.

MALAMOR

Noun

1. Lack of love or friendship.
2. Lack of feelings and affection inspired by certain things.
3. Animosity, abhorrence.
4. A condition caused by a curse or a spell that results in the total absence of love.

CONTENTS

∀

PART I

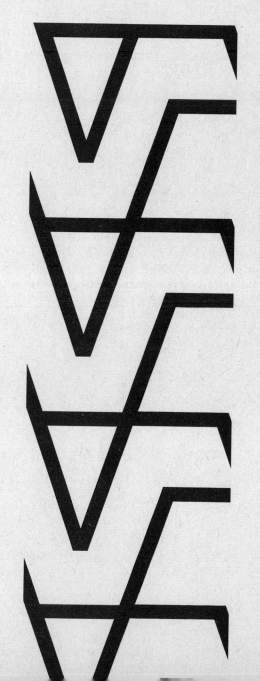

A hero ventures forth from the world of common day into a region of supernatural wonder: fabulous forces are there encountered...

Joseph Campbell, *The Hero with a Thousand Faces*

1 TWENTY-FIVE SECONDS

The phone rang only for an instant before Angela silenced it. Embarrassed to have disturbed the quiet in the Social Sciences library, Angela opened her backpack and put the phone inside, smiling sheepishly at a classmate. Glancing at her iPhone screen, she realized that she hadn't received a call... it was a text. From Patricia Rendon.

Annoyed, Angela frowned. How could Patricia dare to write her after what had happened? Her friend didn't have the slightest sense of contrition or regret. AngelaWland and conduct some interviews. Patricia's betrayal had left her without a topic for her paper and had put her in an uncomfortable position with the professors who urged her to choose another topic of anthropological research. And that was something that she, a nineteen-year-old devoted entirely to her studies, would never forget.

She shoved the phone in her backpack.

Upon leaving the library, the two o'clock sun startled her, setting off a storm of yellow flashes behind her eyelids. She had to take advantage of these unseasonably mild temperatures. Summer was almost over and autumn was rapidly approaching. And when that happened, the venerable hallways of the school filled with shadows and bone-chilling gusts. She made a mental note to tie a light sweater around her waist in case a chilly blast trapped within the school walls surprised her when she next returned to school.

Angela's phone went off again: a short tone that alerted her that she still had an unread message.

She decided to ignore the alert once more and put on some music. From her iPod playlist, she selected *"Sale el Sol"* by Shakira. She barely grazed the touchscreen and the music invaded her head. *"And one day after the storm, when you least expect it, the sun comes out..."* But above Shakira's voice, her own unanswered questions continued to nag her. What did Patricia want? Angela was sure she wasn't going to offer an apology. Of course not, her friend was too proud for that. Did she want to share the impressive progress of her research? That would be the height of insolence, especially because the idea to look into the *Legend of Malamor* in Almahue had been Angela's.

She had by chance stumbled upon some photocopies of notes published by Benedicto Mohr, a European explorer in the 1950's, and she was mesmerized by a story that sounded as incredible as it was fascinating on an academic level. Mohr wrote that towards the end of the 1930's, a young woman who knew the secrets of medicinal herbs and the son of one of Almahue's founders fell head over heels in love. Scandalized, the young man's family forbade him from seeing *that* woman, widely believed to be a witch or a heretic because of her unusual habits: running naked in the forest, and shutting herself up in her house to prepare potions that she supposedly drank in secret ceremonies. The cowardly young man abandoned her to marry another. Spitefully, the alleged sorceress punished her beloved's betrayal by cursing the entire village. From that day on, no one would love again. Ever.

Angela, devoted to the systematic and rigorous studies of societies and human groups, was passionate about the story that had become a legend from the first moment she heard about it. Of course, it had never entered her mind that anything in Benedicto Mohr's notes was *true* but, as a student of Social Anthropology, she was fascinated in a broad view of the biological, environmental and socio-cultural phenomena of the village that believed itself under a spell. So when the moment came to choose a research topic, she didn't hesitate to present an inquiry into the *Legend of Malamor*. She thought about visiting Almahue to interview the inhabitants of that lost village and, with a little luck, talk with some of the elderly men and women who might have witnessed the actual moment of the curse.

She hadn't expected Patricia's underhanded play. She would have never believed that her friend would hack her computer, copy her notes on the *Legend of Malamor* onto a thumb drive and present them as her own the next day.

"A great idea, Patricia! Brilliant!" praised her professor and Angela, sinking in her chair, wanted to die of disappointment and anger.

And now, with its insistent alert, her iPhone continued reminding her that Patricia's message was waiting to be read.

Reluctantly, Angela stuck her hand in the backpack and pulled out the phone. "One new message" read the screen. "Yes, I know!" she wanted to scream at the phone but, out of fear of making a fool of herself again in front of the other students entering and leaving the library, she repressed the impulse. She slid her finger across the screen, opening the inbox. She stopped breathing for a moment when she found a video and not a text message.

Was Patricia sending her an image to upset her even more? Could it be an interview about the witch? Didn't Patricia have any shame?

Play or Delete: the choices offered by the cell phone.

In spite of her fury, Angela's curiosity got the better of her.

Patricia's face filled the screen.

She looked a lot thinner and paler than Angela remembered. "How could she have lost so much weight if she's only been in Almahue for two weeks?" she thought before the blood froze in her veins as she saw the contents of the video.

In the opening frame, Patricia's mouth was open and she had deep, dark circles around her eyes. It was obvious that she was very nervous, maybe on the verge of a panic attack. She was trembling. Twice she tried to talk but her obvious anxiety kept her from speaking. Angela was seized by the imminent threat of tragedy that Patricia's desperate eyes implied. The library hallway and the entire campus disappeared: her eyes were fixed on an unrecognizable Patricia in the video.

"Angela, it's horrible! Horrible!" the phone's tiny speaker played back. "You have to help me! Please! Please!"

Angela put a hand to her mouth, stifling a cry of anguish. What the hell was going on? Despite her anger at Patricia, she wanted to hug her, help her, but she was more than a thousand miles away.

Patricia's eyes opened wider, transmitting a sense of terror that came through the screen. Her disheveled hair was full of dry leaves and twigs. Where was she?

"Come save me, I beg you! You have to look for...!" The video was abruptly cut.

Angela stood frozen. Her muscles turned into stone; her heart skipped a beat. What was the meaning of this? Could it be a joke? The video lasted twenty-five seconds that felt like two hours of horror to her. The mere thought of her friend being in danger at that very moment turned her stomach. What could have happened to Patricia?

When she looked up, she became aware of the fact that, from the other side of the hallway, several students and classmates were looking at her strangely. She wanted to smile at them, as she had done when her phone rang inside the library, yet this time her mouth could only form a grimace that in no way resembled a smile. Giving up on the idea of trying to convince them that she was all right, she turned away from them and dialed Patricia's number. If Patricia had sent her a message, it meant that her phone was working.

Instead of the voice of her friend, she heard a cold, disheartening, "We are sorry. The number you are calling is not in service."

She tried again and got the same message.

Making an effort to pull herself together, she put her iPhone in the back pocket of her jeans and walked out. Everyone watched her unruly red curls bounce as she walked down the hallway.

Even though the last glimmers of summer warmed her path to the bus stop, Angela couldn't rid herself of the deathly cold that gripped every cell in her body. She didn't know what to do or how to proceed. How would she be able to help her friend, especially since she was just a student who wouldn't even be able to get permission to go to Almahue...?

2 INSEPARABLE FRIENDS

Angela Galvez and Patricia Rendon met the day that each turned thirteen. That morning, Angela awoke with the feeling that a new phase in her life was about to begin. Upon opening her eyes, she stayed in bed and looked at the shelf where all of her dolls, with their hair carefully combed and wearing their finest dresses, were arranged by size. But for the first time she didn't jump up to hug and greet them one by one with childish affection. On the morning of her thirteenth birthday, she stared at those dolls for several moments and then glanced down at her sheets with their pink clouds. Angela knew that the time had come to make some changes. She was going to clear off the shelves to make room for her growing book collection. This would also allow her to see the stereo and CDs that she enjoyed listening to. When her mother entered her room with a huge smile, dragging Mauricio, her older brother, so that they could sing Happy Birthday together, she was surprised that Angela, instead of thanking her and asking when her cousins were coming to play, asked for a box.

"It's to store my dolls," she explained. "I need space."

When she got to school, no one greeted her or wished her a happy birthday.

Angela didn't have any close friends. Maybe it was her withdrawn and somewhat solitary personality or her lack of interest in exchanging photos of popular singers and actors with the other girls. She grew up in silence, hidden in the corners of the classroom, paying attention to her teachers and seeking refuge behind a book whenever she had some free time.

Then Patricia arrived.

Miss Hinojosa, the Spanish teacher, introduced her as a new classmate. She explained that Patricia came from a small town to live with her grandmother, and that they should be nice and help her get used to her new environment. In addition, it was Patricia's birthday.

Angela was a bit startled. Until that moment, she didn't know anyone whose birthday was the same day as hers.

Patricia made her way among the desks with an enigmatic smile. It was clear that the newcomer wasn't very worried about being in a group of people she didn't know.

As soon as Patricia sat down next to Angela, they both turned their heads and studied each other's faces.

By the end of the day they were inseparable.

That afternoon, Patricia went to Angela's house and helped her store all her dolls in a box.

When they finished, Patricia asked Angela if she had some eye shadow, so that she could teach her some techniques she had learned from a magazine. She laughed out loud when her new friend said that she had never used eye shadow, or any other makeup. Together, they blew out the thirteen candles that Angela's mother had placed on a chocolate cake, and made a list of secret wishes that they wanted to come true.

That night, when Angela put on her pajamas and laid down for the first time in her grownup sheets, she knew that something had changed; she couldn't yet say she was a woman, but she wasn't a little girl anymore either. Maybe Patricia was to thank, arriving so unexpectedly as the best birthday present ever.

When they graduated from high school, they promised to be friends for the rest of their lives. Under a full moon, each wrote her name next to the other's and together they burned the paper in a ritual that Patricia improvised. The years passed and the two got into Social Anthropology; they were both interested in human science and human behavior through history.

A promise is a promise, Angela said as she remembered the night when she promised her friend that she would always be there for her, no matter what. They had been friends for six years and, although Patricia had betrayed her, she continued to be one of the most important people in Angela's life. How could she ignore her plea?

It was time to deliver on the promise. Angela sighed deeply as she paced her room. She had been thinking for hours about her friend and her unexpected departure to a forgotten village at the end of the world.

What should she do? Where should she begin searching?

She looked at the video once more. Before hitting "Play", she felt another pang of anguish in her stomach.

There was her friend's shaken face again, crossed by dark greenish shadows. Her eyes were wide open and her lips had split from dehydration.

In the background, through the darkness, she could make out what appeared to be a stone wall. A wall almost hewn out of the rock.

Was she in a cave? That could possibly explain the lack of light, and what appeared to be a huge stain of moss on the right hand side of the image.

Angela noticed the dry leaves tangled in Patricia's hair.

Had she been lying on the ground before she made the video with her cell phone camera? Did she have to flee from something, or even worse, someone, crashing through bushes or a forest?

"You have to look for...!" was her last desperate cry before the video stopped. Look for whom? Look for what? Where?

Despite his warning that no one should bother him even if the house was on fire, Angela debated showing her brother Patricia's message. Mauricio had digital expertise, he could hack into anything. He might be able to pinpoint the place where her friend had pressed "Send." Nevertheless, Angela decided not to involve Mauricio because, in the first place, he would not take her seriously; he had traditionally not considered the problems of his younger sister to be of any importance and, in the second place, he might alert someone else about the matter and she might not be able to set the plan she had in mind in motion. It would be best to keep things secret.

She found her mother making dinner. She was stirring a pot with one hand while frying chicken breasts with the other.

"I was calling you, didn't you hear me?" she asked without looking up from the pot. "I need you to set the table, dear. Dinner is almost ready. Call Mauricio."

"May I go with Patricia to her house in Concepción?" Angela asked, realizing that there was no going back now.

"To Concepción? When?"

"We would leave together tonight." Her mother was silent for a few seconds. She knitted her brow, something she always did when she was weighing some important matter inside her head. With the extended pause, Angela began to feel desperate.

"Mom, I need you to answer quickly. Patricia wants to go see her parents and asked me to go with her. You know she doesn't go there very often. It is important."

"And how are you going to go?"

"We'll take the bus."

"Dear, Concepción is more than three hundred miles away," she said, her voice charged with trepidation. "I don't like the idea of the two of you traveling alone."

"Mom, I swear it's really important!" Angela exclaimed as her eyes filled with tears that she couldn't hold back. She couldn't erase the image of her friend's face distorted by fear.

"And you really have to leave tonight?" her mother asked, still not convinced by her daughter's explanation.

Angela held forth about being a model daughter, a brilliant student and a teenager who had never misbehaved, as a last ditch effort to convince her mother. She swore that she would call as often as her mother wanted her to, that she would always let her know where she was at during the two weeks that she thought they would be staying for, and that now, at nineteen years of age, she needed to be trusted.

"Alright," her mother said knowing that she could regret her decision at any moment. "You may go to Concepción with Patricia, but I am going to take you to the bus station. And you will promise to keep in touch and answer when I call you. Is that clear?"

3 PATRICIA MUST BE FOUND

Angela closed the bag and sat on the bed to mentally review her packing. She didn't want to forget anything she would need during her journey. Two pairs of jeans, a few T-shirts, two sweaters and her down jacket seemed adequate for the weather. Her bag also contained a few toiletries, her iPod, and a couple of books to beat boredom: Agatha Christie's *And Then There Were None* and the first Harry Potter, still her favorite. She turned her computer off and put the charger in her bag. She hesitated to take the notebook with all the information that she had gathered on the *Legend of Malamor*. On impulse she took it and put it in her bag, hidden among her clothes. Then she went to her desk, opened a drawer and took out all the money she had. Her bags were packed.

She suddenly felt dizzy and had to sit down on the edge of her bed. She had never lied to her mother, and she wasn't sure that she could stop feeling guilty. But she also knew that she had a good reason to lie: her friend's life was in danger. But what if this was a bad joke? What would she do if she found Patricia, who would never stop laughing at her for being so naïve? Angela hesitated, but only for an instant. She couldn't get caught up in speculation. A sharp pain that drilled into her chest urged her on. She regretted that Patricia had never spoken about her parents. Maybe they would go to the end of the world to find her, like her mother would. But that was not the case.

How would she get to Almahue?

She had never traveled by herself. Patricia's disappearance was forcing her to go further than she would have wanted, to go beyond her own limits, to overcome the fear of leaving her comfortable, safe world.

A knock on the door brought her back. Her mother peeked in as she opened the door. "Are you ready? Shall we go?" she asked. With a lump in her throat, Angela grabbed her bag, her backpack and her coat, and walked to the car. Her mother walked next to her reciting an endless litany of things she had to do. If she didn't do as told, her mother would go to Concepción herself and bring her back.

"Call me from the bus to tell me you are ok. And call me when you get to the terminal. And call me when you are at Patricia's house so I can speak with her mother. Are you listening to me?" she asked, her hands firmly holding the wheel.

Angela said yes to everything but her mind was somewhere else: in Almahue, in Patagonia, more than one thousand miles away from her home in Santiago.

It was insane, absolutely insane. But just like she woke up one day knowing that it was time to remove her dolls from her bedroom shelf, she now knew that she had to leave her fears behind and fulfill her duties as a friend.

When she realized that her mother was looking for a parking place so that she could come along to buy the ticket and greet Patricia, Angela opened the door, and grabbed her bag and her backpack.

"You don't need to come along, mom. It's late. I'd better go by myself, don't worry."

"I want to talk to Patricia and tell her that..."

"Mommy dear, I'm running late," Angela cut her off. "I love you. And thanks... Thanks for trusting me."

Angela kissed her goodbye and, as soon as she heard the door close, she ran into the station. The online schedule showed that the bus heading south was leaving at ten o'clock sharp. She barely had a few minutes to buy the ticket, run to the platform and get on the bus. She found a seat as the bus left the station, and she watched the night roll by on four wheels. The road would end in Puerto Montt. There she would have to find another way to cover the remaining five hundred miles to Almahue.

She didn't let her worries spoil the beginning of her journey. Holding her coat tightly in her hands, she steeled her resolve.

She was going to find her friend no matter what. And that was not the tenacity of an adolescent. For the first time in her life, she felt like a woman.

4 TO THE END OF THE WORLD

"You have to look for..." Angela paused to make herself more comfortable on the bus, reclining her seat and stretching her legs. If she closed her eyes, she could imagine herself sleeping comfortably in her own bed, not sitting in the back of a bus on the never-ending southern highway.

She peeked through a little opening in the curtain. Nothing: it was impossible to make anything of what was on the outside. The entire landscape seemed to have been darkened by a huge brush, painting the night black. She stretched her neck above the headrest of the seat in front of her. Almost all of the passengers were sleeping, some more loudly than others. The driver, enclosed in a sort of a transparent acrylic bubble, was carefully scanning the area lit up by the headlights before it was gobbled by the darkness. Just after leaving Santiago, she had called her mother and reassured her, saying that Patricia was next to her and that she was grateful that she allowed her to accompany her to Concepción. She blew a tender kiss through the phone as she felt the guilt grow inside her.

She turned up the volume on her iPod. "I am" by Christina Aguilera had become a sort of anthem for what she was beginning to live: *"I am timid, and I am oversensitive, I am a lioness, I am tired and defensive..."*

Angela checked the time on her iPhone. It was four fifteen in the morning. They still had six more hours of travel, not even halfway to the thirteen hours she'd be in her seat.

She had never been in Puerto Montt, but it was her embarkation point to Almahue. And she had no idea how she was going to get to Almahue. "I'm not going to think about that now," she said and nestled her head in the pillow they had given her along with a blue blanket. Then, soothed by the drone of the engine, she resumed her reflections on Patricia's last words. "You have to look for..." Look for what? Something? Someone? Where?

Could Patricia's terror have something to do with the legend of the sorceress of Almahue? She had decided to study how a legend affected a community, how an entire community could be ensorcelled by a myth. But Patricia's face showed true terror. Her panic was caused by something that wasn't a product of the imagination; *something* that her friend had seen face to face. "What, a spirit?" Angela couldn't refrain from giggling. If her professors could hear her... their most rational student considering the possibility that Patricia had perhaps seen a ghost.

"How stupid!" she said and curled back up in her seat and turned the music down. She closed her eyes. She could feel the hum of the engine. She wanted to keep thinking about what she had to look for, but an unexpected draft caught her attention, and a sound, like a fan or a bird flapping her wings inches from Angela's face.

"What could that be?" she thought.

Concentrating, she clearly heard the sound of wings getting closer. Could a bird have possibly gotten into the bus through an open window? She thought it was odd that no other passenger had shouted... even the driver continued driving placidly, something that would not be happening if a bird was crashing around the bus trying to get back outside. But there it was: the movement of feathers cutting the night air. Angela opened her eyes.

She didn't even have time to scream.

An enormous black bird was coming towards her, flying down the aisle, its powerful talons pointing at her body, its sharp beak ready to pierce her skin. Its body was covered in feathers, or scales, or some other kind of fur that shined even though the bus's cabin lights were off. Its eyes were most impressive: two deep yellow pools where a pair of round black pupils floated.

Angela wanted to cover her face with both hands but couldn't move her arms. The bird continued bearing down straight at her, cutting threateningly through the air, a bird of prey, an emissary of death.

Just as she gave up hope of emerging unscathed from the enormous owl's attack, she heard above the hooting of the bird, the drone of the engine and her agitated breathing, a voice saying "Young lady, wake up. We're here."

Angela opened her eyes and then snapped them shut immediately against the bright light that entered through the window. It took her a moment to realize that most of the other passengers had already gotten off and that the driver's assistant was at her side, in the aisle, apparently annoyed by her delay.

"Where are we?" she asked groggily.

"In Puerto Montt. You have to get off the bus." Angela didn't want to get off. An unknown fear had seized control of her limbs. She squeezed her eyes shut again, longing to be in her bedroom, wrapped in her soft sheets with the pink clouds, protected by her dolls. She wanted to apologize for having abandoned them at the back of a closet, sentenced to a box. She desperately wanted to turn back the clock and extend her childhood a few more years. But no. That was now behind her. She was in Puerto Montt. And she still hadn't had any news from Patricia.

Once she was in the terminal, she collected her bag and walked toward the street. The first thing she did was to call her mother to tell her that she was now comfortably accommodated in her friend's house but that she couldn't talk to Patricia's mother because she had left to run some errands. She reassured her by swearing she was happy and would keep her updated on all of her activities. She blew kisses through the phone for her mother and Mauricio.

When she hung up, she felt a sharp pain in her lower back from sleeping contorted on the bus. It forced her to walk more slowly than she would have wanted. The sky and the landscape loomed before her, dark gray rainclouds passed across the entire city. The coast along the bay was wide and there were hundreds of people walking around, unaware of her concerns. She stopped to breathe deeply for a few minutes and find her bearings. She looked for her iPhone and dialed Patricia's number. "We are sorry. The number you are calling is not in service."

5 PUERTO MONTT

Angela assessed the enormous metallic span of the ferry *Evangelistas*. On the deck there were almost twenty cars, a pair of motorcycles, a few tour buses and a truck full of sheep that calmly waited to disembark. The prow cut the silver water like a knife, dividing it into two columns of white foam. Ahead, the horizon was one with the sky, both having the same color and texture. The wind was an icy hand that slapped her face, and Angela lifted the collar of her coat and tightened her scarf around her neck.

The end of the day was minutes away and she stopped to witness the instant when the sun was devoured by the mountains. The birds that flew over the canal returned to their nests to wait for a new dawn. Angela scanned the dark green of the Coihue woods, sharply contrasted against the perennially snow covered peaks, and blanketed by shreds of clouds. She could feel the cold in her bones. The gray water seemed more like a foggy mirror than a place full of life and adventures.

She had been lucky when she arrived in Puerto Montt. Although she found herself walking along the waterfront at noon without knowing what to do, she came across a tourist information kiosk. The attendant was a young woman of Angela's age, who was reading a celebrity gossip magazine. Angela told her that she needed to get to Almahue as soon as possible, that it was an emergency.

The young woman put the magazine away and sat down looking very professional. She skimmed through a few brochures and asked Angela how much money she could spend on the trip.

"Not much," she said discouraged. "It must be as inexpensive as possible."

They ruled out the possibility of renting a car or taking a small plane. As they discussed Angela's options, the young woman stealthily looked Angela over from head to toe. The attendant had frequent opportunity to size up strangers. She surmised that despite her assertiveness, this was clearly a young woman breaking out of her family shell.

Angela's best option was the ferry, sharing an inexpensive cabin with another passenger. After a day's journey she would arrive in Puerto Chacabuco, where she could take a minibus to Coyhaique and hitchhike the final stretch. Not a casual jaunt. Angela remembered the horror in Patricia's face stammering for help on the screen of her iPhone. Angela paid for the reservation.

Once she bought her ticket she felt closer to Patricia.

~

A few hours later, Angela entered her assigned cabin. It was at the very end of a corridor lined with doors. There was a narrow wooden berth and a small night table inside the cabin. On the wall next to a tiny closet there was a heater to make the cabin warmer. Who would sleep next to her that night? The voyage to Puerto Chacabuco lasted 24 hours, in addition to the 13-hour bus ride from Santiago to Puerto Montt... She didn't even want to do the math. She only knew that she had been traveling for two days and that she urgently needed a hot shower and a good night's rest. She wasn't mistaken thinking that she had embarked on a journey to the end of the world.

She shut the curtains and, in the semi-darkness, lay down on her bed and gave into the gentle rocking movement. Suddenly a harsh clearing of the throat was heard from the other side of the bathroom door. Angela sat up, alert. Evidently her roommate had entered the cabin before her. She looked around her for a piece of luggage or a bag that would reveal the presence of another person but she didn't find any.

She heard another clearing of the throat, this time harsher than the previous.

"Maybe it was not such a good idea to have bought a ticket for a shared cabin," she wondered worryingly as the bathroom door opened and a silhouette cut across the threshold. It was too dark to make out the stranger's face but she quickly noted the twinkle in the eyes that met hers.

He was not too tall. He had a prominent belly and his body was hunched forward as if he were carrying a heavy weight on his back.

After a moment's hesitation, he began to walk slowly to his corner, leaning on the wall in order not to lose his balance. Angela didn't dare to move or speak until the silence became unbearable.

"Good evening," she said.

The man stood before his bed. Making an evident effort he bent his knees until he was able to sit down on the mattress, his back to Angela. He waited a while for his tired body to recuperate from the effort.

"Good evening," he said without looking at her.

Angela wanted to talk some more but didn't know what to say. Her cabin mate didn't seem friendly; much less someone she wanted to sleep inches away from.

She took off her shoes and massaged her tired feet. She wanted to keep her backpack close to her so she put it under the pillow. Once more she looked at the time on her iPhone. She was hungry but, for reasons she couldn't quite understand, she didn't want to leave her few belongings in that place with a total stranger.

"Where are you going?" the man suddenly said. It took Angela a few seconds to answer the unexpected question. "To Almahue," she said. "And what does a young woman like you have to do in such a far away place?" "I'm going to find a friend," she explained, trying to keep her voice from revealing the fear that was overtaking her. The old man clicked his tongue. He cleared his throat once more as he rested his head on the pillow. Angela was not able to see his face yet. But she didn't dare turn on the light.

There was a moment of silence within the walls of the narrow cabin. Outside, the constant whistling of the wind as it cut through the night sounded like a high note of a flute that wouldn't stop playing. It seemed like the end of the conversation.

"She'll never turn up," she suddenly heard. She was startled. "Excuse me?" asked Angela. "Your friend. She won't turn up. What is lost there can never be found."

Angela didn't know how to answer him. How did the man know that Patricia was lost? She hadn't told him. In fact, it wasn't even something she had considered until this very moment. She regretted not having turned on the light, not being able to see his eyes and figure out if the stranger was a good person. She wished her friend would answer her calls and that she would never have to hear the automatic message again. "We are sorry. The number you are calling is not in service." She wished she wasn't on board that ferry, crossing unfamiliar water in the company of an old man who seemed to be able to read her mind.

"What's your friend's name?" she heard again from the shadows. "Patricia," she answered. The adjacent bed creaked slightly when the man moved. The wind blew stronger outside the porthole. Angela didn't move, waiting for her neighbor to continue talking.

"Go back home," was all he said.

Angela thought that was enough. She didn't have to continue listening to a complete stranger and, let alone, allow him to talk about Patricia and her disappearance. She was going to tell him that the conversation was over when a thump took her by surprise. Something had banged into the glass of the porthole. Through the curtain a shadow could be seen, a small black body cut against an almost equally black background. Startled, Angela opened the curtain. She stepped back, scared by the big yellow eyes that she saw on the other side of the glass. The man stood up with surprising agility. Angela heard him walk back to the door.

"It's only an owl," Angela reassured him, seeing that the bird had upset him.

"No," he answered. "It's the Coo."

Before she could ask him what he meant by that, the old man left. Angela turned on the light. She saw herself alone in a narrow cabin, breathing heavily and with an unspeakable fear in her heart. When she turned to the window, she didn't see anything. Probably the light had scared the bird. The Coo? What was that? She pulled her iPhone out of her bag and turned it on.

She was relieved that there was a weak signal, enough to execute a search. When the Google page finally opened on her screen, she typed "Coo" and "bird" and waited. Several links appeared in perfect order. She chose one from a website about symbolism in folklore. When she began to read, she had to stifle a cry of anguish.

"According to legend, the Coo is an owl with horns and large yellow eyes. When it hoots in a window, it portends a grim death."

6 MYTHS, LEGENDS

After sailing for a day, *Evangelistas* docked at the pier at Puerto Chacabuco. During the last leg of the trip, most of the passengers had shut themselves up in the main hall to watch movies on DVD. To appease her growing anxiety after a restless night, Angela decided to tour the ship from stem to stern. Along the way she managed to engage the captain in conversation. He was a friendly and outgoing man who taught her some nautical terms and showed her the machine room. She spent part of her time watching him maneuver the enormous vessel and communicate with the shore using a radio transmitter. In a short time she was familiar with the transmitter controls. She was on deck all day looking at the horizon, and watching the port emerge out of a shimmering mirage. Several multicolored shacks began to dot the shore and she could feel the frenetic flapping of the birds above her head.

Angela looked anxiously at the rolling hills, covered in green that resembled velvet; they looked so delicate and gentle, yet for her they represented a huge obstacle along the way in her search for Patricia. She had already traveled almost 1,100 miles in three days, and the trip was far from over. Plus she hadn't planned on docking at Puerto Chacabuco after ten o'clock at night. She would have to sleep there in order to resume her journey at daybreak.

As she turned her gaze upon the snow-covered peaks, waterfalls that flowed from the pinnacle's heights like a bride's veil, and vegetation as boundless as it was wild, she again heard the old man's words "It's the Coo."

After the incident with the owl, the man had not returned to the cabin.

Unfortunately she had stayed up most of the night to make sure. But every minute he stayed away was a relief. He didn't exactly make her feel unsafe, but he seemed to know more than he should.

"It's the Coo," she remembered again and a shudder ran down her spine. "Superstitions," she said. As a student of Anthropology, she knew the influence of myths and legends in the daily life of human civilizations, and how important they were to some people. And it just so happened that the part of the world—the Chiloé Archipelago—where she found herself at the moment was influenced by the *Chilote*, and their immense wealth of beliefs in witches, demons, ghosts and marine spooks that terrorized the population.

The mythological beings known as the *Pincoya*, the *Caleuche* and the *Trauco* were part and parcel of the daily conversations of the inhabitants of the region. For them it was normal that an owl with enormous yellow eyes and gray feathers was an evil spirit whose presence presaged death. This consideration almost calmed Angela, who tried to clear her head of the feelings that had lingered since her encounter with the mysterious companion in her room. She had spent several hours scanning the tourists wandering around the ferry but couldn't find anyone who had the same build: a body hunched forward with a prominent belly and an obvious bald spot.

The last hours of the trip dragged out like a film in slow motion. As the crew prepared to throw the lines and finalize the details for the passengers' disembarkation, Angela paced the length of the boat trying to ease her impatience to be on dry land. She called her mother a few times and she even sent her a few text messages so that she could avoid answering her questions.

When she felt the vessel touch port, she picked up her bag, adjusted the scarf around her neck, put her hair in a ponytail, slung her backpack over her shoulder and ran to be the first person to disembark.

As soon as stepped onto the metal gangplank that unfolded from the deck, thunder clapped overhead and an apocalyptic rain began. Sheets of water fell, and Angela struggled down the pier looking for some overhang to protect her. The downpour intensified, blurring the landscape and even erasing the night's blackness. Her goose down jacket wasn't enough to repel the water and Angela began to feel icy drops running down her back.

She took refuge under a tin roof that barely protected her from the fury of the shrapnel-like rain. But even there, curled up and covering her head with both hands, she felt like the frothy mud on the ground was going to swallow her up at any moment.

She wanted to cry.

No one else seemed to be having as much difficulty in the rain, all of them, seemingly, had a place to go. When Angela no longer knew what to do, given that her refuge was as wet as the nearby surroundings, two toots of a horn got her attention.

With the rain and the poorly lit street, she could just make out the vague silhouette of a white delivery van that read "Bookmobile" in black letters. The window rolled down and from the dark interior a hand was signaling her.

"Come on, get in!" someone inside the vehicle commanded.

Without hesitation, she ran. The slippery mud almost caused her to lose her balance more than once. She jumped inside the van, bringing the night's cold and a splatter of raindrops along with her. Behind the steering wheel, a man with red cheeks, a prominent black moustache and a red and black plaid shirt smiled amicably at her.

"We can wait here till it lets up a bit," he said. He introduced himself as Carlos Ule, a teacher. After having taught for many years at the public school in Puerto Chacabuco, Carlos had decided to do more for the region where he was born and that he loved so much. With some of his savings, he bought a used van and turned it into a mobile library. With the support of some government officials, he got several boxes of used books that he arranged in the makeshift shelves in the rear of the vehicle. Once a week he embarked upon an adventure of a couple of hundred miles to visit the most distant and forgotten villages of the harsh countryside. Kids greeted him with shouts of joy and adults would line up to return the novels they had borrowed during his previous visit and take, straight from Carlos' hands, only after paying a tiny amount, a new story to keep them entertained for the next few days.

Angela was impressed with Carlos' passion and generosity; that he was willing to abandon the comforts of his home just to share his love for reading.

The rain was beginning to ease up. "Alright, where should I take you?"

Angela shrugged her shoulders. She explained that her intention was to get to Almahue as soon as possible, that she was meeting a friend to work on a research project, but she had had to spend the night in Puerto Chacabuco.

Carlos's bright eyes sparkled in the darkness of the vehicle.

"What a coincidence!" he exclaimed. "*Tomorrow morning I'm leaving for Almahue.* I can take you if you'd like."

"Oh, my goodness. Yes, please! I can pay." Angela felt like shouting for joy. What were the odds?

"It's not necessary. It would be enough if you could help me organize the books while we're on the road. The potholes make them fall off the shelves."

They closed the deal with a firm handshake. The librarian mentioned that he and his wife rented rooms in their house to tourists and he proposed that, if she wanted, he could take her to see the place. Angela thought that things were finally beginning to go her way. "I'm really lucky," she said to herself as she buckled her seatbelt.

Carlos Ule's house was nestled on a hillside. It was nearly eleven thirty at night when the lights of the van pierced a steep road. They began to climb. The doors vibrated from the effort to make it up the hill, and inside shook twice as hard till they parked by the house. Lights were shining in some of the windows on the ground floor and, even though Carlos and Angela hadn't gotten out, the front door opened.

There, in the doorway stood a short, solid woman with an apron around her waist.

"I have brought a guest for the night!" Carlos shouted as he turned off the engine.

Carlos' wife was named Viviana, and she smelled of freshly baked bread. Angela gratefully inhaled the aroma of spices, wood fire and freshly brewed coffee that greeted them along with the lady of the house.

The couple showed her the room that they were renting, which after the last three days, seemed like paradise to Angela. After travelling for more than 36 hours, finding herself in front of a bed with immaculate white sheets, covered by a fluffy down comforter and four pillows caused Angela to tear up from the sheer joy of it. Viviana crossed the room and closed the curtain.

"Thank you. We wouldn't want the Coo to come in through the window, would we?" Angela joked.

The woman's face froze in a stony grimace. She slowly turned towards the young woman staring at her with a look that was both reproachful and frightened.

"We don't talk about *that* in this house," she muttered. And she left the room abruptly.

7 AN UNEXPECTED BOOK

At six am, Angela woke up to three knocks on her door. That was Carlos Ule's signal for her to get up, wash up and get dressed. They had to be in the van by seven. If everything went according to plan, they would be in Coyhaique by eight thirty. They would make a stop there before continuing on the winding dirt road to Almahue.

The previous night, before collapsing in bed, she called her mother, who asked her all sorts of questions while she did the dishes and fixed herself a cup of coffee. Angela reassured her that she was with Patricia in a busy restaurant in Concepción. Her mother was very happy and sent her regards to Patricia.

Angela felt a lump in her throat. She hated lying. And the fact that she didn't know Patricia's whereabouts or condition only increased her fear and anguish. She wanted to undo the journey, run home to her mother's arms and stay there, feeling that as long as she was by her side nothing could harm her. Before turning off the light on the night table, a lovely wooden lamp crowned with a lace shade, she decided to try one last time. She dialed Patricia's number and waited for a few seconds. When she began to hear the recorded message, she hung up. She would not be able to fall asleep with those words echoing in her brain.

At seven o'clock, Angela was ready for the road. She found Viviana putting sandwiches in a basket; she had also filled a thermos with coffee and filled some containers with rice, meat, and soup. Viviana asked her if she wanted to make a phone call before getting in the van. Angela thanked her and told her that it wouldn't be necessary, showing Viviana the iPhone tucked in her pocket.

Carlos couldn't hold a sarcastic chuckle.

"Do you have the slightest idea where we are going?" the teacher asked. "Almahue is in a tiny valley surrounded by a very high mountain range. There's no signal there."

"But there's Internet, right?" she asked, trying to make her question sound more like a sentence.

Carlos smiled again as he put on a heavy raincoat.

"No. There's no Internet. There's only a public phone that, as I've been told, has been out of order since a heavy snowstorm."

"How do they communicate?" she asked, realizing that she was going to be in trouble with her mother.

"I've heard that there are a couple of ham radio operators, who, in case of emergency, can make calls using a short wave radio that is older than my great-grandmother. That's it. Didn't your friend tell you what to expect?"

When he noticed the look of astonishment in poor Angela's face as she stared forlornly at her modern and soon to be totally useless device, Carlos quickly explained.

"When you enter Almahue, you're going to go fifty, no, a hundred years back in time. Are you ready?" he asked as he kissed his wife goodbye.

The librarian put the basket with the provisions in the back of the van, tightly fastened to one of the bookshelves, and walked to the driver's door. Angela climbed in next to him and they drove off, waving Viviana goodbye, who was quickly eclipsed by the lush vegetation surrounding the house. The gigantic *tepa* trees formed a thick wall of moss-covered trunks. The dirt road leading down to the main road unfolded amongst the various tones of green, still wet and shimmering from the night rain. For a few minutes nobody spoke inside the van. Then, out of the blue, Carlos spoke loudly enough to be heard above the engine's hellish rattle.

"What are you going to study at the end of the world?"

Angela hesitated for a moment before answering. She didn't want to face another disconcerting reply like that of the old man in the ferry.

Considering her options, she said: "I am doing research on the *Legend of Malamor.*"

Carlos didn't answer. Only the sound of the wheels on the pavement could be heard; that and the distant whisper of the wind tousling the crowns of the Patagonian trees.

"Have you heard about that myth?" Angela persisted.

"Of course," Carlos mumbled as he stroked his mustache. He was the caricature of the prim and proper professor. "And it's not a myth."

"Then it's a tale..." Angela replied.

The man grabbed the wheel so tightly that his knuckles turned white under the dry, reddish skin of his hands.

"Do you know the difference between a myth and a legend?" he asked, using his best teacher's voice.

Angela was about to answer that she did, that she was a good student of Social Anthropology, but before she could open her mouth, the librarian began to explain that a myth is a story of imaginary or marvelous events where characters are extraordinary or supernatural. And, pointing his finger up with such enthusiasm that he hit the visor, he went on saying that a legend was an oral or written narrative containing more or less fantastic elements and springing from a real event.

Angela didn't say a word. Was he seriously trying to tell her the tale of the village cursed by a witch was true?

"Of course it's true," he replied when she finally asked him. "And the name of the *witch*, as you call her, is Rayen."

Angela remained silent. That name was an invaluable piece of information. For months, she had studied Benedicto Mohr's texts, and she knew very little about the woman who cast a spell on the village. As she only had a few facts and incomplete photocopies of the explorer's dairy, she had only been able to reconstruct a fraction of the village history. Carlos' gift of the name, and whatever else she could learn from him, provided her with a new a starting point. If only she could tell Patricia.

"Go to the back of the van," Carlos told her.

Unquestioningly, Angela slid between the two seats and went to the shelves. The books were shaking, dancing to the rhythm of the wheels of the Bookmobile. From the driver's seat, the teacher guided her.

"No, the other shelf, higher, there, the one with the green spine," he went on until Angela's hand grabbed the book.

She read the title: *Rayen*. The author was Benedicto Mohr.

"Mohr disappeared mysteriously shortly after the book was published,"

Carlos whispered as if telling a secret. "No one saw him again. His body was never found."

Angela skimmed through the old volume. It was almost two hundred pages long. If she could have it for a couple of hours, perhaps one night, she would be able to read it and return it on time. Or hopefully...

"Keep it," Carlos said as he stroked his mustache. "You are the first person to show any interest in it. So far, no one has wanted to read it."

8 THE END OF THE WORLD

Although Carlos tried to fill the long hours of their trip with commentaries and practical information about Almahue, Angela only wanted to study the book she held in her hands, or prod him for any other piece of information he might have about the legend. When the van turned onto a narrow dirt road and began to penetrate the increasingly lush and abundant vegetation, she tried to immerse herself in the first chapter. But the librarian wasn't going to let her. He was very interested in giving her a detailed explanation of traditional fishing, the major source of income in the village and one of the most ancient activities in the region. He also told her that the fishermen went to sea for days at a time, risking their lives and their vessels in order to return with their nets full of hake, manta ray and conger eel.

Angela didn't have any option but to feign interest and nod a few times. Defeated, she stowed the book in her backpack. She would soon have time to read it cover to cover. To escape the fish lecture, she offered to re-arrange the books. She settled down in front of the shelves. There was *Treasure Island*, *Journey to the Center of the Earth*, *Moby Dick*, *Robinson Crusoe*, and *Around the World in Eighty Days*. From the looks of it, Carlos was a fan of classic adventure stories. Carlos, looking at her through the rearview mirror, began his dissertation with renewed enthusiasm. He suggested that since she had already come this far, she shouldn't leave without seeing the majestic ice walls, one of the main attractions of the region. She could also spend some time observing the unique flora and fauna on horseback.

"For example, the giant rhubarb you see over there is called *nalca*," he explained, pointing at some enormous green leaves the size of an open umbrella. "Have you ever eaten *curanto*? I'm so hungry!"

Angela offered to get some sandwiches out of the basket and Carlos enthusiastically thanked her. It was almost one. They had been travelling for six hours. After devouring the last crumb and drinking a thermos of coffee, both surrendered to placidly observing the last part of the journey.

At the end of the road, illuminated by the weak light of early autumn, Angela saw a thin thread of silver appear. It took her a few moments to realize that it was water. As the truck approached, the twinkling liquid mirror grew and became an extensive fjord. *Chilco* and fuchsia thickets lined the road, painting the pristine countryside. Angela saw a building off in the distance.

It looked like a dollhouse. And it was almost identical to the one that her father had built in their backyard when she was six years old. Unlike hers, this one was made of dark wood. It had a window frame that was painted the same red as its pitched roof. A smokeless chimney seemed to be waiting for someone to take pity on it and start a wood fire to justify its existence. "Who could live in a place so close to the road?" she asked herself. But a few yards ahead, she realized that it wasn't a house at all, but a clever billboard announcing the village: "Welcome to Almahue," it said in white letters.

"We're here," confirmed Carlos. "I hope you find Rayen, who, according to some people, still lives hidden in the forest."

The strength of her sense of destiny had increased with the numbers on the odometer. Angela knew that her trip to the end of the world would change all of her short-term plans. Not only that; she was sure it would change her life as well.

9 THE DEEP FOREST

The trees are her strongest allies. Fierce vertical soldiers, they protect her from intruders who wish to enter her territory. They watch her sleep, shade her days and shelter her rest. They don't ask questions. They have gotten used to her presence, her footsteps that barely touch the ground, that move quietly among the dry leaves and branches. They let her live there in a wooden belly, knowing that she will never harm them. Sometimes, at night, she speaks to the moon. It's always the same story: an innocent young woman who was deceived in the worst way. The story ends with a broken heart, a vow of vengeance, and flight to the highest peak in the region. From there, protected by the indomitable vegetation, she will see that no one is ever happy again. She has learned to disguise herself in the form of mist and dew. That's why the few that dare climb to where she is can't see her. Her body is concealed by the vapor rising from the humus that covers the soil. Time has hardened and cracked her skin like the trunk of a hundred-year-old tree. Her long, gnarled fingers resemble the branches of a tree waiting for the spring shoots and blossoms. Her eyes have grown used to seeing beyond the forest that surrounds her; she can fly over the channels and fiords that break up the continent in hundreds of islands; sometimes she spies through the windows on the unhappy people that live under her spell. She hears them yell words full of hatred and despair at each other. Hiding in the shadows she knows so well, her mouth is a slit of satisfaction; she forgot how to smile a long time ago.

She knows she has infinite power. She only needs to sink her feet in the ground and her toes become roots that stretch for miles and miles. She feeds on the same deep underground currents that carry the minerals and energy that nourish the earth. Suddenly, her body shivers, vibrating with the intensity of an erupting volcano. It grows and reaches the crowns of her guardians. She opens her arms and calls for lightning; she opens her mouth and thunder shakes the earth. The wind roils her hair in swells, creating universal darkness and hurricane winds. As long as no one loves again, she will continue being Rayen, the most powerful woman who ever cried for a treacherous love.

10 THE TREE IN THE SQUARE

The dilapidated van with "Bookmobile" written on its side panel entered the seemingly deserted village. The streets of Almahue followed the arm of the sea; a small congregation of houses faced the Patagonian fjord as if in worship, turning their backs to the lush vegetation of the mountains.

From her seat, Angela saw a handful of weathered wooden houses. Some were covered in moss and vines; others had roofs raised like turrets, as if trying to rend the heavens that were on the verge of spilling their contents. There were also some beached and colorful rowboats like an idyllic postcard. The water was quiet like a mirror reflecting the silhouette of the snowy mountains. There was no wind, no waves. She could tell that it was very cold just by looking at the bluish rocks, the sharp glare of the puddles that marked the route, and the breath exhaled by a handful of grazing sheep.

The rattling of the vehicle ceased when Carlos turned off the engine, and the hinges groaned as they opened the doors. Angela took a look at the screen of her iPhone. "No service." How would she keep in touch with her mother? With a discouraged sigh, she jumped out of the van only to find herself ankle deep in a mud puddle the color of weak coffee. She was grateful for her waterproof boots and made a note to herself to be more careful each time she took a step. She shook her legs and wiped her feet against a fence. When she opened her mouth to say something, a blast of frigid air froze her tongue and nostrils. Amused, the librarian smiled. This was always the first reaction that strangers had when they came to the village.

"Where is everyone?" asked Angela when the feeling came back to her face.

Just as Carlos was about to respond that he didn't know, his eyes opened wide, giving away his forgetfulness.

"How could I forget?" he exclaimed. "Today is the burning of the witch!" He turned and headed towards one of the mountains that boxed the village. Angela followed.

Walking through the silent dirt streets, she could see a grocery store, a bakery, and a post office. They were all empty and closed. She crossed what she thought was a deserted soccer field with its rickety wooden goals and a scoreboard that someone standing on a ladder had to change by hand.

The town square was a platform made of cement with some benches and four weather-beaten, cast iron railings arranged around an imposing tree that Angela couldn't identify. Its trunk was as wide as a circle of twenty men. In order to hold the colossal weight of its branches, the mostly visible roots had raised part of the pavement and buried themselves in the ground like tentacles. What impressed her the most was that in spite of its bearing and how magnificent it appeared upon first glance, it was weak and parched. A strong gust of wind would be enough for the tree to come crashing to the ground. Its branches appeared dull and dead; all except for one. A sprig at the top, facing the sky and its pressing gray clouds, shined with intense green leaves freshly varnished by the rain. The only healthy branch on the tree, as dead as it was alive, reminded her that hope is the last thing to die.

Angela was spellbound by the totemic presence of the trunk and its dying foliage. But, when she saw Carlos disappear into the vegetation behind an old house she ran to catch-up with him.

She almost stopped; she thought she had seen a woman's silhouette hidden by the curtains in one of the windows of a very old dwelling. She shook her head trying to erase the image and followed Carlos into a forest of *calafate* bushes and ferns that obscured everything but his vest. The cold cut her cheeks like a knife and she could hear the dry crackle of branches.

All of a sudden, she heard a muffled uproar.

Surprised, she strained her hearing, trying to locate the source of the sound. It reminded her of the boisterous crowd at the only rock concert she had ever attended, with Patricia, of course. Hundred of shouts combined into a single intense voice.

What was going on in the village? What was the burning of the witch?

She tried to ask Carlos but he surged ahead of her, not hearing. She climbed the hill that separated her from the commotion and stopped dead in her tracks at the spectacle before her. There was a multitude in a small valley; hundreds of men and women holding torches were jumping up and down. The flames flickered above their heads like an ocean possessed of fire, fed by the villagers with their altar candles and torches of gasoline-soaked rags. In the middle of the mob there was an enormous, crudely erected wooden witch. It must have been four stories tall. Someone had painted a mean looking mouth with thin, cruel lips. Its eyes were two yellow circles with pupils as black as coal. Its eyebrows and nose were simple straight lines. The statue inspired fear and respect simultaneously.

Angela noticed that Carlos had joined the crowd.

He had hoisted a torch and was shouting and uttering litanies about curses, spells and incantations that should be reversed.

Everyone knew what to do. They were all making the same motions. Yet, no one appeared to be comfortable with the situation. Some people were angrily shoving each other. Others stopped shouting at the witch to assault those around them. Angela saw a woman slap a man who had accidentally bumped into her. He then responded with obscene gestures and loud insults.

"What's going on?" muttered Angela, shocked by the insanity of the fire, the yelling and the ill-tempered people.

Suddenly, at the command of one voice that rose above the rest, everyone turned back to the wooden witch.

The ones closest to it held their torches in front of them. The boards caught fire as a plume of black smoke rose to the sky.

The crazed crowd began to applaud as the flames licked the effigy until they reached its head and engulfed its furious and terrifying face.

Angela saw the group divide when the burning structure lurched forward. Suddenly everyone was silent. No one breathed for what seemed like an eternity while the figure collapsed upon itself, becoming a pile of charred rubble.

A roar of satisfaction shook the zone and the echo of the howling flew to distant shores to tell what had happened.

Some people cried, others fell to their knees and the most enraged kicked the wooden ashes as if to finish off the witch's corpse.

Angela wanted to return to the village before they did the same to her.

But she couldn't move. Unexpectedly, she was pushed forward and almost at the same time, she was thrown in the other direction. Her head struck a rock on the ground. Her mouth filled with the metallic taste of blood.

As she tried to stand up, a new jolt threw her flat on her face. She saw her iPhone plummet downhill and disappear in a crack that had opened like a slash at the base of the mountain.

She could hear the far-away commotion of people who, like her, suddenly felt that their lives were in danger. The ground convulsed like an injured animal, trying to shake off what was bothering it. The crash of rocks added to the noise of splitting tree trunks.

A new fissure appeared like a slithering black snake, zigzagging towards Angela, who screamed in horror. If she didn't move quickly, she would be devoured like her cell phone.

But the shoving prevented her from standing up. She closed her eyes as if the darkness could save her from death. But instead of falling into the earth, someone yanked her violently. She heard agitated breathing as two hands took her by the waist. Afraid, she squeezed her eyes shut even tighter. The pain of the blow to her head drained the color from her thoughts, her consciousness, and the rest of her body.

After traveling for four days and this most aggressive welcome, she gave up and allowed those hands to take her away, as far away as possible from her misfortune.

11 SURVIVING

There's Patricia. She smiles with a perfect row of white teeth. As usual, she scrunches her nose a little bit. It seems that she is trying to say something. But she remains silent. She only smiles.

Will she come closer or is she going to stand there, almost distant?

Patricia doesn't move; she doesn't do anything. Her feet are buried in the stony ground. The earth has swallowed her feet. Her legs sink to the ankles. That's why she doesn't move; she can't. That's why she is so silent; she is concentrating, trying to escape.

She is not smiling anymore. Instead, her mouth twists in anguish.

"Patricia, can you hear me? I came here to look for you. I heard your message asking for help and I've come to the end of the world to bring you back home. I never thought I would find you like this, the way I see you now... Can you hear me? Say something!"

When Angela tries to come closer, her friend's body begins to shake as if hit by a strong wind, not from the outside, but from the inside. She moves back and forth, faster and faster. She opens her arms and stretches them to impossible lengths.

Patricia grows bigger, taller than the crowns of the trees.

The roots that sprout from her feet squirm on the ground like wooden snakes that fasten her to the earth. She opens her mouth and with a bellow fills the ocean with foam, shreds the clouds in the sky, and makes the confused birds crash into one another rather than face the huge typhoon she has summoned. Her face has turned into a mask of burning sticks with two yellow eyes, cruel and thin lips, a nose, and barely defined brows. Like a quilt made of dry leaves, her hair spreads over the mountains forming towering new peaks.

The earth crumbles into islands as the roots destroy everything in their way. "Patricia! Patricia! It's me! Your friend! Can't you see me down here!" Her shadow is bigger than the landscape; the sky is too small for the huge tree. The only branch with green leaves hangs menacingly over her head. "Patricia? What are you doing?" And before she can run, the branch, cutting through the air like a whip, falls on her head and blurs her vision. Angela opened her eyes, terrified. A sharp pain stabbed at her left temple. "Be careful. You'd better stay down," said the voice next to her. And then she saw her savior. He had a heavy shirt of an indistinct color, faded by the wind and use. The rain must have washed it a thousand times. Locks of black hair fell on his dark olive eyes that looked at her with concern. Pink lips were the only color on the stranger's face. A face that was as attractive as it was enigmatic.

"You hit yourself on the head. If you want I can get a doctor..." Angela realized that he had taken her to the town square. She was leaning on a metal bench under the enormous, nearly dead tree. She trembled as she remembered the vision that followed her fainting: the terrible vision of Patricia turned into a monster of nature battering her with wooden arms. Why would her friend want to hurt her? And where was she?

She sat up with difficulty, resting her back against the bench. "What happened?" she asked. "There was an earthquake," the young man said as he sat next to her. "A huge one." "Is it normal to have huge earthquakes in this area?" she asked. "Not before. But now it is," he replied. Angela could not stop staring at those generous lips. The young man must have been twenty-five years old. Maybe a little bit older. He had strong hands with short nails. When he talked, the skin around his eyes wrinkled a little bit, enhancing the expressiveness of his face.

"You helped me?" The young man looked down.

"Charming," Angela thought. "He is both handsome and shy." "Thanks. You saved my life." He nodded and gestured with his hand as if saying: "It was nothing." He stood up clearly wanting to leave and, thus, end the conversation. Angela thought about following him but she decided not to. A sudden dizzy spell turned the ground into water.

"What's your name?" she asked trying to sound nonchalant.

"Fabian."

"I'm Angela, Angela Galvez." Fabian gestured with his hand again but Angela couldn't figure out what he meant by it. He backed up a few steps and put on a knitted wool cap that hid his jet-black locks.

Angela felt someone's eyes on the back of her head, running down her neck. Uneasy, she turned around just as a cat jumped on her legs, leaping to another bench. Taken aback by the animal's unexpected attack, Angela screamed. The cat was as black as the night and it stared at her from a distance with insolent yellow eyes. She turned to Fabian as if looking for help in the event of a new feline attack but he hadn't noticed anything.

"I just arrived in town," she said pulling herself together. "I don't know anyone here. Do you know where I could spend the night?"

"At Rosa's," he answered. "She has a room for rent."

"Could you take me there? I still feel a little dizzy," which wasn't entirely true but for some reason Angela wanted to feel Fabian's hand on her waist again.

The young man nodded. "He's a man of few words," she concluded, even more pleased with him.

There was something about Fabian that she found tremendously appealing: a sort of mystery, a concealed invitation to a dark existence, to a secret story. Angela's sense of adventure was suddenly awakened. After all, she was a student of Anthropology researching this town. What better way to do it than through direct observation of one of its inhabitants?

Slowly, she stood up. She didn't want to aggravate the throbbing pain in her head. Fabian held her by the arm. His hand was warm. She could feel it through the sleeve of her coat. Angela looked at him just when he looked up. For a brief instant their eyes met.

Suddenly, the branches of the tree shook as if jolted by a gust of wind, but the air was still. Several yellow leaves fell on Angela and Fabian, turning into dust upon touching the ground. The cat shrieked and arched its back and, for a moment, its black fur looked like deadly spikes. With great precision, it jumped onto a branch.

"What a shame it's dying," Angela said, looking up at the tree as she leaned on Fabian and they began walking.

"When that tree dies, this whole village will be swallowed by the earth," he replied.

Angela stopped.

She had to turn around to look at him. Was he joking? But Fabian's eyes reflected a profound fear and inexplicable yet real anger. Judging from the gleam in his eyes, he felt he was telling the truth.

"Do you know about this place, stranger?" Angela did her best to make her face noncommittal.

"It's Rayen's curse," he went on. "She cursed the village before she disappeared. When that tree dies, all of us will die with it."

Angela looked up. The only living branch in that hundred-year-old tree stood out against the gray sky. The cat's tail became visible for an instant and then disappeared among the branches.

"This is the tree where Rayen's father experimented with grafting. He harvested apples, pears, and sometimes plums. That's why people got scared... you don't play with nature. According to Don Ernesto that was the cause of the tragedy," Fabian said, almost out of breath.

He regretted having said too much and became silent.

Angela noted that his body was trembling, especially when she looked him in the eye, but she couldn't overcome the urgent need to look at that face. She felt the earth move under her feet. She had the same feeling whenever she met someone who would be important in her life... just like the day she met Patricia. But this time her intuition was even stronger. Notwithstanding the uncontrolled galloping of her heart, Fabian was the most attractive man she had encountered in her nineteen years.

The wind moaned as it blew through the branches of the tree.

The frightened young man looked up. His face contorted in pain. His body writhed for an instant before he pulled himself together.

Angela saw despair in his eyes, not only for himself but also for all who came before him. Fabian had inherited a fear with which he had learned to live. Quietly, he moved away from her. He bit his lip so he would not speak another word. He fled leaving a wake of fear and confusion behind. Angela could hear the faint noise of the wind blowing through the branches that seemed to clap when Fabian ran away.

12 REASON TO BE

Rosa's house... How to find Rosa's house? Angela was about to start walking in no particular direction when she heard the clatter of tin cans and turned her head. At the end of the street, Carlos appeared in his van, gesturing to her from behind the steering wheel.

Angela approached the vehicle. The librarian hit the brakes and the halt of the van sounded like the groan of a dying animal.

"What happened to your head?" he asked, shocked, as he got out of the car and saw the wound on her left temple.

Imitating Fabian's gesture, she moved her hand as if to say "it's nothing." Even so, Carlos reached through the window, rummaged around in the glove compartment and produced a white box that had a red cross on its cover. He insisted that she sit in the passenger seat while he moistened a cotton ball with disinfectant.

"Wow, what a welcome, huh?" he commented while gingerly dabbing disinfectant on her skin.

"Do you know where I can find Rosa's house?" asked Angela. "On the next street," Carlos responded. With the blood cleaned off her forehead, Angela grabbed her bag from the rear of the Bookmobile. There was so much she wanted to ask Carlos about what she had just witnessed, but he had to return to Puerto Chacabuco and it was getting late.

As she hugged him for the last time, she smelled the dried wood, the freshly baked bread and the fragrant spices from Viviana's kitchen, and remembered how good they had made her feel after her endless journey.

"Thank you so much for everything."

"Take care, Angela. Take good care," Carlos insisted.

She watched as his van, threatening to fall apart at each curve, drove away with its treasures, becoming a tiny white spot in the green landscape before it finally disappeared. Angela began to walk in the direction that Carlos had indicated, leaving her footsteps tattooed in the wet ground.

~

Rosa's house turned out to be the ancient building where Angela thought she had seen a silhouette of a woman framed in the window behind the curtains. The house had two floors and high pointed roofs. The paint was peeling off because of age and inclement weather. Angela had the impression that the building was leaning to the side, just like the elderly people that curve, little by little, due to their fragile bones. A sign next to the main door read "La Esperanza. Handmade rugs."

"*Esperanza*," Angela thought, "Hope... I sure hope I find Patricia."

She thought about checking again for a signal, but as she searched for her iPhone in her pockets, she recalled with horror that it was lying at the bottom of a crevice, most certainly destroyed. She felt more alone than ever, unable to communicate with her mother or her missing friend.

After knocking a couple of times, she thought she heard sounds on the other side of the door.

Footsteps came closer, slowly and without rushing. Creaking hinges announced the door was opening; perhaps, given the slowness of their movements, it was someone very old. Nonetheless, on the other side of the door, there appeared a thin young woman with very fine and straight hair and a face that looked more like a medieval painting than a girl from this century. She was almost ethereally pretty. Her black hair fell with perfect symmetry on both sides of her face. Her eyes were a glassy opaline. One delicate hand with long immaculate fingers rose into the air and came close to the recent arrival.

"Who's there?" she asked with a voice that sounded like the tinkling of a glass bell.

"I'm looking for Rosa," responded Angela, still surprised by the delicate, blind woman in front of her. "I've been told that there are rooms available to rent here."

The lady of the house stepped forward. She lifted the same hand and put it on Angela's forehead, barely grazing her skin. She slid her fingers along the curve of her cheek, leaving a warm trail where her fingertips had touched. When she arrived at Angela's chin, she stepped to the side, clearing a path inside.

"Come in. Make yourself at home," said Rosa.

Angela went into the living room and immediately had the sensation that she had gone back in time one hundred years, exactly as Carlos had forecasted.

When Rosa closed the door, the interior was plunged into a thick semidarkness, barely interrupted by the weak beams of sunshine that filtered through holes in the wall or the shutters that covered the windows, pointing like long yellow fingers at the dusty furniture.

It struck Angela that everything was excessively neat and in its place after the earthquake. In fact, it looked like nothing in the room had been out of place in years.

The long wooden floorboards creaked with each step that Angela took but didn't make any sound when Rosa moved. The owner's hands felt their way along the walls, confidently guiding her along a path so frequently walked.

A mixture of smells, particularly parsley, rosemary and chamomile, welcomed her.

Rosa and Angela walked down the hallway that led to the rear of the building. They stopped in front of a closed door that Rosa opened with a key she had taken from her pocket.

"Welcome," she said smiling and her colorless eyes showed a trace of sweetness.

Angela entered the room. It had a double brass bed covered with a wool comforter that was decorated with lovely geometric designs. On one side of the bed was a huge armoire with beveled mirror doors. A dark wooden table, a chair, and a night table completed the cozy furnishings. A bare bulb hung from the high ceiling.

When she walked towards the center of the room, one board creaked more than the others. One of the armoire doors opened slightly and reflected the image of a man on the other side of the window.

Frightened by the unexpected sight of the stranger, Angela gave a little jump.

Upon turning, she discovered that it was a scarecrow in the garden with a flour sack face. Its arms were open and it had a hat with a large black feather. The wind played with its tattered clothes and made it sway like a lonely creature dancing in the middle of nowhere. Angela decided it wasn't a very pretty image to look at, especially when she was by herself at night. She decided to keep the curtains drawn.

A thunderclap shook Rosa's house from its foundations to the turret on the roof. It began to rain and the old mansion was filled with noises.

"If there's a leak, let me know," Rosa said from the door, still smiling. "Are you hungry?" she asked straight away, as if guessing what her new houseguest was thinking. Angela hoped her meek 'Yes, please' conveyed her gratitude.

The kitchen was as dark as the rest of the rooms. A warm aroma rose from an enormous wood stove. Angela saw how Rosa moved around the space with astonishing efficiency and precision. Without hesitation, she opened the cabinet doors and found glasses, plates and silverware. She was heating up a delicious-smelling lamb stew accompanied by rice perfumed with a sprig of basil that she herself had cut from one of the many planters that filled the shelves.

Angela cast her eyes on the long wooden plank that held more than one hundred containers made out of clay, tin, plastic cups and anything else that could hold soil and a plant. An infinite variety of leaves, stems, and flowers were crammed in a warm fragrant embrace. She asked herself how Rosa managed to keep them healthy and fresh; each appeared to be recently fertilized and pruned.

While Angela savored the meal, Rosa went over to one of the windows and, in a gesture of consideration for her guest, opened the shutters allowing the light to percolate in. Angela looked up and discovered that she could clearly see the rain falling through the bare branches of the enormous tree in the square.

A woman shouting at a man suddenly distracted her. He was making gestures of extreme annoyance raising his hands only to let them fall immediately, clearly rebuffing her. She had her hands on her hips and it looked like sparks were shooting from her eyes. Neither seemed bothered by the drenching rain. They only seemed to be interested in showing how deeply each resented the other.

"Apparently no one in this village can love…" Angela murmured without realizing whether she had said it aloud or not.

"I see you've heard Rayen's story," Rosa said.

"Yes. That's why I'm here. I came to do some research on her legend," Angela responded staring at her.

"And you're also looking for your friend, aren't you?"

Angela stopped in mid-bite and didn't say a word while she tried to sort out her thoughts.

How did that woman know about Patricia's disappearance? Did she have something to do with it? Was Rosa whom she had to look for?

"She stayed here the first night she was in Almahue, in the same room that you have," Rosa answered before Angela could ask her.

"Do you know where she is?" Angela stood up and approached Rosa.

"I don't know. The next morning, when I went to her room, she wasn't there." Angela passed a hand across her face. She was dazed by the new information.

The image of Patricia in the house in which she now found herself made her feel closer to her friend.

"How did you know I knew her?" Angela wanted to know.

"Because she also told me that she had come to the village to do research on Rayen's legend. And then she started crying and told me about a friend that she loved dearly and had betrayed out of utter ambition."

Another thunderclap made the plants jump on the shelves and the glasses and silverware inside the cabinets chatter. A flash of lightning cut a bright slash across the sky and, for a fraction of a second, filled the kitchen with shifting shadows.

Angela shivered when she saw one of the shadows jump from a corner and land silently close to her feet. Looking again, she was relieved to discover that it was a black cat. Arching its jet-black back and purring, it went between the stove and the wall. Could it be the same cat from the square? It was impossible to tell; she thought all black cats looked alike. At least this one, in contrast to the other, didn't show any interest in her.

"Why do you think she left without saying anything? I'm sorry to interrogate you, but it's very important," pleaded Angela.

"Perhaps she was frightened when I told her that Rayen and her father lived in this very house in the middle of the last century. Do you believe in coincidences?" Rosa asked.

Before Angela had time to think about her answer, the blind young woman declared "I don't. Everything happens for a reason. I hope you enjoy your dinner."

Saying nothing more, she left the kitchen.

13 NO LOVE ALLOWED

The first thing that stood out when entering the attic was a curious round window. From it, like through an enormous eye, everything that happened in the village could be seen without leaving the room. A wooden bed with a tall, carved headboard was against one of the walls. On each side of it were elegant night tables. On one of them was a bronze table lamp with a frosted glass shade struggling to illuminate a space populated by shadows. Finally, there was a magnificent roll-top desk with a green mat and lots of drawers where he kept his most valuable memories: a collection of pens, a few old photographs, and a couple of athletic trophies. In a corner, next to the bathroom door was a cast iron wood stove finished with beautiful bronze details and a tempered glass door through which the burning logs could be seen.

Judging by the silence, the attic appeared uninhabited. But Ernesto Schmied, almost ninety-years old, hadn't left the room for three decades. One day he asked to be moved to the attic of his childhood house: the house where he was born, where he married, where his only son was born and where he expected to die when his time came.

Acting upon Don Ernesto's request, his son Walter set up the attic, a big abandoned room, barely lit by a strange round window, and which could only be accessed by a steep and creaky ladder. For several days, a group of men cleaned, organized and moved Don Ernesto's clothes, bed, tables, and the noble desk where he worked for so many years. They built a small washroom with a porcelain basin and an antique mirror. After a week of hard labor, everything was set for the patriarch to move into his new room. He ordered all his meals served in his room because he was never going to leave it and he would never go down to the dining room. Walter was indignant at what seemed an unacceptable decision. But Silvia, Walter's wife, didn't even try to convince her father-in-law to share the table with them. Without ever asking what he might prefer to eat, she ordered each of his meals to be taken to his room on a tray.

Thus, Ernesto Schmied locked himself and waited for the day that death would be kind enough to take him far, far away to pay for his sins, especially the one that tormented him the most. It was the least he could expect after all the horror he had caused.

Each night, when he closed his eyes, he was haunted by his guilty conscience. Almahue knew no love because almost seventy years ago, he didn't dare to stand up to his family. He was sure that there was no power on earth that could forgive him for what he had done. All that was left for him was to spend the rest of his life atoning for the pain he had inflicted on the woman he loved.

Every morning when he woke up, he dressed himself slowly. He adjusted his suspenders, carefully tied his tie, put on his shiny black patent leather shoes, applied English cologne to his thinning hair and brushed his mustache and his brows. Once he was ready, he approached the round window. He leaned on the polished handle of his cane and from this vantage point, he painfully stared at the enormous tree in the square for hours. That was why he moved to the attic. It was from there that he had an unobstructed view of the tree. He was flooded by memories. Each dying branch broke his heart; each withered leaf reminded him of Rayen's enraged words as she looked at him straight in the eye: "I curse you, Ernesto Schmied! I curse you and all your descendants!"

Rayen's voice. How was it possible that he could still hear it so clearly?

Three knocks on the door brought him back to reality. He turned around and cleared his throat before saying: "Come in!"

Fabian peeked through the doorway and smiled sweetly at the old man as the grandfather clock struck seven.

"May I come in?"

"Of course. You are always welcome," he said shuffling away from the window and gesturing him in.

Fabian helped Don Ernesto sit down in a worn leather chair and handed him a glass of water covered by a delicate linen napkin. Don Ernesto slowly sipped the water.

The veins in his hands stood out against the neatly starched cuffs of his shirt. "I wanted to know if you were scared by the earthquake," Fabian asked.

"A little shaking won't hurt these old bones," Don Ernesto smiled bitterly.

"I'm glad you came to see me. I was wondering when you would show up."

"A stranger came to town, Don Ernesto," Fabian said after a pause. "Well, that's something!" said the old man nodding.

"And it seems she's trying to find out about Rayen," Fabian said. Ernesto Schmied looked Fabian in the eyes.

The young man avoided looking back at him and looked down, knowing that his voice was betraying him. The old man knew right away that Fabian's concern with the stranger didn't have to do with her research on the sorceress but, unfortunately, with something else. Don Ernesto knew Fabian since the day he was born, twenty-six years before. On that day, the Schmied's cook, Elvira Caicheo announced to everyone's surprise that not only was she pregnant, but she was about to give birth. No one had even noticed she was expecting.

From the moment that Ernesto first saw the little boy wrapped in plain sheets, still a little bit purplish from labor, he had felt a surge of grandfatherly devotion. He never minded that the cook never revealed the real father's identity.

"Are you sure?" asked the old man.

"I am, Don Ernesto. I sent her to Rosa's house because she needs to stay for a couple of days."

The man leaned on his cane. The handle shined in the half-light. He got up with much effort and walked across the attic on trembling legs. Fabian wanted to help him but Don Ernesto refused with a wave of his hand. He walked to his desk and rolled up the wooden cover hiding the drawers. He opened and closed them until he found what he was looking for. He remained still for an instant looking at the contents of the drawer, hesitant, breathing rapidly.

"Don Ernesto?" asked Fabian worriedly.

But the old man again cut him off with a gesture. He pulled out a black notebook from one of the drawers. The cover was worn and the corners were dog-eared. It was tied with a black ribbon that kept the pages from falling out. He turned to the young man, who was looking at him expectantly.

"Do you know what's in here?" he asked. Fabian shook his head. "Everything is here. Everything," he whispered in a faint voice. "From the day I met Rayen until..." He didn't finish. After almost a century, the pain was the same. He stared at the notebook for a moment, searching for courage to continue. "Tomorrow you will look for the stranger at Rosa's house and bring her here," he ordered. "She might be interested in reading what I wrote."

"As you wish, Don Ernesto."

The old man was going back to his seat but stopped. Slowly, he turned his head to the young man who was sinking in the shadows as night took over the attic.

"You better not fall for that girl, understand?" he said, trying to sound firm.

Fabian could feel his face burning again and was grateful that it was too dark for the old man to see his blushing cheeks. He couldn't allow the turmoil in his heart to take over. That's why he ran away, leaving her alone in the middle of the square. That was the only way he could prevent things from getting out of control. But how could he stop such a pleasant and natural impulse? One he had never felt before.

"Your life is at stake here," Don Ernesto declared and his eyes turned somber. "It's all my fault. I'm sorry."

The young man approached the old man. Affectionately, he put a hand on his shoulder to show him he need not apologize. He was surprised to feel how thin he had become. Fabian could feel every bone through Don Ernesto's coat and shirt.

"Fabian, I'm serious. You can't fall in love with the stranger."

"Don Ernesto, there's no need to..." he managed to say.

"I know why I'm saying it, damn it!" he cut him off severely. "I know you. I've seen you grow up and become a man. I can see in your eyes that she made an impression on you. Now listen to me. If what you are feeling turns into love you will die."

~

The grandfather clock sounded the half hour with a harsh gong. The echo bounced around the walls for a few seconds. And although he tried hard not to think about it, Fabian felt like he was listening to the music at his own funeral.

14 AWAKENING

The first night that she slept in the enormous house, Angela couldn't stop imagining Patricia curled up in the same unfamiliar bed, covered by the same wool blanket, her head nestled in the feather pillows and her eyes wide open trying to overcome the darkness. As hard as she tried, Angela couldn't fall asleep and spent the first hours of the night startled by any noise that interrupted the silence of the bedroom. It hadn't stopped raining since the afternoon and the water continued to run down the window. The curtain lit up with every flash of lightning that drew mysterious shadows on the wall and illuminated the silhouette of the scarecrow.

Angela estimated that Rosa's big house must have at least six bedrooms. "Which one was Rayen's?" she wondered. "And her father's laboratory?" She remembered having read in one of Benedicto Mohr's entries that the girl's father, a mysterious European by the name of Karl Wilhelm, was an accomplished botanist who had arrived shortly after the village was established. He moved there with his only daughter, whose unusual name had probably been chosen in homage to the language he was learning in the continent where he had recently built their new home.

Holed up for long hours in his laboratory, Karl experimented with plants, combining different types of saps, changing the composition of seeds, and stimulating the stems and branches with fertilizers he invented. "This is the tree where Rayen's father experimented with grafting. He harvested apples, pears, and sometimes plums," Fabian's words came back to her, coming full circle; now she understood why the botanist had horrified Almahue's small population at the end of the thirties. The man had challenged nature and he settlers found this unforgivable. Angela was certain that was the reason they started calling Karl Wilhelm's daughter a witch. If her father was capable of altering the natural cycle of life, it was likely that his offspring had inherited the same powers and evil arts. The girl was just a victim of the intolerance and ignorance of the time.

Thinking of Rayen, she remembered the book that Carlos had given her. Where had she put it? It was in her backpack, resting on the chair on the other side of the room. The idea of getting out of bed and crossing the entire room in the dark and the cold gave her goose bumps so she gave up on the idea. She would begin reading in the morning, with the sun shining on the other side of the window.

~

Angela was dozing lightly as morning broke. When she opened her eyes, the four walls of her room were bathed in the soft yellow light of a new day. One of the armoire doors was open. As she sat up, she saw the reflection of her face peeking out from the covers and, behind that, the window where she could make out the scarecrow, waving at her from the garden with his extended arms.

"That's the last thing I need," she muttered, sitting in the bed. "That puppet is visible from every corner."

She imagined Patricia running through the branches and brambles of a forest being chased by the scarecrow. She got up and firmly closed the door of the closet. She wanted it to stay shut and stop surprising her.

She took the book out of her backpack and went out into the hallway. She wanted to ask Rosa about the shower and where and when was breakfast served. She didn't even know what time it was. Her watch had died along with her iPhone. She'd have to take care of this as soon as possible. Did Almahue have a watch store? Besides, where was she going to get a new telephone to keep in touch with her mother? She could imagine her nervously sitting by the phone hoping that it would ring at any moment to bring her news of her daughter's activities while she was supposedly in Concepción. Sighing in resignation, she decided this was something she was going to have to take care of quickly.

The long hallway was empty and dark. The only problem with temporarily living under the same roof as a blind person was that she would have to get used to turning on the lights as she went. Otherwise she would have to get used to living in the gloom. And she didn't like that at all.

"Rosa...?" she called. No answer.

She drew her pajamas around her because it was much colder outside her bedroom than she had thought. She walked a few steps, feeling her way along the wall to find a light switch. She pressed the button but no lights turned on. She tried a couple more times to no avail. Something creaked at the other end of the corridor.

"Rosa? Is that you?" No response. She tried to convince herself that the wood made sounds when it expanded or contracted with changes in temperature and humidity, and that it was normal for old buildings to be filled with strange sounds that were impossible to identify. Despite repeating it to herself over and over, like a mantra to overcome her fear, Angela couldn't convince herself as she walked down the hall. "Rayen and her father lived in this very house," Rosa's words came flooding back to her ears.

She felt like running back to her room, jumping back into bed and hiding under the covers until her prolonged absence prompted Rosa to come looking for her. Nonetheless she proceeded, holding the book tightly against her chest. She got to a corner and, to her right, was able to make out a new hallway. To her left, she felt to see if there was a door. Her hand touched the doorknob. She could see a ray of light shining on her bare feet from underneath the door. Just as she was going to open the door, a new creak, this time behind her, made her blood run cold. There was no doubt; someone... something... was approaching. Could it be the cat? No, the animal was small and never had made a noise like this. She imagined the faces of Rayen and Karl. A shudder ran down her spine. She turned the knob and entered the room. She stopped in her tracks when she found herself face to face with Rosa who, peaceful and unaware, was weaving long strands of wool on a vertical loom.

"Is that you Angela?" she asked, turning her head towards the recent arrival with her dead eyes.

She was going to answer yes when she felt a hand on her shoulder.

The scream died in her throat as she realized the warmth and sweetness of that perfect hand. Collecting herself, she turned to see Fabian's face. He smelled like the forest, like freshly cut wood. He was bewildered by her proximity and the enormous smile with which she greeted him.

"Good morning to both of you. Will you join me for breakfast?" said Rosa.

15 BREAKFAST

The raucous whistle of the teapot announced that the water was boiling. With her delicate hand, Rosa served three cups of a fragrant infusion of mint and lemon verbena that she had harvested from different pots. She handed them to Angela and Fabian who were sitting at opposite ends of the table. Angela noticed that the young man didn't dare look at her. Not only that, he did everything he could to avoid eye contact with her. She took it as a compliment. It was obvious they were desperately attracted to one another. But for Fabian it was far from pleasant. Apart from a totally uncontrollable desire, he felt a stabbing pain that made his heart stop and his body double over, he felt paralyzed. Such was the power of the curse. He could barely breathe but, when he felt that he was about to faint from lack of oxygen, his lungs miraculously filled with air like bellows, revitalizing his blood, his heart, and his muscles. "Don Ernesto," he thought to himself. "If only you were wrong."

"Did you sleep well?" inquired Rosa as she sat between them. "Yes, very well, very comfortably," Angela answered. "What are you reading?" Rosa asked as she took a bite of her bread with butter and fresh cheese.

It took Angela a few seconds to understand that she meant the book in her hands. Rosa's milky eyes didn't seem capable of sight, yet how could she know about the book if no one had mentioned it until that moment? "Is she really blind?" Angela asked herself. "Or is she lying to everyone?"

"It's about Rayen, the sorceress from Almahue," she answered.

"And what do you think about the story?" Rosa asked as she sipped her herbal tea.

"I haven't started it yet."

Rosa cracked a smile. Was she laughing at her? She turned to Fabian who didn't say anything. She couldn't see his face because he was looking down, his eyes fixed on the steaming cup in front of him. Suddenly something touched her foot under the table. Angela jumped up and screamed, scaring everyone. The black cat emerged from underneath her chair, distant and disdainful, sauntered across the kitchen and hid behind a cabinet.

"Please forgive Azabache," Rosa said. "He likes to play jokes on newcomers." Angela could only grin. It was difficult to hide that she hated the animal. Interrupting the awkward silence, Rosa began to tell them that she was finishing a new rug.

She told Angela that the process began with dyeing the wool with natural pigments obtained from flowers and roots. Then she would spin the skein to form threads that she knotted one by one on a huge loom. Once the rug was woven in the stretcher, she would cut around it, knot the edges and eliminate any flaws. After combing the wool, she shaved it to make it even. The last stage was the stiffening, which consisted of applying water-soluble animal glue. This adhesive gave the rug its rigidity.

"Do you design them all yourself as well?"

"Yes. Rosa is the best artist in town," Fabian spoke for the first time with a tiny voice.

Once again, he didn't look at Angela but he could feel his eyes coming back at him. His heart rate increased and his ears buzzed. For a fraction of a second, he considered looking up at her beautiful eyes, trying to lock with his, but he gave up. His life was at stake. No one had ever overcome *Malamor*. No one. The village cemetery was full of unfortunate ones who challenged the curse and died suffering terrible pains, body and soul. If he couldn't resist looking at that young woman with red hair and fair skin, he was about to become one of them.

He stood up, turning away from her.

"Don Ernesto asked me to come get you," he said looking at the wall and feeling totally stupid.

"And who is Don Ernesto?" Angela asked.

"The village patriarch," Rosa answered from her side of the table. "That's a real surprise... it's been a long time since he has called for anyone. He's probably going to tell her about Rayen," she concluded in a knowing tone.

"And what does he know about the sorceress?" Angela asked.

Fabian and Rosa bit their lips and remained silent. Angela was now certain that she had put her foot in her mouth. Was there anyone in Almahue that wasn't related to the sorceress in some way?

"Don Ernesto is the only living person in this village who knew Rayen," Fabian said very seriously.

"I'm going to get dressed and I'll be right back."

Out of the corner of his eye, Fabian looked at the reddish glow she left behind as she disappeared through the door. He couldn't avoid letting out a sigh. He quickly tried to hide his feelings in front of Rosa but he realized his situation was worse than he had imagined. He couldn't stop looking at Angela's face. In order to dodge death he would have to be more careful, although perhaps he didn't mind burning in hell for her. A kiss would be well worth the sacrifice.

16 WELCOME HOME

When Fabian and Angela crossed the square on their way to the Schmied's house, Angela couldn't take her eyes off the line of people that had formed a long human chain, from the well to the enormous tree. They passed buckets full of water hand-to-hand and the last one in line poured it on the roots and exchanged it for another. In spite of the coordinated execution of the movements, the mood was not good. Some were yelling insults that others, even more angry and annoyed, returned. When Angela, surprised by the spectacle, stopped for a moment to watch the collective fury and the teamwork, Fabian stopped and approached her from behind.

"Once a day they organize a group to try and keep it alive," he explained. "Are they that scared of the legend?" Angela asked him. "It's not a legend, it's our reality," he answered, looking off into the distance. Angela had lots of questions but the biggest one was why Fabian wouldn't look her in the eyes. Fabian wanted to talk to her about *Malamor,* he wanted to tell her about the merciless invisible spear that pierced his chest every time he thought about her or felt her nearby. The spasm that tormented him wasn't a legend; it was every bit as real as the imminent death of the tree in the square; as each earthquake that was more violent than the last.

She was going to ask him another question but Fabian kept moving forward without waiting for her. Annoyed, Angela threw up her hands. She watched him go farther down the street. There wasn't anything about this taciturn and stubborn young man that she didn't like. In fact, she was amused by his efforts to keep his distance and his inability to keep his ears from turning crimson every time they spoke. For a few seconds, she contemplated his swimmer's back, his shirt stretched across the breadth of his frame, the somewhat coarse cut of his hair at the back of his neck, his sailor's sway as he walked.

Before she ran to catch up, Angela took one last look at the long line of Almahue citizens that were straining to water the tree. She felt her throat suddenly tightened when she saw a short man, hunched forward with a prominent belly and a clear bald spot. It was *him*. Of course it was him; the old man from the ferry, the one who told her about the Coo for the first time, the one that seemed to know much more than he should.

The old man looked at her with beady eyes that were surrounded by taut and shiny skin, too small for the size of his skull. She felt like going to meet him, emboldened by the idea that he might have news about Patricia. But some shouting caught her attention. Two men were fighting apparently because one of them had dropped the bucket, spilling the water. Instead of separating them, the others in the line began to argue with the person closest to them, taking sides over the two fighters. The din was increasing in intensity and Angela was scared that the situation would escalate to tragic proportions, considering the aggressive mob.

She looked again for the old man but didn't see him anywhere; he had disappeared. A hand took her by the elbow and pulled her back.

"Let's go!" Fabian ordered and she let him take her away.

The Schmied's enormous house was at the end of a dead-end street. It dominated the street with its three floors, various roofs at different levels and its well cared-for collection of windows and turrets. A thick coat of yellow paint covered the wooden exterior and the doors and garden fence were white. Angela's attention was drawn to a round window at the upper vertex of the roof, a big Cyclops eye that looked down on Almahue from above. She walked towards the front door but Fabian turned down a side path.

"I have to enter through the kitchen," he announced. "Wait for me here; I'll be back to open the door for you."

Before she could reply, he took off around the house.

Angela was taken aback by the situation; what did it mean? Could the Schmieds forbid him from entering through the front door? What kind of people allowed only certain visitors to enter through the front door, while ordering others to enter through the kitchen? Immersed in her thoughts, she didn't notice that Fabian had already opened the door and was waiting for her.

"Come in," he said.

Angela entered an elegant parlor with parquet floors and subtle lavender wallpaper. A chandelier swayed above their heads and delicately illuminated the room. Angela felt like she had stepped into a period film where the decoration divulged ancient ancestry and a booming economy. She felt like her worn jeans and her heavy coat clashed with the scene around her.

"Do you live here?" she asked surprised. "My mother is the cook in this house," Fabian replied. "I live here with her." Angela understood the situation, and felt closer to this young man who would do anything to avoid looking her in the eye. She imagined him sleeping at the rear of the residence, in a narrow and damp room, while the others enjoyed excessive luxury for a village like Almahue. A throb of injustice lodged itself in her chest and made her frown.

"Do we have a visitor?" she heard behind them.

When she turned around, she saw an attractive woman in her fifties, her hair gathered in a bun and wearing a long dark skirt from beneath which only her shoes were visible.

"Well, I've never seen you," she said as she came to the bottom of the staircase. "Silvia Poblete Schmied," she introduced herself and Angela wondered why she would recite her full name instead of simply saying "Hello."

Angela responded with a nod. "My name is Angela." She knew that the woman in front of her was responsible for the fact that Fabian couldn't use the front door. Her taut hair, the tension in her features, the arrogant tilt of her neck and chin all defined Silvia as the strict and severe owner of the house.

"Don Ernesto sent me to look for Miss Angela," interjected Fabian.

"That is impossible. My father-in-law hasn't wanted to see anyone in many years," Silvia answered without taking her eyes off the recently arrived girl. "I'm afraid that there has been a misunderstanding," she declared approaching the door.

"What are you saying woman?" A white-haired man entered the parlor. He was dressed in a heavy overcoat with lots of pockets. He had a woolen scarf around his neck and the end of his nose was red with cold.

"Well, look who the cat dragged in!" exclaimed the woman. "Would you mind telling me where you've been?"

With a slight limp in his right leg, the man approached Silvia and smiled at Angela.

"Welcome to our house. I'm Walter Schmied," he said formally. And then he turned to his wife, without answering her question. "Don't be a bad hostess. How long has it been since we've had a visitor?"

"She says your father sent for her," she said defensively. "Fabian, take eh... Excuse me, what is your name again?"

"Angela," she answered feeling much more warmth towards the man of the house.

"Very well. You may take Angela to my father," he commanded. Fabian nodded and with his head motioned Angela to follow. Somewhat disapprovingly, she understood that Fabian was employed by a family that only saw him as a servant. She realized that Fabian's use of the word "Miss" to address her, and his inability to look her in the eye, were to be expected from a man raised to be deferential, despite what was in his heart. Lost in these reflections, as they began to climb the stairs, she felt the warmth of his body.

They were just turning on the first landing when she heard Silvia nagging from downstairs.

"I don't know you anymore, Walter! You're completely responsible for this. Our downfall will be your fault!"

Angela followed Fabian down a long hallway. She tried to keep her mouth closed but was unable to do so. When the opportunity presented itself, she mumbled in collusion: "What an unpleasant woman! I don't know how you put up with her."

Fabian didn't respond and kept walking.

"And on top of everything, he's discrete and loyal," Angela thought and, for reasons that she still couldn't understand, she was sure that Fabian was much more of a rebel and more dangerous than he appeared. And it was precisely that mystery that made him impossibly attractive.

A door slammed behind them and they stopped.

Startled, she turned to see a man around thirty years of age leave one of the rooms. His eyes and nose strongly resembled Walter Schmied, and his arrogant and distant expression that of Silvia Poblete. He was the perfect combination of both, the absolute summation of his parents.

"Aren't you going to introduce me to this charming visitor?" he said, his gaze fixed upon her, smiling like a ladies' man and winking as he came closer.

"Oh boy," Angela silently complained to herself. The last thing she needed was this pretentious fool.

"Egon Schmied Poblete," he introduced himself, in the same way his mother had, using all of his names and lineage.

She returned the greeting without much enthusiasm. Egon stood next to her. The overpowering aroma of his cologne made her throat tickle. As if by instinct, Fabian came closer to Angela. She could feel his arm against her body and a wave of warmth flowed through her.

"I am so lucky. In less than three weeks, I've had the opportunity to meet two lovely strangers," Egon exclaimed with a forced smile. "What could I have done to deserve such a..."

But, surprisingly, he didn't finish his sentence. Angela noted a glimmer of fear in the eyes of Walter and Silvia's first-born son, a regret that led him to back up a few steps and clench his teeth.

"Excuse me," interrupted Angela anxiously, "but who's the stranger you're talking about?"

It took a few moments for him to reply. Angela noticed that Egon's hands were shaking. "A couple of weeks ago, we had a group of Argentine hikers visiting, and among them was an attractive tourist. She also had red hair, just like you. And, well... there was a special chemistry between us... if you know what I mean," he answered mischievously raising his eyebrows to conceal his nervousness.

An uncomfortable silence came to rest among the three of them. No one seemed to know what to say.

"Don Ernesto is expecting us," Fabian interrupted after the extended silence.

Fabian took Angela with him in the direction of the stairs that led to the attic.

Egon was left alone in the middle of the hallway, with a frozen smile and a thread of sweat that trickled down his temple. He almost made a tremendous mistake, but fortunately neither of them seemed to notice. He had to be on guard. The last thing he needed was a moment of carelessness that could cost him his life, should he mention Patricia Rendon. He promised himself to watch every word, especially in front of suspicious strangers. He also had to be more proactive... starting now.

He wiped the fake smile off his face allowing the dark glimmer to return to his eyes. With an affected gesture, he ran his fingers through his slicked-down hair and went back to his room.

~

Angela felt the pleasant warmth before she entered the attic and saw the wood stove glowing in the corner, its long aluminum chimney rising through the slope of the ceiling. The hardwood furniture, walls and bookshelves were covered with photographs and piles of books. "Cozy," Angela thought.

"Don Ernesto..." Fabian muttered as he entered. Angela saw him at that moment, she had mistaken him for the shadows on the walls: a delicate figure who silently emerged from the darkness surrounding the round window where he was standing.

Don Ernesto Schmied set his blue eyes on Angela and, with his ninety-year-old smile, welcomed her.

"So you're the one who has been asking around about Rayen," he whispered almost inaudibly.

She nodded, moved by the elegant image of the fragile, elderly man who approached her with the help of his cane. He extended his time-marked hands with their prominent veins and he patted her on the back with infinite tenderness.

"It's a pleasure to meet you, Angela. I have been waiting for you for many, many years," he said emotionally. "May I get you something?"

~

Rosa's house was completely silent, except for the brushing of the wool fibers as they rubbed against each other in the loom. The hallway was dark as usual, seemingly resting from the bustle of the morning. Angela's room, however, was humming with activity. First, the door slowly creaked open. A frigid gust of wind blew inside, ruffling the curtains and the edge of the comforter. The wood groaned from the rapid change in temperature. A book, left on the night table, opened. Rayen read the first page. The windowpanes opened, and a little whirlwind pushed the backpack onto its side, unlatched the larger bag, removing the few articles that it contained, and brushed one of the doors of the armoire open just enough to reflect the scarecrow with its stitched smile, which remained impassive as the book flew out the window like a paper bird and disappeared forever into the storm clouds.

17 IT SEEMS LIKE YESTERDAY

"It was just a matter of time before someone got interested in this story," Don Ernesto Schmied said as he sat down in his leather armchair. "I didn't want to die without knowing that someone would keep Rayen alive."

"Don't say that!" Fabian confronted him with a glimmer of sadness in his eyes. "You still have a lot of time."

"That's not true, my boy. This body can't withstand much more."

He turned to Angela, who was watching him in silence.

"Could you tell me how you learned about *The Legend of Malamor*?" Angela told him about her first encounter with those photocopies, more than a year earlier, at the library of the School of Social Sciences. Fascinated by the subject, she searched for more information and was able to find other documents written by Benedicto Mohr. Her research advisor contributed some readings, especially on the subject of Mapuche and Patagonian mythology.

"Benedicto Mohr!" the old man said, gesturing with his hands. "He was a man of good intentions... But he never really knew the truth. He made up a lot of things to fill in the gaps of his work."

"Did you know him?" Angela asked, fascinated.

"Of course. Mohr lived in Almahue for some time while he was writing his book on Rayen. After finishing it, he disappeared and no one heard from him again."

"I have that book," Angela said.

Don Ernesto raised his eyebrows, looking pleased. He nodded and rested his hands on the arms of his chair.

"Well... you're more prepared than I thought. It is not easy to find that book," he said.

"Let's just say that I've been lucky," she replied, smiling at him with satisfaction.

Fabian could not hide a sigh of admiration for the young woman who held her own in a conversation with the patriarch. He was surprised by the calmness of her voice and the poise with which she addressed Don Ernesto as if she had known him all her life. Despite the fact that she was in a remote town, in a strange house, and in a rather bizarre situation, she managed to kindly answer all of Don Ernesto's questions. "A kiss from her is well worth the price of having to endure the symptoms of *Malamor*," Fabian thought. Suddenly, an unequivocal spasm hit him in the pit of his stomach. A scorching volcano exploded in his rib cage, accelerating his breath at an unnatural rate. As casually as he could, in order to avoid drawing attention to himself, he leaned against one of the walls and stood still, letting the cold sweat that bathed him from head to toe evaporate from his skin.

Don Ernesto gestured to Fabian.

Fabian shook off what was left of the spasm and quickly went to him. He supported Don Ernesto by the elbow and helped him stand up. The old man's bones cracked like nutshells when he straightened his back and walked to the desk. Angela watched him move forward one step at a time. With great calm, he opened one of the drawers and reached inside.

"For a long, long time I've been waiting for someone to whom I could give this," he whispered taking a black notebook out of the drawer. "I'm sure you can understand, it couldn't be someone from Almahue. I couldn't give it to someone who is under the spell of *Malamor*... like the rest of us."

Angela took the notebook without saying a word.

Filled with curiosity, she untied the ribbon that held the pages together and opened it. In the first page, she read: "February 28, 1939". Her heart skipped a beat. She raised her eyes and saw the old man looking at her with a sweet smile.

"Yes. It's all there, my love story with Rayen."

For a while Angela stood still, shocked and unable to utter a word. Was it true, then? The famous legend, the one about the spurned witch that put an evil spell on a whole town, was not a folk tale handed down from one generation to the next? And what about Patricia? Was she in danger?

"You? You were the lover that rejected her!" she exclaimed, unable to believe what was happening.

"Yes, I was. And, trust me, I'm not proud of it," the old man replied. "Not a day goes by that I don't think of her. I remember her as if our last moments together had been yesterday."

Angela felt the black notebook, with its approximately one hundred pages written in perfect calligraphy, throbbing in her hands. She wanted only to get to Rosa's house, jump into her bed, and, there, under the covers, devote herself to reading Ernesto Schmied's manuscript. She heard wood crackling in the stove.

"I need someone to finally break the spell," the man implored, lowering his voice almost to a whisper. "This village has suffered too much because of me. Angela, I want love back in Almahue. Will you help me?" he asked.

Angela didn't know what to say. She didn't believe in magic spells, how could she possibly help the old man?

Her head was spinning.

She saw Patricia's desperate cry, her mother waiting for her next reassuring phone call, Rayen's powerful presence, her long trip across the country, the landscape at the end of the world, Fabian's eyes, Fabian's mouth, Fabian's hands, the way her heart beat when he was close to her, and Don Ernesto asking her to save an entire village from disappearing into the maw of the earth.

Stumbling, she looked for a wall to lean against.

Fabian ran to her aid, held her, and kept her from collapsing.

It was then that she looked through the round window as the afternoon faded into evening. And she saw it, its big yellow eyes fixed on her, its owl feathers blowing in the wind, its short beak violently tapping the glass as if wanting to come in.

"The Coo!" she gasped.

Her first reaction was to run away, find the main door and leave. But she couldn't. The Coo was coming for her. Could it be that it was following her, first in the ferry and now in Don Ernesto's room?

She had to escape.

She began to walk out of the room.

In the hallway, a hand held her back.

She turned around and found herself face to face with Fabian, his bright eyes looking deeply into hers.

"I will not let anything bad happen to you," he whispered in her ear.

He drew her closer.

His mouth brushed her nose and the curve of her cheek. Angela closed her eyes and allowed his scent of smoked wood wash over her like a rainstorm in the forest.

Despite the bad omens that haunted him, Fabian kissed her passionately, giving in to the burst of pleasure. For a brief eternity, there was nothing but their lips, their arms tied in an unbreakable embrace, their wild hearts beating as one.

A tremor made the hallway creak.

Two shouts were heard downstairs, and a roar came from the street, accompanied by the sound of heavy steps-people running and pushing.

"New leaves! The tree has new leaves!" Angela looked out a hallway window to see the crowd approaching the Schmied residence. They raised their arms, applauded and congratulated each other. Smiles brightened their faces.

"The tree has new leaves!" she heard people say.

Angela looked up over the multitude. Her eyes scanned the neighboring houses and the surrounding greenery until they came to rest at the top of the monumental tree in the square. Next to the branch that was still alive, she saw a twig with three or four fresh leaves, barely unfolded, but already blowing in the afternoon wind.

"Someone is in love!" a woman yelled as she jumped for joy next to the fence of the Schmied house.

When Angela turned around to celebrate the news with Fabian, she found him on his knees. The young man raised his head with great difficulty. His face was pale, drenched in sweat.

A deathly shadow covered his eyes, making it hard for him to keep them open. He tried to speak but his body collapsed on the parquet floor like a marionette whose strings were cut. Don Ernesto was right. His life was at stake.

∀ → O

PART II

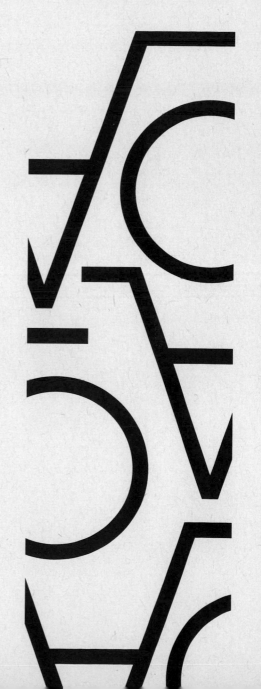

... for now it appears that the perilous journey was a labor not of attainment but of reattainment, not discovery but rediscovery. The godly powers sought and dangerously won are revealed to have been within the heart of the hero all the time.

Joseph Campbell, *The Hero with a Thousand Faces*

1 HOSTILE VILLAGE

The doctor's assessment was definitive. After a careful examination, he said that Fabian was suffering from acute anemia. This explained the rapid heartbeat, the fatigue, the vertigo, the inability to concentrate, the difficulty breathing and the paleness. Although his words seemed reasonable, Angela, Don Ernesto, and Elvira knew that the doctor was wrong. Fabian's ailment had nothing to do with blood diseases. He was suffering unmistakably from *Malamor*, which was why Elvira treated Angela so harshly when she found her son lying on the hallway floor upstairs. She didn't say a word as they took him downstairs to put him in bed and call Dr. Sanhueza at the only clinic in town. The moment she confirmed that her son was breathing, she bitterly asked Angela to leave them alone without even thanking her for calling for help. For Elvira, the stranger was the only one to blame for her only son's condition. She had captivated him with her presence!

Nonetheless, Elvira had to acknowledge that the young woman was beautiful; that she had a unique face, fair and freckled, and framed by hair of a color she had never seen before. Elvira could see the effect Angela had had on Fabian. He felt the urge to be around her from the first time he saw her. Angela had to be kept as far from Fabian as possible, no matter what.

As she walked out of the Schmied's house, Angela looked up at the round window. Through the glass, she saw Don Ernesto waving goodbye like a ghost about to disappear in the twilight. She waved back, holding tightly onto the notebook he had given her.

The townspeople had taken over the streets of Almahue. They were shouting and cheering in joy and relief at what seemed the first setback to the curse. A second branch, shiny and green, sprouted full of life at the top of the tree. Families gathered around it. Elders played dominoes or cards while others toasted, and the little ones ran and hid behind the trunk.

For a moment, the peaceful tableau persuaded Angela that the kiss had been worth it. Then she remembered the pain in Fabian's face as he was lying on the floor, looking at her in agony. She felt a knot in her stomach. All that joy was the result of someone's suffering. The new branch sprouted because Fabian had the courage to defy *Malamor* and follow his heart. He dared to kiss her without regard for his life.

Angela felt like yelling at them that they shouldn't rejoice when Fabian was suffering. His passionate kiss, the way he looked in her eyes, the terse yet irresistibly sweet words he whispered in her ear, "I won't let anything happen to you." She felt the shivers as she realized that Fabian was in love with her. She was certain now. He was in love with her.

She had to control herself in order not to run back to Fabian's room and hold him even if the whole world crumbled. But she didn't. She was afraid his health would worsen. Would she ever see him again? Would Elvira allow her to come near him, if only to say goodbye when the time came for her to go back to Santiago? She almost choked. She had not planned on running into someone like him in Almahue. In fact, she couldn't let anything get in the way of her original plan: to find Patricia sooner rather than later, and she had already let herself become so distracted. What could she do?

A shadow flew over Angela's head. When she looked up, she saw a huge bird with white feathers flying in circles over the square. Its stylized shape and its gracious movements reminded her of a heron, with its big, bright, smart, black eyes, although she wasn't able to tell what kind of bird it was. It glided for an instant, grazing its long legs against the crown of the tree, flying up and then down. It headed towards Angela as if it wanted to attack her, grab her with its claws. Then it made a guttural sound, a loud screech that gave Angela goose bumps as she moved to the other side of the street to avoid the encounter.

A group of children accidentally hit her as they ran by. Don Ernesto Schmied's notebook fell on the ground and disappeared between their feet in a cloud of dust. Angela screamed and hurried to recover the notebook, pushing anyone who was in her way.

A little girl cried out as Angela attempted to liberate the book from under her little boot. Everyone in the square turned to the stranger kneeling and struggling with a seven-year-old girl.

Hundreds of eyes looked at her severely. Nervous, Angela stood up. She slapped the dirt off her pants, not oblivious to the hostile observers. The bird had disappeared. In the most friendly and graceful manner possible, she recovered the notebook, put it inside her pocket and stroked the girl's hair awkwardly. The girl cried even louder to keep attracting attention.

Two women and a man made their way through the crowd and approached Angela with unfriendly looks on their faces. Something told her to leave the place right away. She had witnessed how things in Almahue could get violently out of control and she didn't want to take any chances. She stepped back. Her muscles were tense and her heart beat erratically.

When she turned around, she saw another group walking towards her with confrontational attitudes. She tried to appear nonchalant, but that wasn't going to work. Nothing could change the fact that she was there alone, boxed in by the unfriendly people in the square. There was nowhere to run.

She clenched her fists preparing to defend herself for as long as her strength would allow. She estimated that there were over twenty people coming at her. Nature seemed to hold its breath, waiting to see what would happen.

The circle became threateningly smaller and smaller. "Stop!" someone suddenly ordered. The unexpected command made everyone halt in their tracks. Angela saw Walter Schmied looking very serious and composed. His mere presence dispersed the crowd. Limping on his right leg, he walked towards Angela. "Come with me," he said leaving no room for discussion. Angela had no choice but to take his arm and walk with him. The challenging eyes bored into the back of her head. Things were not settled yet between Angela and the people of Almahue. "I won't be able to walk in the streets," she complained anxiously as she realized that now it would be even harder for her to find her friend or a telephone to call her mother.

After the alarming episode with the villagers, she practically had no chance of finding allies who could help her locate Patricia. She felt Walter's reassuring hand pat her gently on the forearm.

She realized that she would have to trust her intuition and leave that place as soon as possible.

2 PEACE

Walter and Angela stopped in front of Rosa's house. A sign reading "La Esperanza. Handmade Rugs" hung directly above their heads. Angela took the set of keys that Rosa had given her on the day she arrived and opened the door.

"Would you like to come in?" she asked Don Ernesto's son.

He shook his head. With a nervous gesture, he looked at the façade. His eyes darted from the high pointed roof to the window frames. It was clear that he was overcome by hidden emotions. His eyes were moist and he had to turn so she wouldn't notice.

"Did you know that this is the oldest house in Almahue?" he asked, trying to make his voice sound as natural as possible.

"Yes, they've already told me. Here is where Rayen lived with her..."

"Those are old wives' tales!" Walter interrupted aggressively. "Is that why my father sent for you? To fill your head with his nonsense?"

Angela froze when confronted with the man's outburst. He then breathed deeply and continued as if nothing had happened.

"What did you discuss with him?"

Angela decided not to say anything about the notebook she had in her pocket. Apparently communication didn't flow easily in the Schmied family. Why would Walter want information about his father?

"I came to Almahue to look for a friend," she replied with her best smile. "And Don Ernesto offered to help me. That's why I went to see him."

Then she told him about Patricia's disappearance, about the video she had received, about her trip, about the few clues she had, and about how worried she was because her schoolmate didn't look good in the images she had sent.

As Walter listened to Angela, he shook his head in disbelief.

"We should act immediately! There's no time to waste! I will personally speak with the chief of police to form a search party. Don't worry about anything. Your friend will appear before you know it," he concluded with great conviction.

For the first time, Angela felt as though an important step had been taken to solve the mystery of Patricia's whereabouts. Excited, she hugged Walter, who patted her reassuringly on the back. She then asked him if he had a cellular telephone that she could use. When he nodded and handed her his phone, she smiled for the first time since she had come to Almahue.

"But I have to warn you that there's almost no signal here. I only use the phone when I travel, it's no good in Almahue... sometimes the only thing you can do is send a text message."

For her mother's sake, Angela decided it was worth trying. She wrote: "Hi, it's Angela, I'm borrowing a phone, mine fell down a hill! We're going to the mountains with Patricia's parents. I'm very well. I'll call you when we get back." This would allow her to be out of touch for a few days. Optimistic, she hit "Send" and prayed that the message would arrive at its destination.

"Thank you," Angela said with tremendous relief. "Thank you very much."

Walter puffed up his chest and nodded, taking on the posture of a hero who had won a battle. He said goodbye and walked away but then suddenly stopped. He turned back toward Angela and looked at her. He took a deep breath, hesitated for a moment, "My father... did he, uh... did he tell you anything about me?"

Angela didn't understand what he meant but didn't have the chance to ask. Walter came closer to her with fear and anger in his eyes.

"Whatever he said about me is a lie! Do you understand? After my accident, he changed with me. A lot!"

"It wasn't my fault... It wasn't my fault, dammit!" he exclaimed and he kicked a garbage can.

The tin fell on its side, spilling its contents onto the sidewalk and the street. Angela watched in silence. Walter didn't say anything about the garbage. He just looked at the damage he had done. He adjusted his scarf and his heavy coat. "Don't worry about your friend. We're going to find her," he said and walked down the street whistling.

~

Angela entered Rosa's house as confused as she was tired. Too many things were happening all at the same time. It was dark inside and everything was silent. The wooden floor creaked as she walked to the door of her room. She stopped dead in her tracks; the door was open. And she remembered having locked it before she left. Had Rosa entered to leave a set of fresh towels?

She pushed the door slowly, peeking her head cautiously through the doorway.

The first thing that caught her attention was a blast of cold air that hit her full in the face. Something had happened because the radiator usually kept the room warm.

Then she saw the damage. The window was wide open, the curtains flapped like flags in the wind. Her clothes were out of her bag and scattered on the floor, so were the sheets, the comforter and the contents of the armoire. Her backpack was lying under the bed, open and with clear signs of having been tampered with.

Angela was dumbstruck. It dawned on her to look for the book that Carlos Ule had given her. She couldn't find it anywhere.

Her suspicions were warranted. Someone was following her, someone who didn't want her to continue investigating. She looked out the window and was spooked by the scarecrow that seemed to be laughing at her with its stitched mouth.

She didn't have to think twice to understand what had happened. Someone didn't want her reading that book. She took Don Ernesto's notebook from her pocket and squeezed it tightly. She would have to be more clever, more astute and, above all, much braver.

"I'm not afraid! Did you hear that? I'm not afraid of you!" she furiously shouted to the outside.

When she heard the echo of her voice off the peaks that surrounded Almahue die down, she slammed the window shut. Only then did she allow herself to accept the fear that overwhelmed her, and she trembled from the challenge she threw at the wind... Someone would take her up on it.

3 FIRE IN THE FOREST

The night stretches into the forest, crawling along the ground while moving the dry leaves and turning the trees into darkness. The wind whirls between the trunks, whispering as it passes around the branches, shaking the foliage. The bonfire is not perturbed. It keeps burning in shades of black and red.

Every night, at the designated hour, nature salutes the woman who emerges from the shadows. She reigns over everything that surrounds her. Her loose hair blazes, her eyes are two bottomless wells that swallow whoever dares to look at her. Her feet drag the long roots that keep her upright. Her hand stretches forward. Something gets trapped between her fingers. It seems like a bird flapping its wings with the fury of nature. It's a book with green covers. On the cover, *Rayen* can be read.

The woman is silent. A flurry of images and memories collide inside her mind. The persistent European explorer searching for her, the persecution of the villagers, her beloved father's face, Ernesto Schmied's smile, Ernesto Schmied's hands, Ernesto Schmied's promises... The blood that still runs through her veins boils when she thinks of him, the world's greatest traitor. She lets out a loud, visceral cry of pain. She raises her arm above her head, the pages of the book shake in a last flutter of life. The book falls into the flames that embrace it, wrinkling each page until it becomes an unintelligible heap of ash.

The fire dies out. The night ticks on, until the new day forces it to go to sleep. The woman folds into herself. The wind is her loyal accomplice. It whispers news she hadn't heard.

When she learns the tree in the square has sprouted new leaves, her body begins to vibrate until it loses its shape. The situation is worse than she thought. The stranger is a threat who must be annihilated, as Benedicto Mohr before her. As she sinks her roots into the soil looking for nutrients and minerals to ease her discomfort, she closes her eyes in order to see him once more. "Ernesto Schmied," whisper the leaves in the forest. "Ernesto... Ernesto..."

4 FRAGRANT KITCHEN

After she straightened up her room, Angela decided not to say anything to Rosa about the strange robbery. If someone didn't want her to read Rayen, she was going to have to deal with that by herself. She didn't want to involve more people with her problems. It was already enough that Fabian was very ill because of her. She didn't want to make Rosa feel responsible for the theft.

She tried to think about something else. She was grateful for the fact that Walter Schmied had lent her his telephone. That calmed her down. It had been very smart to tell her mother that she was going to be with Patricia's parents for a few days in the mountains. Now she just hoped that her mother received the text message. "When you enter Almahue, you're going to go fifty, no, a hundred years back in time." Carlos Ule's words suddenly came back to her. The teacher wasn't exaggerating. She was overcome by a feeling of extreme isolation. She had never felt more alone.

Attracted by the noises she heard from her room, Angela went to the kitchen. The light hanging from the ceiling was on and Rosa moved hastily among the table, the wood stove, and a large basket of fresh vegetables. She had placed a large quantity of herbs, leaves, stems, and roots in her workspace.

"It's so good that you're here," Rosa said without turning to her. "Come, help me, it's getting late."

Rosa asked Angela to select a fresh sprig of rosemary, a final ingredient in the medicinal potion she was concocting for Fabian.

While Rosa was busy grinding a cinnamon stick by hand before it macerated in a cup of alcohol, Angela looked at the myriad of pots and containers that made up the herb garden. Rosemary? She wasn't exactly sure what it looked like.

"I'm going to make an infusion of lemon balm, rosemary, herb-of-grace, valerian and sarsaparilla," she said as she checked the kettle. "This will help Fabian manage his vertigo, the spasms, the palpitations, and the fainting spells."

"If Fabian is going to recover, he has to break Rayen's spell," replied Angela staring at the shelf.

Rosa was quiet for a few moments and then she sighed.

Rosa approached her and, with a kind gesture, asked her to step aside. Rosa extended her hand, cut a few long, delicate leaves that looked like pine needles, and went back to the table with them in her hand. She smelled her fingers and smiled, satisfied.

"I need a tablespoon of crushed rosemary, boiled in two cups of water. Did you know that it's very good for anemia?"

She continued explaining that lemon balm has a smell very similar to lemon and different from the herb-of-grace, that has a slightly spicy taste. Her hands moved quickly, cutting and energetically stirring while she warned that sarsaparilla was a powerful tonic but had to be administered by an expert because too much could cause violent vomiting.

The kitchen was filled with a thick steam that stuck to the walls and released its heavenly perfume. The enormous kettle bubbled on the burner while Rosa threw in the different leaves that she had skillfully crushed.

"May I ask you a few things about Fabian?" Angela said, overcoming her shyness about beginning such a conversation.

"What do you want to know about him?" Rosa answered dipping a spoon in the boiling contents of the pot.

Angela instantly regretted having brought up the topic. Merely having asked the question revealed her feelings. She also felt guilty about his state of health and was afraid that Rosa would react just like Elvira or perhaps like the other residents of Almahue.

As the conversation flowed, the skillful chef went over to a plant with a very slim stem and a bunch of blue flowers at the top. With a practiced movement, she uprooted it, exposing three tubers similar to carrots. She cut them with a sharp knife and put them in the sink to clean. Angela watched in awe, so sure and precise were Rosa's movements, it was almost impossible to believe she was blind.

"I don't know what you want to know, Fabian is the best man in the world," stated Rosa as she scrubbed the bulbs with a brush. "And I only want the best for him."

"And that's not necessarily to stay with me," Angela thought sadly. "He is condemned to die for love, and I will remember him for the rest of my life as something that might have been." Dejected, she looked for a place to sit down. Azabache left from under the table, looked her in the eye, and unlike other occasions, came close to her and rubbed against her leg. Even the cat was paying his condolences for the impossible love that afflicted her heart.

"These are monk's hood roots," Rosa said changing the topic abruptly, and holding the tubers. "I am going to mix them with saffron and aloe. It's a magnificent potion to protect oneself and repel bad spirits."

Angela asked herself why Rosa went to so such lengths to explain each of the procedures. Was she trying to teach her some of her skills?

"I need you to open the second drawer from bottom to top and bring me what's inside," she said.

Angela obeyed. She approached the cabinet and opened the drawer. Inside she found a spotless white linen napkin folded in quarters.

"Pick it up very carefully, please," Rosa said, solemnly.

As she held it in her hands, Angela realized that there was something between the folds of the cloth. It was light and sleight. Intrigued, she set it delicately on the table. Rosa immediately separated the four corners of the cloth exposing what appeared to be a wavy leaf of lettuce.

"This is chicory," Rosa said. "If you pick it before sunrise on the feast day of St. John the Baptist, and you say the right words, you will have a powerful amulet against diabolical snares and spells."

"Why are you telling me this?"

"Because all is not lost, Angela. I might be able to help Fabian and you might both have what you yearn for," she answered with complicity, her pale transparent eyes glittering. "At least for a couple of days."

Angela's jaw dropped, surprised by her words. Could it be that this thin and fragile woman was capable of overcoming *Malamor* by mixing herbs and chopping roots?

"I don't understand. If you can prepare potions to reverse Rayen's curse, why haven't you used it before?"

"Because I didn't have the most important ingredient of all. And now, for the first time, I do," she said. "May I have your hand?"

Angela held her arm out towards Rosa who gently took hold of one of her fingers. With an agile movement that left a metallic glint in the air, Rosa stuck something in her fingertip. Angela watched as a red drop flowed from her skin. Rosa guided her towards the boiling kettle and let the blood drop in.

"Thank you," she muttered while Angela put her finger in her mouth.

"My blood is the most important ingredient of all?" she asked, still astonished. "Why?"

"You are not yet ready to understand but I assure you that very soon you will understand everything. Trust me," Rosa said and she turned around, stirring the contents.

A knock on the door startled Angela. Azabache purred between her legs, raising its tail and stretching its front paws. Who could be visiting them at this time of the night?

"Just in time. Would you be so kind as to open the door?"

The cat walked next to her in the dark hallway to the front door. Opening the door, she came face to face with Elvira Caicheo. Neither one knew how to react. After what seemed like an eternity, Angela stepped back, clearing the way.

"Is Rosa here?" Fabian's mother asked.

Angela nodded silently, trying not to appear rude by looking her straight in the eyes. The woman entered with confidence, knowing that she was entering a friend's home. Her delicate and resounding footsteps announced her arrival to Rosa, who continued preparing infusions. After greeting her, the Schmied's cook studied the series of glass bottles of different colored liquids lined up on the table.

"This is the bugloss syrup," Rosa explained pointing at one of them. "It's good for heart palpitations. Your son needs to take a glass at bedtime. And this other one is an extract of alcohol and cinnamon. A couple of teaspoons are more than enough to control the fainting."

She then explained what had to be done with the chicory amulet. It should be well-protected and hidden in Fabian's bed, underneath the mattress where he slept every night. She had to make sure that the white cloth remained spotless. Rosa assured her that, with a little bit of faith, things would begin to improve. She also gave her the concoction of lemon balm, rosemary, monk's hood, valerian and sarsaparilla... a green juice that Fabian should drink in large quantities several times a day. Moved, Elvira thanked Rosa for each of the potions and carefully placed them in a cloth bag hanging from her wrist.

"Rayen isn't going to win this one," Rosa reassured Elvira, taking her hands into hers and stroking them. "Fabian is strong. Besides, now he has a reason to fight."

Upon hearing these words, Elvira turned towards Angela who was looking at them from the doorway, her fingertip still throbbing from the puncture.

The woman hardened her gaze and in two large strides came face to face with Angela.

"Get out of here, leave my son alone. Don't you see you're going to kill him?"

"Elvira... please," Rosa asked, trying to calm her down. "It's the truth, she has no business being here!"

"I came to find my lost friend. And I'm not leaving Almahue until I find her."

"The girl that was here a couple of weeks ago? If you want to know where she is, talk to Egon, Don Ernesto's grandson. I saw them together a couple of times. But leave my son alone or it will be your fault that we bury him!"

She hugged Rosa and kissed her goodbye on each cheek. She held the bag with the bottles to her chest and left the kitchen. They could hear her footsteps moving away down the hallway until she left the house with a slam of the door.

Angela was relieved that Rosa couldn't see her. Her eyes were full of tears and her chin trembled. She was so sad that she was on the verge of weeping. She tried to be angry with Elvira but deep down she knew she was right. Because of Rayen, Angela could be the executioner of the man she loved.

5 THE JOURNEY WITHIN

The first gulp burned his tongue. But, with complete faith in Rosa's abilities, he took another gulp, a larger one. It was his only chance to get out of bed.

"Careful, not so much!" warned Elvira, sitting by his side.

The young man felt the warm liquid running down his throat and into his stomach. An indescribable fragrance, a mixture of lemon and pepper, of roots and sugar, of cinnamon and alcohol came through his nose and filled his lungs. In an instant, his pores opened and he could feel a bolt of energy charging his heart. A wave of fresh blood made its way through his veins, causing a tingle in his limbs. A strong vibration like a drum roll lifted his back from the mattress. He could hear the sound of water running through the pipes in the house. He could hear the humming of electricity through cables and light bulbs. He opened his eyes and saw his mother's body turn into dry leaves that the wind blew away. All the dogs in the world howled and barked at the same time. Then he felt an upward thrust and he was floating in a pitch-black space where he didn't need eyes to see what surrounded him. His skin shined like gold, especially the skin over his heart, where a kaleidoscope swirled to the rhythm of the waving shapes. A ray of light ran towards him in the darkness. He could feel its warmth. From afar, the rhythmic beating of the drum droned on. He turned his chest to the yellow glow that penetrated his skin like a luminous dagger. He couldn't feel his body but lightning bolts were passing through his chest. Despite the darkness, he could see his heart, a small bundle of pulsating flesh that suddenly projected forward. It was covered in a thick and sticky layer of tar that leaked poisonous ink. Touched by the light, the dark matter began to melt, faster and faster, and it became thinner and thinner until his heart twinkled with the clear light of a newly born star. The color of the muscle was so intense that it blinded him momentarily.

Red. He was submerged in a vibrant red bath that cradled him like a newborn baby. It was blood, but not his; it smelled different, it tasted different. At the end of that scarlet ocean, a distant little spot grew bigger and bigger. Or was he approaching it? The light drew him in. He was going to take off. He was about to become who he used to be. He was coming home.

He opened his eyes. The furniture stopped shaking and everything around him went back to normal. He turned his head and saw Elvira's worried eyes. She was still holding the glass with what was left of one of Rosa's potions.

Fabian was sweating from head to toe, burning with the heat that came from his chest. He sat up. He was still confused. His heart beat with a new vitality. He thought about Angela and smiled. He waited for the stabbing pain but it didn't come. He remembered the kiss, the sweet smell of her white skin, the bewitching color of her eyes and he felt like laughing out loud, jumping out of bed and dancing in the moonlight. There was no trace of the weakness that had crippled his knees and squeezed his lungs, reducing them to broken and useless bellows. He felt full of love. He was experiencing something unknown and invigorating.

His mother didn't say a word. She left the glass on the night table and stood up. She could see the triumph on Fabian's face: it was as if he had been reborn. And, despite the immense joy that she felt knowing that her son was healthy again, she feared that Rayen now had a ferocious enemy, one who wouldn't stop until he defeated her and freed Almahue from its chains. She didn't protest when he asked her to leave him alone. She knew there was no use in contradicting him, so she leaned over and kissed him on the forehead. Then she left the room with a heavy heart.

Not knowing what else to do to stop a tragedy from taking place, Elvira Caicheo prayed for Fabian's life.

~

Angela covered herself with the comforter. She fixed the pillows under her head, moved her legs to warm the sheets and looked for a comfortable position to start reading. Before she had put on her pajamas and jumped in bed, she had taken the *The Legend of Malamor* folder out of her backpack.

School seemed so distant now, with its stone buildings. And, of course, she remembered Patricia. Where could she be? Maybe it would be better to forget about the research, go to the police, file a complaint, and leave the matter to the authorities.

But a deep and disquieting intuition warned her that she should go on looking for the truth of the curse of *Malamor*. Her instinct pushed her to review the history of the village, to go back to the moment when everything for Almahue went wrong. And when she found it, she was sure that Patricia would show up.

She only hoped that it didn't take her too long. She was running out of time.

The best way to avoid the melancholy caused by Patricia's disappearance and Fabian's ailment was to immerse herself in Ernesto Schmied's notebook, plunging deep like a scuba diver. Suddenly she felt a weight on her legs and the mattress was slightly shaken. Scared, she looked over the notebook and found Azabache's face staring at her from the foot of the bed. The cat turned around a couple of times and lay down peacefully, licking its paws.

"It seems I won't be sleeping alone tonight," she murmured in resignation.

She took a deep breath, sent a kiss to her beloved wherever he was and began reading the first line.

In that exact moment, an old man with a bald head, a prominent belly and a body curved to the front moved behind the scarecrow in order to spy on Angela through the lit window. The same window where she, on the other side, started reading a line that said "February 28th, 1939."

6 FEBRUARY, 1939

The woman's bare feet quickly run over the dry leaves. They skillfully avoid the obstacles along the way: some fallen branches, a narrow stream, and a couple of rocks with sharp edges. With just two strides they disappear, swallowed by the foliage. Other feet come after hers; they are a man's and they are shod in elegant ankle boots. Ernesto Schmied stops for a few moments, panting from the effort of the race. He leans his nineteen-year-old frame against the trunk of a tree and tries to calm the uproar of laughter and the fatigue in his lungs and heart.

"Now I'm going to catch you!" he shouts breathing deeply. "Besides, this isn't fair, you're barefoot and I'm in these stiff boots which were not made for running!"

Ernesto is in the middle of a clearing in the forest: a perfect circle of trees and lush vegetation. His blue eyes are blinded when the sun shines directly on them.

"Rayen, Rayen, where are you? Rayen!"

Nobody answers. Only the persistent murmur of leaves and animals hidden in the forest can be heard.

His heart skips a beat, frightened because he doesn't know the source of the buzz that surrounds him. In the distance, he can hear the sound of the ocean as it plunges into the fjord from which Almahue rises. He hears the song of the high foliage blowing in the wind, the crash of the branches that fall to the earth, rocks rolling down the hills only to be swallowed up by cliffs, the sand that is pushed to and fro by the ocean currents, the frantic flapping of the birds as they disappear in the clouds that graze the mountain peaks.

Pristine nature surrounds Ernesto, who feels like the first man in the world.

In order to hide the sudden tremor in his hands, he runs his fingers through the blonde tangle of his hair and tucks his shirt back in.

"Oh, I see... you want to play," he says with feigned naughtiness in his voice. "Very well then, we'll play. You want me to find you? Here I come!"

Ernesto enters the forest. Light is falling in diagonal columns, clearly delineated by the humid steam rising from the earth. There, inside the forest, the world is lush and green like the bottom of the sea. The enormous nalca leaves form an organic ceiling and ferns that look like octopuses with hundreds of tentacles brush his face and mess his hair. There is a constant hum of insects, thousands of wings and legs in movement.

"From the moment I met you, I knew that you were different from every other woman in Almahue. That's why I like you, Rayen!" he exclaimed. "Why are you hiding if we're alone? Where are you?"

Ernesto stops. He has heard something. Someone is walking behind him.

He turns around happily but his smile freezes in bewilderment. No one is there. Disturbed, he frowns. When he turns around again, he comes face to face with a young woman that cuts him off. She seems to have materialized from behind the veil of the afternoon light.

"Surprise!" she shouts.

Stunned, Ernesto instinctively steps back. The heel of his boot catches on a root and he falls to the ground on his back. He stays there among the leaves sticking to his clothes, watching her smile.

"I thought you were behind me. I felt someone walking up from the rear..."

"That's how I like you. At my feet," Rayen says taking a step towards him. And from above, she blows him a kiss and whispers, "I love you so, so much."

The young man invites her to lie down next to him.

Rayen smiles coquettishly, her eyes are full of reflections of honey and sun. A dimple on her cheek peeks out from behind her hair, wild as the tops of the trees that surround them. She kneels by Ernesto and caresses his face. Her hand smells of freshly cut grass.

"I have to go now. My father should be done already..."

"I'll talk with him, relax. Stay for just a few more minutes." Rayen stretches out next to Ernesto, who holds her. He buries his nose in the nape of her neck, savors her lips that taste of fresh fruit and her cinnamon colored skin that drove him wild from the first moment he saw her.

"You're never going to leave me, right?" she muses.

"Leave you? I'd have to be crazy. And there aren't any crazy people in my family," he says intensifying his caresses.

"I mean it, Ernesto... I don't want to have to flee from this village with my father. Not again..."

Ernesto doesn't answer. His mouth has found the seashell that is her ear and it stays there, enjoying this unexplored territory.

"I don't want to have to leave," she pleads.

"The Schmied's are the founders of Almahue. No one will bother you when they know you are with me..."

"I want to live forever among these trees, Ernesto. This is the place where I want to grow old, where I want to die!"

Rayen gets up, leaving him on the ground. She opens her arms and turns her face to the intense blue sky. A soft breeze blows, toying with her simple clothes and dancing with her tangled hair.

"I belong to the earth. My father is right when he says that we were born from the clay, from the sap of the trees and the plants. We don't need anything else to heal our bodies. We're nature's children! I feel it Ernesto...! I feel that this place belongs to me, that you belong to me. I feel it here...!" she exclaims, placing her hand on her chest.

A stronger gust shakes the foliage and moves the dirt that surrounds them. Ernesto shields his eyes from the brisk wind. He looks for Rayen among the dancing leaves but doesn't see her. Uneasy, he tries to lift himself but a voice coming from somewhere else, stops him.

"I want to live here...!"

He has to turn his head around to discover that she is at his right, much farther away than he remembered seeing her. How did she get there? She still has her arms open, her eyes closed and her face to the whirlwind that seems to surround only her.

"As soon as I stepped into this village, I knew I wanted to stay here forever! And the same thing happened when I met you, Ernesto!"

Rayen is like a sprite that flickers around the dense vegetation. The sounds of the forest become louder and louder, almost deafening. The sunlight has disappeared completely. Thick rainclouds close in over their heads, swollen by the water that will soon pour mercilessly down upon them.

"Even if I wanted to, I couldn't abandon you, my love! It's impossible to leave you or to let you leave me!" she shouts and her voice echoes off of each trunk. "I want to grow roots! I want to belong to a place!"

Ernesto tries to get up but the wind pins him down. The cry born in the thicket reaches its apex and becomes a groan from the belly of the earth. A violent shaking throws Ernesto on his back. He is unable to protect himself from what he imagines to be a violent earthquake. But suddenly, everything is quiet. The wind dies down and the whirlwind dissipates. Nature is again silent. Ernesto opens his eyes and discovers that Rayen is only inches from his face.

"You're never going to leave me; right?" she asks with a smile in her eyes and on her lips.

Ernesto looks at her in silence. He doesn't dare to answer.

~

Using a sharp scalpel, the botanist makes a small incision in the green flesh of the stem. A drop of thick white sap wells up and drains leisurely into the little ceramic dish. Karl Wilhelm nods in approval. This will be enough. Then he sets down his instruments and cleans his hands on his apron. With a finger, he adjusts the round glasses on the bridge of his nose and checks one last time. Everything is as it should be. The test tubes are in symmetrical rows, just like the flasks filled with different colored liquids and an endless number of small pots with flowers and plants of all sizes and shapes. An enormous microscope occupies a place of honor on his workbench. It is a modern metal contraption, painted white, with powerful magnifying glasses and several interchangeable lenses brought from Europe with great effort.

Three months have gone by since his arrival in Almahue, and although the community still doesn't feel completely comfortable with his presence, he is sure that will change very soon. He can be of great use to the newly founded village where there is still so much to do.

He walks to the window and slides the curtain a bit to the side, just enough to check that no one is spying on him. With a sigh of relief he closes it again. It just might be a better idea to cover it with wood, as his daughter had advised. Perhaps this would keep the curious at bay. He knows the rumors that things which defy nature are happening in his laboratory. But he is not going to waste time with gossip, nor is he going to defend himself from cowardly attacks launched behind his back. He will do the same as he had done when they surprised him collecting lichens in the alley, or when they found him high up in a tree extracting the pulp of an apple. He will smile innocently and be on his way without looking back.

He takes off his apron and puts on a heavy cloth jacket acquired in colder climates. He goes out to the street. Before beginning his regular afternoon walk, he stops for a few seconds and studies the house that he purchased at some expense. It is a two-story residence with a high pointed roof. It has recently been painted blue, allowing it to stand out from the exuberant vegetation that surrounds it. He nods in satisfaction. He is sure that this is a good place to raise his beloved daughter Rayen, the only woman in his life.

His steps take him to the central square, only a few yards from his home. It is packed dirt covered with moss and calafate. At its center stands a monumental tree with a robust trunk full of streaks that foretell a long and healthy future. Karl studies it for a moment. It's perfect. It is a work of art. And it's exactly what he needs to carry out his plan and win the appreciation of all of Almahue's inhabitants.

A group of women walk arm-in-arm towards the beach. Upon seeing him standing there by himself lost in reflection, they immediately stop. One of them nods a weak greeting and leads the others away from him. He hears them chattering as they move away.

"They say he has animals locked up in cages. And that he tortures them."

"My God! Something must be done about that!"

"I heard he was creating a plant that breathes and eats animals."

"He has no respect for anything..."

Karl Wilhelm silently watches them walk away. His situation is perhaps more complicated than he would like to admit. Outsiders always stir up suspicions and doubts among the locals, especially when they devote themselves to tasks that are barely understood. He might just have to act. Perhaps it's time to start going to church or to invite some officials to tour his laboratory.

~

The sound of galloping stirs him from his thoughts. Ernesto Schmied comes down the dusty road on his shiny horse. Rayen is seated behind him, holding onto his waist. She has the broadest and happiest smile that has ever been seen in the village. The botanist waves at them.

Ernesto stops the animal who whinnies when the reins pull up on its muzzle. She jumps to the ground to hug her father.

"I am so happy to live here! This place is marvelous!" Ernesto dismounts and greets Karl with a solemn nod of his head. "Mr. Wilhelm," he says respectfully. The man returns the greeting and turns to his daughter. "Are you ever going to wear shoes?" he asks her without any hint of reproach. "Never! I love to feel the clay, the moss, even the stones on my feet! It makes me feel alive!" The girl runs to hug the trunk of the tree in the square. She closes her eyes. The wood shares the secrets it has witnessed during the past years. She listens knowingly to the sap flowing below its deep wrinkles. Some passers-by whisper comments. Two women carrying a basket full of fish make the sign of the cross upon seeing her, scandalized and upset by the scanty dress that reveals her long, pretty legs almost to the middle of her thigh.

She returns to Ernesto, hangs on his neck and gives him a loud kiss on the cheek.

"I'll see you tomorrow, my love," she whispers in his ear. A pleasant shiver runs down his spine.

"Until tomorrow," he answers.

The young man approaches Karl and extends his hand in farewell. Once again the botanist adjusts the eyeglasses that have slipped down his nose and hugs him affectionately. For some reason he trusts this boy with his intense blue eyes and unruly hair who already carries himself like an adult. He is pleased that his daughter has chosen him. They both watch him mount his horse and gallop away.

~

That night, Rayen and Ernesto have the same dream. Both are playing in an enormous meadow of four-leaf clover. Now and then, they stop to look at each other with loving eyes and swear that they will never part.

The next morning, Ernesto wakes up with the certainty of having made a sacred decision, the confidence of destiny.

He doesn't know how mistaken he is.

~

He has to find the exact moment to announce his decision. With an anxious heart and a slight stitch in his gut, Ernesto takes Rayen to the lagoon, a crystalline reservoir that swells during the spring thaw and freezes in the winter. Upon arriving, she observes the place with wide eyes. The landscape celebrates the couple's arrival, dispersing the impertinent clouds and allowing the sun to shine. Before Ernesto can tell her what he had been thinking, Rayen takes off her dress and dives into the lake.

"Be careful! It must be freezing!" Ernesto shouts as he watches her disappear below the surface.

But she doesn't care about the warning.

After a few seconds, she surfaces with a glowing smile. Her skin glistens. Ernesto cannot remember anyone so audacious, much less nude. She is a formidable woman. She is different from every other one he has met in the boring soirees organized by his mother to find him a wife. None of them had captivated him the way Rayen has. None of them could stop the world from spinning with a smile.

After a few strokes, Rayen approaches the shore. Ernesto collects her clothes and runs to prevent her from getting chilled by the cool breeze blowing in from the snowy peaks. When he arrives, he averts his glance out of modesty. He has never seen a naked woman.

"Look at me, I know you like to look at me," she challenges as she slides the light fabric over her body.

Ernesto takes hold of her hair that is still dripping ice-cold water, and lifts it to expose the nape of her neck. He hugs her from behind, kissing her neck, licking each of the drops that twinkle on her skin. He gently turns her to look her in the eye. The hour is near. It is time to be brave and tell her.

"I want you to marry me."

Rayen keeps her eyes closed as if she hasn't heard her precious lover. A light wind blows along the shore of the lake, wrinkling the surface of the water and drying the girl's skin with its whisper.

"The more I think about it, the more I look for a reason to change my mind, the answer is always the same: I adore you Rayen. I want to grow old with you."

A couple of tears slide down her cheek and he hurries to wipe them away with a kiss. She embraces him tightly. Her thin arms squeeze him as strongly as those of a man.

"You're not toying with me...?" he hears the question in his ear.

"The Schmieds never lie, much less toy with something as serious as marriage! Some day I'll inherit my father's fortune and I want to offer it to you. I promise that you will have a good life with me, my love..."

At that point, the botanist's daughter steps back, pulling away from him. She opens her eyes, they sparkle like aquamarine. In their intense color, the boy sees the reflection of his own expectant expression.

"From the moment we met, my heart has been yours. I knew that we would become one from then on," Rayen says as she takes his hand and puts it on her breast. "I felt it here. Deep inside."

"But you haven't answered me yet."

"Of course I want to marry you!" Ernesto smiles, triumphant and relieved. He will be able to sleep soundly again.

He has taken the step that turns a boy into a full-fledged man. When he tells his father, he will be proud. Ernesto is sure he will approve his decision to settle down with such a special and unique woman.

Rayen celebrates. She hugs the trees. She falls to the ground and sinks her hands in the soil. She can't believe she is going to put down roots and have her own family in this far-away place. Her destiny is already written, although, unfortunately, it doesn't appear to be what they think.

~

Karl sets a ladder against the trunk of the huge tree in the square. He is wearing a spotless white apron with his name proudly embroidered in red thread. He has set his working tools on a folding table. Underneath the warm summer sun glitter a few knives, some different sized scissors, a flask filled with a whitish liquid, and a syringe with a very long needle. The botanist whistles a simple tune as he climbs a couple of rungs to reach the desired height, the exact spot where the trunk divides in two and extends upwards. There, it forms a crease in which the man begins to work. He uses a small saw to cut a vertical slit and then makes a horizontal cut. He climbs down the ladder and changes instruments. He uses a metal hook to pry out some of the bark. He pauses to wipe the sweat from his shiny forehead and dries his face to keep his round glasses, which constantly threaten to fall, in place.

His gloved hand delicately caresses the wound that he opened in the trunk of the tree; a small pulpy, humid triangle that begins to spill its sticky sap.

A group of passers-by has stopped to watch him. Speechless and curious, they stare at the odd fellow that goes down the steps and looks for a syringe. He checks to see that the needle is firmly attached. Then he puts it into the flask and with a single draw, begins to fill the glass tube with the thick white liquid. When he collects the necessary amount, he climbs back up to the hole he has opened in the wood.

"There, there, this won't hurt," he murmured affectionately. "Trust me."

With a quick and precise movement, he buries the needle in the center of the incision. Instantly the branches shake, detaching a few leaves that fall to the ground. Karl caresses the trunk as he continues to administer the liquid to the tree. When he finishes, he removes the syringe and replaces the piece of bark to cover his work. Now the sap must do its work and heal the cuts. Then no one will see a trace of the graft.

Suddenly, a woman's voice disrupts his concentration. "What do you think you are doing?" The botanist discovers that an angry woman with her hands on her hips is standing by the ladder. People who have decided to intervene surround her. He goes down the steps until he is face to face with her. He knows the type. He had already seen many of them. They are the ones who avoid looking at him in the street, or detour when they are on course to run into him at a corner.

"How can I help you?" he asks in a polite manner.

"If nature wanted crazy people injecting trees, it would have made them with skin and not wood," the woman bitingly blurted out. "What are you doing to the tree? Are you trying to kill it? By whose authority do you inject that tree, saw off its limbs? The tree is perfect as is."

"Nature also makes mistakes, ma'am."

"Miss!" she corrects and raises the tone of her voice, insulted. "And what you are saying is heresy. Our Father is the creator of the world and everything that surrounds us and only He can..."

"Excuse me, miss," Karl interrupts in the middle of her speech and calmly adds, "I have very important things to do."

"You offend God, closed up in that house. We've been watching you. You've never been to church. You have no wife, no family other than your odd daughter. You receive strange parcels. And now you think you can experiment on this tree -a creation of God- with impunity. Why should we allow it?" The woman's tone becomes measured, but her eyes belie her fury.

The botanist stops.

For the thousandth time, he slides his glasses up his nose and stares at her, serious and inscrutable.

Everyone has goose bumps. They cautiously step back, avoiding the eyes that hide behind the round lenses. Karl lifts an arm to the sky and points to the clouds that block the afternoon sun. His body tenses as if he was going to jump. And when it seems like he is going to scream at the top of his lungs, he tamely opens his mouth and says, "To be ignorant like the simplest creatures is the greatest offense that you can commit."

The woman huffs at the insult. Those accompanying her look at each other shocked by his audacity.

"Did you just call me ignorant?" she sputters.

"So it would seem," the botanist responds, his voice hardening.

Chaos explodes in the square. The residents confronting Karl Wilhelm all talk at the same time, attracting passersby who approach to get in on the gossip and rapidly add to the chants and the insults.

As the crowd surges, the scientist calmly begins to put his instruments away.

"This man is disgusting, just like his daughter."

"What do we even know about them? Why they don't want anyone to see what goes on when they are closed up in their house?" questioned another, his voice rising above the rabble.

"Heretics!"

"Sorcerer!"

Karl stops. It never takes much to get to this point. Very slowly, he turns to see who has called him a sorcerer. When he finds him, he just returns an ironic smile that curves his lips. When Karl Wilhelm confronts him, the six feet tall, pot-bellied man carrying a fishing net on his shoulders points at him with a shaking hand, not daring to get any closer than necessary.

"Yes! He's a sorcerer! I have seen him sniffing around the pier, collecting things in the middle of the night, surely to make his potions!"

Various people nod their heads and swear to have seen the same thing time and time again, but in different places in the area.

"And his daughter is a witch! I have seen her ride bareback, almost naked!" someone else exclaims.

"And if that were the case?" The botanist answers, inciting an even greater commotion.

The women shout, frightened. Some cross themselves while others, terrified, fall to their knees, bowing their heads. The fisherman throws down his net and wipes his eyes, drying the cold sweat that clouded his vision.

"You're going to leave the village. You hear me? You and your daughter have been warned! We are decent people. You don't belong."

"People who respect God!" shouts an old woman hiding behind the broad shoulders of the fisherman.

"Sorcerers! Sorcerers!"

As they all shout in unison, Karl closes his bag. Without losing his composure, he begins to walk towards his house, the oldest house in the village, he locks the door, and closes the living room curtains.

A roar runs through the streets of Almahue. He can still hear it from inside, better safe than sorry. As soon as he can take a break from his research, he will look for planks, nails and a hammer to barricade each window of his house, even though the villagers will take this as proof that he's gone crazy.

He holes up in his laboratory. The echo of the insults bounce off of whitewashed walls that smell of formaldehyde. In spite of the chaos he caused in the community, he smiles lightly with satisfaction. He only has to wait until spring for his work to appear in its splendor. And when this happens, the village will be humbled by his powers. These poor fools will discover that he twisted the arm of the mother of all living things—that he conquered nature.

And if they want to call him a sorcerer, let them do so.

For now, he would return their rudeness by laughing at their ignorance, with a hint of the magnanimity a god reserves for mortals. He caresses the back of his darling pet, a shiny black cat who purrs like a spoiled child, while it rubs against its master's leg.

7 TIME TO INVESTIGATE

When Angela opened her eyes the scarecrow was smiling back at her in the armoire mirror, somehow it was open again. "Have I been sleepwalking?" she asked herself as she jumped out of bed to slam it closed. She walked to the window and looked out at the garden, trying hard not to fix her eyes on the straw man with open arms and strange hat. She felt like he was spying on her. The morning sky was gray, like a dirty chalkboard, covering the sun and degrading it to an opaque and hazy light.

Closing the curtains, she saw the footsteps in the fresh mud. She brought her face closer to the window and saw that there were several tracks around the scarecrow. They all had the same shape. Some even reached the wall of the house very close to her window. Who had been spying on her last night?

She was gripped by fear. She felt vulnerable, exposed. She imagined a mysterious being stalking her at night, the same stranger who stole Benedicto Mohr's book. She checked that the window was still locked and that there were no traces of mud on the floor. At least, he hadn't entered the room.

She would have to anticipate her stalker's moves. The fundamental thing was to protect Ernesto Schmied's precious notebook. She saw it on the bed, opened on the last page she was reading before she fell asleep. Karl's story was awesome. As she was reading it, she felt she was there in February 1939, witnessing the moment when the botanist grafted the tree in the square.

Where to hide it? Angela pushed the night table to the side. Using the handle of her toothbrush, she plied a floorboard until it popped up on one end. She slid the notebook under the board, popped it back into place and returned the night table back where it was. No trace. Feeling more at ease, she put on her coat and went down the hallway to look for Rosa.

Angela found Rosa in her workshop, sitting quietly at the loom full of colored wool threads. She watched with admiration the speed and precision with which Rosa's delicate white fingers tied rows of knots, giving life to a new rug. Rosa was an artist, skillfully creating patterns and symbols of different colors. A rug that was hanging on the wall caught Angela's attention. She assumed it was on display, it didn't seem destined to be packed like the rest. It was brown, red, and black wool. At the center, it had a circle from which other circles and triangles of different sizes sprung. Some were crowned with crosses, arrows and other symbols that Angela wasn't able to recognize. It was very peculiar, totally different from the rest and not very aesthetically pleasing. Maybe that was the reason no one bought it, forcing the owner to hang it as a sample of her work.

"Good morning," Rosa said unexpectedly as she stopped working.

Angela entered the workshop. Azabache ran to her legs. She leaned forward to pet the cat's back, which curved with pleasure when she touched it.

"Did you know Rayen's father also had a black cat?" she asked Rosa. "I read about it in Don Ernesto's notebook."

"Of course I knew," Rosa said as she resumed weaving.

"Any news from Fabian? Have you talked with his mother to see how he's doing?"

"Fabian is about to knock," was all Rosa said. At that very moment his powerful knocking echoed through the house. Angela looked at Rosa in awe. Did she know Fabian was about to arrive or did she simply sense it? She decided not to waste time figuring out a logical answer. In Almahue, nothing seemed to follow sensible rules. She ran down the hallway followed by Azabache. When she opened the door, she came face to face with Fabian. He appeared fully recovered from the ailments that had almost killed him.

"You are alright!"

"Thanks to Rosa." Overcome by impulse, Angela held Fabian with all her strength. Her body reacted emotionally to him. She smelled the scent of recently cut wood, the forest and the cool air. She wanted to stay there, protected by the strong arms that embraced her. They looked at each other for an instant.

Angela remembered Rayen's curse and felt dizzy knowing that she was to blame for Fabian's pain. She pushed him away and stepped back. Azabache purred, announcing Rosa's emergence from the dark hallway.

"Don't worry. You may hug him. Fabian is now immune to *Malamor* thanks to the potions he drank."

Rosa's words surprised the young couple.

Visibly moved, Fabian walked towards Rosa and took her hands in his. He was not able to say a word. He could only give her a sincere and tender hug that the she humbly accepted.

"You must thank Angela who provided the only ingredient that was missing: a drop of blood from a stranger in love."

Angela's mouth hung open in astonishment.

Rosa had said the words "in love." It was so obvious that even a blind woman could tell. Angela felt so embarrassed that all she could do was to blurt out questions.

"Are you more powerful than Rayen? Could you make potions for everyone? Does this mean that *Malamor* has come to an end?" she asked without stopping to catch her breath.

"No," Rosa answered. "It's not that easy. The antidote only lasts for a few days and, in order for it to work properly, the person who drinks it must also be in love. Fabian is the only one that meets all the requirements."

Now it was his turn to react to Rosa's words. Despite his efforts to hide behind the shadows in the hallway, Angela saw the look on Fabian's face and a feeble twinkle in his eyes, those beautiful eyes that had been dark for so long. But, of course, he didn't say a word. Were they not going to talk about the kiss at the Schmied's? Did he want to keep his distance?

Angela saved the day once again by breaking the awkward silence.

"I need to talk to Egon Schmied. Could you take me to him?" she asked Fabian, who didn't dare look at her.

"What do you want with him?" he asked with a stronger voice.

"I need to ask him a few questions about Patricia. Is he home?"

"No. He is at the shipyard right now. I'll take you there." As they left the house, the cat ran after them. Angela stopped it.

"You're not going anywhere, Azabache. You stay right here with Rosa."

Angela handed Rosa the clearly bothered cat. She cradled it as she warned Angela.

"Be careful, Angela. You will face great adversity."

"How do you know?"

"I can see it. Please, be careful," Rosa replied with conviction.

Her intuition told her that Rosa was right. She only needed to remember the footprints by her window.

8 WALTER SCHMIED

"Tell me about Walter Schmied," Angela asked as she strode next to Fabian.

"What do you want to know?"

"I don't know. Tell me everything you know about him." Fabian blinked, putting his thoughts in order. After taking a deep breath, he began to speak. "Don Ernesto has a very bad relationship with his son. It's because of Walter's accident."

"When did it happen?" Angela wanted to know.

"Seven... eight years ago. He disappeared one day. By nightfall he hadn't come home. Silvia was beside herself. She went up and down the stairs crying hysterically and no one could calm her down.

Angela could easily imagine the stiff woman having a hysterical attack. She couldn't avoid a mocking smile although she felt guilty to take pleasure in Silvia's pain.

"Three days went by and there was no news about Walter. They had given him up for dead in Almahue. Then someone found his scarf in the forest. They organized a search party, I joined. We went to the mountain, following the route to the forest.

"And Don Ernesto?" she asked.

"He never left his room. He wasn't doing well at all. My mother stayed with him the whole time. He got so weak that we didn't think he'd make it," Fabian said without hiding the pain that his words caused him.

After a pause, he went on with his story. The search party scoured the forest until they discovered footprints, heavy work boots like the missing man wore and, without any other clues, they followed the path in the mud.

That's how they got to the cave. The footsteps ended at the other side of an opening in the mountain, a vertical fissure that had been caused by numerous earthquakes. Despite being the youngest of the group, Fabian offered to enter the cave first, carrying only a lantern. The air inside stunk of rot. He had to make a great effort not to vomit.

The rock ceiling forced him to tilt his head. He thanked the heavens that he wasn't claustrophobic, especially when the tunnel grew even narrower and his shoulders grazed the walls. The intermittent noise of water dripping in the puddles, the fluttering of bats' wings and the movement of rodents in the darkness didn't scare him.

After several yards, the light from his lantern illuminated a larger and higher vault. Hundreds of stalactites hung over his head. Frightened, he thought he saw red eyes by his feet. He imagined that a snake was coiled to strike and puncture his ankle with its fangs. But upon illuminating the place he realized that he stood before the dying embers of a bonfire.

"Someone was living there?" Angela asked, mesmerized by the story.

Fabian explained that, in the first place, he was puzzled to see the remains of the fire. Then he set about lighting every centimeter of the cave in search of hints that would help him understand. Suddenly, a hand appeared before his eyes. Terrified, he was relieved to see that the hand was attached to an arm, and the arm to a body. That's how he found Walter Schmied, unconscious on a pile of rotten leaves and surrounded by half-eaten fruit. He was covered in scabs.

"Help! I need help!" Fabian shouted.

After a little while, the men extracted Walter. After examining him, they confirmed that he had some bruises, as if he had fought with a wild animal. His right ankle had a compound fracture that had begun to fester.

"But I don't understand," Angela said with a frown. "If he had a fractured ankle why did he hide inside a cave instead of returning home? Or... did someone bring him there?"

"His were the only tracks," Fabian answered. "From the looks of it, he went into the cave himself."

"And what was his explanation?"

"He didn't remember anything."

Silvia fainted when she saw the sorry state he was in and Elvira went to the kitchen to boil water to clean his wounds. They put him in bed and Egon ordered that Dr. Sanhueza should be called. He arrived with his nurse. He set the ankle with a sudden pull that made the bones sound like a nut crushed by a stone and put a cast up to the knee. He examined one of the wounds and came to the conclusion that no animal had attacked Walter. There were no traces of tooth marks or scratches, only cuts made by some sort of knife.

"So, what was it then?"

Fabian shrugged his shoulders. "They never found out. The worst part was when Don Ernesto came down from his room to see Walter. Don Ernesto didn't recognize him. Can you imagine? He didn't recognize his own son," Fabian said raising his voice. "From that moment on, their relationship was strange, damaged."

He told her that the old man closed himself up in his room and never left again.

Walter Schmied was never the same either. He had sudden mood shifts and he didn't care to leave his house. Every time they lit the fireplace he began to shout and shake. When he became upset he was disoriented and spoke in a strange language that no one could understand. In fact, he was frequently very aggressive and exhibited superhuman strength. Little by little, he regained his composure and behaved as if nothing had happened, his injured ankle healed, but his limp was a constant reminder of the accident.

Suddenly Fabian stopped walking and turned towards Angela. "We've arrived," he exclaimed, pointing ahead at a gate that read "private property." Above them was a hand painted sign with enormous letters that read "Almahue Shipyard." There were two large structures built almost on the shore, and from the middle of one of them, a scaffold extended towards the sea like a pier. Several vessels were moored to the quay and beached shipwrecks were waiting to be repaired.

The hustle and bustle of the workers and the seagulls welcomed Angela and Fabian. The smell of the salt air and varnish intensified as they entered. They had to walk to the back of one of the buildings to find Egon's office; his closed door bore the word "Private" on it, painted in gold letters. Walking through the workshop, Angela saw the beams of a vessel that looked like the ribs of a giant wooden dinosaur.

"Come in!" they heard after Fabian knocked on the door.

Egon worked in a small, windowless room with a big desk that took up almost all of the space. The walls were covered with framed photographs of yachts, cruise ships, catamarans and different vessels, clearly an obsession for Walter's son. On a side table, there was an antique amateur radio surrounded by a collection of colorful ships in bottles.

Angela remembered that Carlos Ule had told her that, in case of emergency, there was a short wave radio in Almahue and, apparently, the manager of the shipyard was one of the operators.

Egon received them, peeking out from behind a stack of papers and invoices that he was checking unenthusiastically. Upon seeing Angela, he quickly stood up and passed his hand through his hair in a practiced gesture.

"Well, what a pleasant surprise!" he exclaimed as he approached Angela, who wrinkled up her nose at his intense cologne.

He greeted Fabian with a cordial but distant nod.

Angela tripped on something and had to grab Egon's arm so that she wouldn't fall. Her shoe had caught on the metal ring of a wooden hatch.

"That's the entrance to an old cellar. I'm constantly hurting my foot when I step on it. And to what do we owe this unexpected visit?" Egon asked showing a row of perfect teeth.

"I've come looking for information about Patricia Rendon," Angela said, getting right to the point.

Egon was silent. His face paled and he casually leaned on the edge of his desk to keep from falling. He had been so discreet. He thought that nobody had seen them. Where had he made his mistake?

"I don't know any Patricia Rendon, I'm sorry."

"You know very well who I'm talking about," she said to him, emboldened by the effect that her words had on him. "The best thing would be to tell me what you know about what happened to her. And the sooner the better."

"I think there's been some mistake..."

"Patricia was here a week ago and now she's missing." As Angela said this she confronted Egon, cutting him off when she realized that he was thinking about leaving the office. "You were seen with her a couple of times."

Egon took his cellular phone off the table and put it in his pocket. He ran his fingers through his hair one more time, not to smooth it but as a distraction.

"I'm sorry, but I am seen with a lot of women, Fabian here can testify to that. I hope you can find your friend, but I really can't help you. Now, I have a lot of work." Egon smiled beatifically and headed towards the door. Angela defiantly blocked his way. "I want to know where my friend is."

"I don't have any idea who this Patricia Rendon is, but I wish you all the luck in the world finding her. And now, if you don't mind, I really have a lot of things to take care of." Egon slid out of the office, vanishing in the rush of the workshop.

Angela turned towards Fabian, who stood mutely in the corner.

"He's lying," she angrily declared.

"How do you know?"

"Because he couldn't hide it. But don't you worry; this is far from over. Are you willing to help me?"

"You can count on me. What do you want to do?"

"Go to the Schmied's house."

They left the office, the overwhelming scent of Egon Schmied's cologne still clinging to their clothes.

9 HIDING PLACES

"You have to look for... whom... what?" Fabian asked. For every step he took, Angela had to take three.

"I don't know! I can't show you the message because my iPhone fell down a crevice during the earthquake the day they burned the witch, remember?" she answered as she sped up. "What matters is that, before she disappeared, Patricia tried to get in touch with me to tell me she was in danger. And the last thing she said was that I had to look for someone... or something. She didn't get to finish her message," Angela tried to sum up the best she could.

Fabian stopped. He remained silent for a few seconds as he rubbed his cheeks in the chilling wind.

"When we find out what Patricia meant we will know where she is," Angela concluded.

"The first thing we should do is to get your phone back."

"It's probably broken..."

"We will know when we find it, right?" he said, drawing attention to the obvious.

"How will your friend call you if you don't have your phone?"

"Not only that... I need to talk with my mother." Angela shook her head. She felt isolated. She started walking towards the Schmied's house.

It only took Fabian two strides to catch up with her and by the third stride he was ahead of her. "Is he really not going to say anything about the kiss?" Angela asked herself. "Is it possible that he is so tight-lipped?"

"The effect of the potion only lasts a few days," Angela remembered

Rosa's words as if they were a death sentence. If she wanted something more serious with Fabian they had to defeat Rayen as soon as possible.

"But, look at me thinking about all this romantic nonsense while Patricia is still nowhere to be found!" she reprimanded herself and hurried up.

They passed by the square, some people were still rejoicing over the new leaves on the tree. Angela heard them talk about the party they were going to organize to celebrate the miracle. After seventy years, a sudden sprout of life in a tree that only knew how to die was worth celebrating.

When they saw her cross the street, many looked at her, their faces reflecting disgust and disdain. They didn't want her in Almahue. They didn't trust her.

Feeling followed by more eyes than she wished, Angela reached Don Ernesto's house. Instinctively, she walked to the front door but Fabian signaled her to follow him. He pointed to the back door and motioned for her to keep quiet by putting his index finger to his lips. She nodded and followed him around the house to the kitchen door.

Fabian opened the door slowly, checked that there was no one around, and let her in. Pots bubbled on the imposing stove hinting at the delicacies to be served at dinner. There were several baskets full of potatoes and other vegetables and grains that Angela couldn't recognize but found very appetizing. She was distracted by a braid of garlic that hung from one of the ceiling beams. She stopped before a collection of jars with perfectly handwritten labels holding walnuts, almonds, pine nuts, hazelnuts, sesame, and a bunch of other nuts. She heard someone whisper her name.

Fabian was waiting for her in the hallway that led to the stairs. "We're lucky that no one is here. We'd better hurry up!" They went upstairs. Fabian stopped in front of a closed door and indicated that they had arrived. With her mind set on Patricia, Angela opened the door and entered Egon Schmied's room. The place was meticulously organized, sparsely furnished and decorated.

Several paintings of sail boats and nautical themes hung on the walls. The bed was narrow and covered with a down comforter that touched the floor. Under the window, there was an improvised desk holding a few books, a bronze lamp, and an old computer.

"An IBM ThinkPad 700C!" she exclaimed in awe.

Fabian turned around and nervously signaled to her to keep quiet. Angela nodded contritely and pointed to the heavy relic.

"My brother had that laptop back in 1998... Apparently Egon, besides being a liar, is old school."

She quickly concluded that there were not many hiding places in the room. Perhaps her urge to search his things was futile. What could Egon possible hide in a place with hardly any furniture and so few drawers?

"What are we looking for?" Fabian whispered. He wanted to leave the room as soon as possible.

Angela said that she didn't know but that they should search the drawers, under the mattress and inside the closet to see if they could find something.

"Something like what?" he asked again. But this time Angela didn't answer. Fabian shrugged his shoulders and looked under the bed.

Angela opened the closet door. A cloud of perfume hit her right in the face and she sneezed. The occupant knew no moderation. He probably used a half a bottle of perfume every day and his clothes had an intense and pervasive scent. She searched through his sweaters and pants. Nothing. Everything was in perfect order. No hint of anything out of place or suspicious.

The unexpected creak froze them. It came from the hallway, the sound of footsteps approaching them. Angela saw the terror in Fabian's eyes as he desperately looked for a place to hide. Stealthily, almost tiptoeing on the wooden floor, the couple stood with their backs against the wall. Angela felt Fabian's warm breath close to her ear and heard the pounding of his heart like a low drumbeat, warning them.

Horrified, they watched as the doorknob turned.

With a decisive movement, Fabian pushed Angela into the closet. She landed between the hanging clothes and a divider. She almost hit the back wall when Fabian rushed in and silently closed the door. They held their breath, trying not to make any sound. She felt Fabian holding her hand in a protective way. She wanted to kiss him but the circumstances didn't seem appropriate.

Through a crack, they saw Silvia Poblete enter the room. Egon's mother walked to the center of the room, raising her brow, scanning the place with a severe look. She approached the bed, put one of the pillows in its place, ran her hands over the comforter to smooth it, aligned a couple of books, moved the lamp a half an inch, and centered the computer. When she finished, she nodded, pleased.

Then she looked at the closet door. Inside, the intruders intuitively stepped back as she approached. The owner of the house stood in front of the closet. Bothered by the crack that partially revealed the inside of the closet, she held the knob. She was about to open the door when she heard Elvira, "*Señora Silvia...!*"

The woman stood still. Then she turned around and saw the cook peeking through the doorway.

"Could you come with me for a moment? I would like you to taste the rice."

"Why? Is it too salty again?" Silvia answered testily. "For God's sake, Elvira! Lately, I have to supervise everything you do..."

With a slight but audible sigh, the sole purpose of which was to show how upset she was at being interrupted, Silvia walked back to the hallway. Before closing the door behind her, she took a last look at her son's room. Angela and Fabian started breathing again. They felt they had aged a hundred years. Carefully, Fabian opened the closet door and peeked out.

"Let's get out of here, *now*." Angela was about to admit that was a fine idea when something caught her attention. There was a metallic shimmer on the floor of the closet, a small shiny surface that caught the light. She leaned over the shoes and boots. Her fingers got hold of a cellular phone. Her heart skipped a beat. It was a brand new Motorola. She had no doubts.

All of the blood drained from her face. She looked at Fabian terrified. She couldn't say a word.

"What's wrong?"

"This is Patricia's telephone," she whispered. "It's my friend's telephone!" She turned the phone on but the battery was very low, with only one bar lit.

With trembling hands she went to the Outbox. The last dialed number was hers. And there was the video message. She pressed "Play" and held the screen in front of Fabian's eyes.

"Angela, it's horrible! Horrible! You have to help me! Please! Please! Come save me, I beg you! You have to look for...!" Patricia cried once more.

Fabian was paralyzed for an instant. He tried to make sense out of what he had just seen.

"This is worse than I thought," was all he could say.

"I knew Egon had something to do with her disappearance. I told you. That reeking idiot lied to me!"

"We have to go to the police."

Angela was going to put the phone in her pocket but she had an idea. She turned it on quickly again and entered the multimedia folder. She chose "Pictures." Fabian watched her pressing the buttons quickly.

On the screen, she saw the list of the last photos taken by her friend. There were views of the mountains, a panoramic view of the fishermen's wharf, and a photo of Egon with a big smile. Angela chose one, a selfie of Patricia standing by the scarecrow in Rosa's garden looking directly to the camera. With her other arm she was signaling to the scarecrow pointing directly to its heart.

"Why? Why?" Angela wondered. "Come with me," she told Fabian, putting the phone in her pocket. Fabian held her by the arm and stopped her. Now he was as pale as she was. "Do you see it?" he asked. "Egon!"

"I don't get it," Angela answered. "You have to look for... Egon!" he said in a low voice. Angela rushed down the stairs with Fabian.

When they got to the parlor the front door opened and Walter Schmied walked in, wearing his scarf, whistling and letting in the afternoon cold. He smiled when he saw Angela.

"Where have you been? I'm so glad to see you! I just organized the first group of men to search for..." he managed to say before Angela ran by without even looking at him and rushed out the door, followed by Fabian.

Angela ran, oblivious to the frozen puddles on the ground and the people yelling insults at her. She didn't mind that her lungs threatened to collapse from the effort of breathing the frigid air. She had just realized that she was more scared than relieved having found Patricia's phone in Egon's closet.

And she was also thinking about the scarecrow.

10 THE SCARECROW

It was completely dark when Angela returned to her room. She was sweating in spite of the cold, and she had to catch her breath after her sprint. Fabian had returned with her to Rosa's, but he was unfazed. "Either he is in great shape or the potions prepared by Rosa are more powerful than I thought," Angela said to herself as she walked to the window. She opened the curtains. Outside, the twilight outlined the silhouette of the scarecrow.

There it was, waiting for her.

She turned to look at the armoire door. It was open again, reflecting the effigy that no longer struck her as dangerous or hostile. It had become an unexpected ally in her search.

"Listen to me, we have to go to the police!" Fabian kept repeating. "Now!"

But she didn't answer him. She was too busy unlocking the window. With a decisive movement, she opened both panes. The freezing wind entered the room, messing up her hair and overcoming the feeble warmth produced by the heater.

As Fabian looked on dumbfounded, Angela jumped up onto the windowsill. She sat there for a brief moment with her feet hanging outside. Then she hopped down, falling onto the frozen mud, the footsteps from whoever was spying on her still visible.

Fabian followed her out, even though he didn't understand why they weren't already at the police station. Considering the strange things that were going on in Almahue, he wasn't about to let her go to the end of the dark garden by herself. No one had ever disappeared, much less a visitor. As soon as the sun came up, he would go to the police station to alert Lieutenant Orellana that Egon Schmied Poblete had kidnapped Patricia Rendon.

And, if he didn't believe him, he would show him the video message.

Angela came face-to-face with the scarecrow, surprised at how much larger it was than appeared from the window. She took Patricia's telephone out of her pocket and looked at the photo again. Patricia was definitely pointing to the scarecrow's heart.

"Help me!" she thrust the phone into Fabian's chest.

Angela used both hands to search through the scarecrow's old shirt. She found a hole, inserted her finger and ripped the fabric to get at the straw. She plunged in her arm practically to the elbow, feeling the hard stalks of the stuffing scratch her skin.

Fabian took her by the shoulders and gently pushed her aside. "Let me try? My arm is longer." He rolled up his shirtsleeve and buried his arm in the hole that Angela made. "What are we looking for?" he asked.

"I don't know... I don't know!" she answered sincerely.

A piece of paper grazed Fabian's fingertip. He squeezed his lips together and buried his forearm a bit more. He extracted a sheet of notebook paper that had been folded in quarters.

"A message from Patricia," she said with an overwhelming certainty that surprised even her.

Fabian shone the light from the phone onto the note. As soon as she unfolded it, Angela recognized her friend's handwriting: big strokes and capital letters. It was obvious that it had been written hastily, and that the strokes were shaky.

KARL WILHELM CAVE

Angela frowned. She should have finished reading the rest of Don Ernesto's black notebook. What was Patricia trying to say? When she turned the paper over, she discovered a sketch of a map. A cross marked the beginning of the route. Underneath it she read "Almahue." A straight line continued to the north and ended at another cross underneath which read "Forest." From there, another section, this time to the right, indicated different landmarks along the road until it arrived at a final destination marked by five bold letters: "RAYEN."

"I need two favors from you," she told Fabian, straining her eyes to see him in the darkness of the moonless night.

"Whatever you want."

"Tomorrow, when Egon has gone to the shipyard, steal his computer." And, before he could object to the dangerous request, she added: "You're going to bring it here because we are going to use it. And then you'll come to the forest with me. Let's see what we discover if we follow the map."

Angela gave a couple of thankful pats to the gutted scarecrow and they went back into the house. That night, Angela had an inescapable appointment with Ernesto Schmied's black notebook.

11 UNDERGROUND

She was shackled. The metal manacle was wide enough to cover her entire left forearm. A short heavy chain held her to the wall. There was no way to escape.

She had lost track of the time she had been held. She couldn't tell the difference between day and night and she was no longer able to feel her body rhythm. The hours went by in eternal darkness. The only window to the outside world had been bricked up. Her cell was a small rectangle very close to the ceiling, she assumed she was in a basement.

Her eyes were closed most of the time. The air was stale from having breathed it over a thousand times. Fresh air came only in those brief moments when the door opened and light flooded the tiled shallow room. The short chain that held her close to the tile wall prevented her from turning around to see her jailer. The light only lasted for the duration of the visit. The jailer didn't say a word, didn't touch her and didn't bring her food either. The jailer stood in silence for a few minutes then left through the same staircase. Once the door was closed, she was covered by darkness again. Only a faint yellowish line illuminated the wall, a ray of light that came from above. She imagined it coming from the bulb that lit the way to the basement. Then the faint light also went out. Her captor was gone.

She didn't want to admit it, but she was beginning to lose all hope. There was no use in fooling herself much longer. She was sure that the news of her disappearance had caused a little scandal among her family and her friends. Her parents had probably flown from Concepción to Santiago to talk with the police, but no one would come to the end of the world that had become her grave.

She had only one chance, and it was remote at best: that the video message had reached Angela. But the signal was very weak and she had no time to check if it was delivered to the number she had entered by heart with a shaky hand. No sooner had she pressed the "Send" button than she felt the blow on the back of her head and lost consciousness. When she opened her eyes again she was already in that place where she could barely see her hands.

Patricia was scared. Very scared. She couldn't understand what she had done to end up a prisoner, buried alive in a basement with no food or water. Screaming was in vain. After shouting at the top of her lungs for endless hours she realized that no one was going to hear her. She was alone, totally alone.

But the worst part, worse than the painful grip of the manacle, the uncomfortable position she had to sit in, the cold and rough floor and the spasms caused by the hunger and the fatigue, was the memory of having betrayed her best friend. "What goes around comes around," she thought.

She tried to fall asleep in an effort to evade the guilt and the fear for a couple of hours before waking up once more in a nightmare.

12 SEPTEMBER, 1939

*E*rnesto Schmied spurs on the horse. His eyes are fixed on the distant horizon, blooming with the arrival of spring. He likes to ride his horse full gallop along the nearby valleys when the setting sun seems to light red and violet flames on the glaciers and the perpetual snows on the hilltops. He saddles his horse and chases the shadows of the twilight. He feels free. Accompanied only by his horse, on these long rides he thinks about important things. Some day, the Schmied's only heir will inherit his father's livestock business: more than two thousand head of cattle and already worth a fortune. Modernity is coming for the big cities, and he is not going to let Almahue be left behind. Ernesto knows that the time has come to show that the investment in his education was not in vain. A few months shy of his twentieth birthday, he has to start a family and assume the responsibilities his father, now old and weary, is about to pass into his hands.

Rayen. The power that she exerts over him is impressive. He fell at her feet the moment he set eyes on her. He spends days on end chasing the echo of her laughter. He treasures her caresses. He could recite by heart every loving word she has said to him. She will be the mother to his children, the grandmother of his grandchildren.

Nonetheless, something has undermined the courage he needs to tell his parents about his decision. Every time he is about to tell them that he wants to ask for the botanist's daughter's hand in marriage, the premonition of an outright rejection makes him flinch. He tells himself that he will find a better moment to declare his intentions. But seven months have already passed and *his fiancée is beginning to lose patience.*

"Have you spoken with your parents?" she asks as they take a walk on the beach.

"Not yet. I haven't found the right moment..." Ernesto confesses.

The young man spurs on the horse again. The sun hangs on the transparent line that separates the ocean from the sky. He relives his last encounter with Rayen. She didn't say a word after his admission. She simply let go off his hand and began walking ahead of him. He fixed his eyes on the frigid ocean, small islands and noisy seagulls.

"Please, understand," he begged. "My father has been very busy with the family business. Did I tell you that he is going to build a shipyard?"

But she doesn't want to understand anymore, much less excuse her lover's hesitance. Ernesto comes near her and holds her in his arms.

"A Schmied will always keep his word. I will talk to my family, and to your father too. Don't be scared. I'll never abandon you."

"I want a beautiful wedding."

"And you will have it. Trust me."

"I want us to marry in the forest!" Rayen exclaimed, breaking his embrace and smiling radiantly at him. "I want us to marry under these trees, on this bed of leaves, surrounded by nature."

Ernesto remained silent. He knew that was impossible. He imagined his mother's reaction when she heard such a proposal.

"Why are you looking at me that way? What did I say?"

"Nothing, nothing. Go on..."

"Promise me that we will get married in the forest! Isn't it a wonderful idea?"

"Coward," Ernesto tells himself.

"You are a coward." He holds the reins tightly. The horse pants with him as they lose themselves in the shadows of the end of the world. He pictures Karl Wilhelm's face silently nodding, agreeing with every word his daughter says, his elusive eyes hiding behind his round glasses. Who was that man? Could he get along with his father, the authoritarian and conservative patriarch? They were so different.

"When are you going to talk to your family?" Rayen asked once more.

"Soon..."

"When?"

Ernesto shakes his head trying to hush the unanswered question. "Coward," he repeats to himself. "Coward, coward, coward" he goes on until he and his horse disappear into the night.

~

The horse heads for the Schmied residence at the end of a dirt road, a three story house with inclined roofs and well-kept windows and gables. The wooden walls are painted yellow while the doorframes and the fence surrounding the garden are white. The day they christened the house, Otto Schmied, Ernesto's father and one of the first Europeans to arrive in the region, expressly requested that no one ever change the color. A round window at the apex of the roof, like the eye of a Cyclops overlooking the village, is one of the few modern touches.

Ernesto ties the horse and cleans his boots before entering the house. He walks into the elegant foyer. A chandelier hangs over his head dappling its delicate light on the space. He is about to climb the stairs when he hears a woman's subtle laughter in the living room. "We have guests," he thinks. He walks to the door of the living room but halts when he hears his mother's voice.

"Yes, my son is turning into a very attractive man."

"I saw him yesterday riding his horse," says a voice he doesn't recognize.

"Ernesto loves horseback riding."

"He was with the daughter of the sorcerer. Both on the same animal," the guest finished up reproachfully.

Ernesto pushes the door open with the intention of putting an end to the conversation. The unexpected creaking of the door forces Mrs. Aurora Schmied, his mother, and her guest, a big woman with generous, rosy cheeks, to stand up.

"Good evening," the young man said bowing his head. "Look at yourself, Ernesto," Aurora reprimands him as she kisses him. "I'm sorry. I was riding my horse," he says as he straightens his hair with his fingers and tucks his shirt in. "Do you remember Filomena Mora?" Aurora asks as she turns to her guest. "And her daughter?"

Ernesto turns around and sees a young woman staring at him from the other end of the room. No sooner do their eyes meet than she lowers her head in a gesture of modesty and respect. In her eyes, nonetheless, a flame of admiration for the young man burns. She is wearing an elegant navy blue dress with a high neck. Her arms are covered with a shawl. She wears her hair back in a low bun. Her whole body denotes repression and lack of liberty, a sharp contrast to Rayen, who exudes freedom from every pore.

"Good evening, miss," Aurora's son greets her flatly.

"Her name is Clara," Filomena cuts in the conversation and knowingly nudges Aurora.

Clara bows her head and clutches her shawl closer. Ernesto understands what the young woman is doing there. His parents are thinking about a match for him.

"I'm going to clean up. I'll be back," he says and exits the room.

Aurora gestures to Philomena to wait a moment and goes after him.

"Is it true that you know the sorcerer's daughter?" she asks with a trembling voice. "I heard that you have been seen together more than you should."

"The sorcerer's daughter, as you call her, has a name: Rayen," Ernesto answers sternly.

"No one with a name like that can come from a decent family. I don't want you to see her again," she orders.

"Mother, I am an adult," he says without raising his tone.

"But you still live in this house and you're still my son! I don't want you near that woman."

They remain silent for a moment. The chandelier sheds its fragile light on them. The distant gong of the grandfather clock strikes half past eight. It is time to serve dinner.

"I don't want to talk about this anymore. Or do you want me to ask your father what he thinks of your friendship with that person?" His mother finishes up holding him by the arm.

There is nothing else to say. She puts a stray lock of hair back in its proper place, along with a vapid smile, the rigid mask of a high-class woman who always appears in control. She pats her son on the shoulder.

"Go get cleaned up. We'll wait for you," she says and hurries back to the living room where Philomena and her daughter await.

Ernesto climbs the stairs two at a time, his temples pounding. He enters his room and slams the door. His eyes burn from the indignant tears he has been holding back, from the anger that runs through his veins. He goes to the window and looks outside. A perfectly full moon shines in the sky: a white dish on an immense black tablecloth.

"Rayen."

He can see her hair blowing in the wind; he can hear her laughter at the sight of any little wonder in nature.

"She only wants to put down roots," he says to himself. "I love her," he sighs, and his breath leaves the trace of his words in the window.

He is sure that the sun will never rise again for him. From now on he will live an eternal night. "Coward. You are a goddam coward." And he falls on the floor all curled up like a child that doesn't want to wake up.

~

"Witchcraft!"

There is a commotion around the tree in the square. Everyone points at the branches. Some cross themselves and cry, others put their hands to their mouths and look away. They are scared and they can scarcely believe their eyes.

Clara Mora makes her way through the crowd. When she reaches the center of the square she wraps her woolen shawl closer.

"We all saw him ruin the tree!" a woman leading the crowd cries out.

"Yes! He injected something in its trunk!" another woman adds nodding after each word.

"He is a sorcerer! There's no doubt about it! He and his daughter must leave the village right now!" exclaims an old lady, turning to Clara for approval.

"How I wish they would leave Almahue!" Clara says to herself. She wouldn't have to see her running barefoot on the beach, chasing seagulls or riding with Ernesto to the forest... always laughing... so vulgar, so immodestly dressed. The best thing for everyone in the village, especially Clara, would be for Rayen and the botanist to pack their belongings and leave forever.

"They must leave! They must leave right away!" she shouts with conviction.

All heads turn to her. Many praise her boldness and applaud her vehemence. Clara, who is barely seventeen, feels the rush of the crowd's approval. She is the youngest person there, and the only single girl who could marry the Schmied's son. She has a lot to lose if the outsiders stay. With that in mind she finds the courage to lead the commotion.

"We don't know what they did to the tree, what could they do to us? How much evidence do we need that they break from the natural order?" she asks, her eyes wide open and her arms outstretched to add a dramatic flair to her question.

Her words have the desired effect. Panic spreads through the crowd. Some embrace the person next to them and others pray out loud. The leaves of the tree rattle. Clara feels the energy of the mob coursing through her veins. The realization of her power in the crowd is shocking, and fuels her conviction.

"We don't know what they want, do we? It is not to live in peace, that much is clear. It is not to live by God's plan, they have said so themselves, and we see the fruit of their separation from God before us. I fear for the children of the village, that they should be forced to bear witness to these heretics, to be forced to live among them. I believe we should act on God's authority!"

The result of her harangue is far better than she expected. Dozens of voices unite in a single battle cry that shakes the main street from north to south, deciding the fate of the botanist and his daughter.

Clara allows her hair to be undone by the September wind. No one is going to judge her modesty under those circumstances. On the contrary, whatever she does will be praised by the growing mob desperate for a sign to assault the Wilhelms house.

Ernesto Schmied appears on horseback amid a cloud of dust. Upon seeing the mob, the young man rides to the square at full gallop. He frowns. He has a bad feeling about what is going on. He stops and makes his way through the crowd until he reaches Clara.

"What is going on here?"

"Look at what that sorcerer did to the tree!" Clara points furiously.

Ernesto looks up and for an instant feels the earth under his boots melt into water. It is not possible. His eyes must be deceiving him. Magnificent bunches of apples, oranges and pears hang from a single branch. Perplexed, he shakes his head. Rayen. Where is his Rayen?

"If God wanted a single tree to bear different kinds of fruit, he would have provided for it!" a man shouts as he approaches Ernesto.

"Witchcraft!" a woman concludes joining the crowd, firmly holding a rosary between her fingers.

"This is botany! There's no sorcery here, it's just the work of a scientist!" Ernesto tries to explain knowing that anything he says will be totally useless.

The crowd doesn't want to listen.

The botanist has gone too far. The number of people gathering in the square multiplies. A few crude weapons can be glimpsed in the hands of some villagers.

"This is the devil's work! We must throw the botanist and his daughter out of this village!" someone shouts.

Ernesto is desperate. He opens his arms trying to hold back the human wave that floods the street towards the Wilhelms house.

"Rayen and her father have the right to live wherever they want!"

But no one is listening.

The angry footsteps leave tracks in the mud. Ernesto knows that he has very little time. He manages to get to his horse, who breezes through the few streets that lead to their destination.

In front of Rayen's house, Ernesto jumps off and runs. The rabble approaches. He starts banging a window hastily covered with boards.

"Rayen! Rayen! Open the door! You and your father must leave! Rayen!" he screams at the top of his lungs.

The front door is ajar, he enters and locks it behind him. The hallway is very dark. He gropes around for a chair to block the door. A cat's meow startles him. When he turns around, the animal arches its back in the dark, its big yellow eyes wide open and alert.

"Rayen! Rayen!" he shouts as he runs to the bedrooms followed by four very quiet legs that move silently across the floor.

Stumbling through a door, he lands in Karl Wilhelm's laboratory. He scans steamy test tubes, burners, the monumental microscope, and the sharp, shiny instruments identical to those used by surgeons. On the table by the boarded window is a long row of pots with plants he has never seen before. Huge petals that open and close looking for insects, robust stems that puff up to the rhythm of a vegetable breath, serrated leaves that could cut a piece of meat, and floating pistils that follow moving objects.

Ernesto is paralyzed at the sight of these creatures of formidable colors and unsuspected proportions planted in small clay pots. A sudden touch on his shoulder startled him.

"What's going on?" It is Rayen's voice.

He turns around and she jumps in his arms. He holds her tightly against his body, feeling guilty for being such a coward, for his inability to stop the crowd.

"You and your father must leave Almahue! Now!" Ernesto says catching his breath.

"Why? What is happening?"

Breaking one of the boards that shuttered the window, a rock falls at their feet. Rayen, terrorized, screams. Ernesto takes her by the arm and pushes her under a table to protect her.

"We don't want witches in this village!" the crowd yells from outside. "Go away!" "Get out of here!" Ernesto manages to get under the table right before a new volley of rocks hits the windows. From his hiding place he sees beakers, test tubes and flasks destroyed. Meowing wildly, the cat dodges the onslaught. Rayen grieves when a plant falls off the shelf. Its leaves shake in agony until a whitish liquid exudes from the folds of the petals. The mob is outside the house, frantic and delirious. One of the burners falls on the floor. Its small flame sets fire to a curtain. The fire grows, forming voracious tongues that lick the ceiling.

In that very moment, Karl Wilhelm enters what used to be his laboratory. He stands in the middle of the room, his glasses balancing on the tip of his nose, his arms hanging uselessly at his sides. The smoke blurs shapes and distances. Rayen coughs. Ernesto takes her in his arms and runs frantically to the door, screaming at her father to follow him.

But the botanist is paralyzed. The last thing Ernesto sees is a flame approaching bottles of alcohol on a shelf. When they explode, Karl Wilhelm disappears, engulfed by the inferno.

Ernesto runs away from the house as fast as he can, holding Rayen in his arms. Her eyes are shut. She has fainted. Ernesto enters the forest seeking the shelter of the trees to shed their protective and benevolent shadows over them. From there he can see the smoke and he can hear the voices of the frantic crowd, now trying to put out the fire that threatens to consume the house. Rayen's chest moves slowly up and down. Ernesto puts her listless body on a bed of dry leaves. He wants to cry, he wants to bang himself against the trees, to feel that at least he is atoning for his inability to stop the violence. He knows his family is looking for him and that things will get more complicated if he disappears. But, what about Rayen? What about the life he had offered her? What will she do now? He wipes the dirt off his face with the back of his hand. He can hear the distant shouts from Almahue, the church bells tolling to announce the tragedy. His father must know by now. He is probably down there, with his people, extinguishing the fire.

Cradled by the humus that covers her like a lace blanket, Rayen remains motionless.

"I am sorry, my love. I am really sorry. I am a coward and cowards have no choice."

Ernesto Schmied then runs as if his life were at stake, dodging trees, stumbling, falling down and getting back on his feet, yelling insults to himself, swallowing his tears of impotence and anger. "Coward, coward, goddam coward!" The echo of his words resonates in every rock, every leaf, every cloud, and every creature that dwells in the forest. A coward is swallowed by the landscape.

13 NOTHING IS WHAT IT SEEMS

"Karl Wilhelm. Cave. Karl Wilhelm. Cave. Karl Wilhelm. Cave." What did Patricia mean by those three words hidden in such a way that only Angela could find them? Why did she use a trick they had seen in a movie? During their summer vacation, they had seen a movie, a moderately entertaining story of adventures and explorers. At the climax, the hero hides a valuable map inside the clothes of a mannequin and sends a text message with a photo pointing to its exact location. Patricia thought it was a great idea and, for the next few hours, she mentioned several times that if she ever had to hide something valuable she would do it that way. In the movie, a murderous gang of emerald dealers wanted the map and were chasing the hero. But who was chasing Patricia?

As morning poured in through her bedroom window, Angela woke up energized. She had decided to hide Patricia's cell phone under the night table, next to Ernesto Schmied's notebook. She had already checked all the photos and messages and was reasonably sure that it held nothing else of use. She left it on top of the black notebook that she had read late into the night.

She imagined the botanist's laboratory in flames and shuddered. "So that's how Rayen's father died, in a fire set by the intolerant people of Almahue," she said to herself.

"Where was Karl's laboratory?" she wondered.

It had a window to the street, not to the back yard like hers. From what she saw, the house was professionally and expertly remodeled. She couldn't tell what part of the house had burned down. She was anxious to know how the story ended but now she had other things to do. Come nightfall, she would get back to the journal and, with a little luck, finish it in a couple of hours. She carefully put the floorboard back in its place and got dressed.

Right on schedule, a knock on the main door announced Fabian's arrival. Followed by Azabache, who hadn't left her side all night, Angela ran to the door. Fabian rushed in, holding a package wrapped in a blanket. Pressing his lips, Fabian went directly to the kitchen.

"Where's Rosa?" he asked worried.

"I don't know. In her workshop, I guess," Angela answered, concerned by Fabian's tone.

He placed the package on the table and unwrapped it to reveal Egon Schmied Poblete's old laptop.

Angela smiled.

"We don't have much time," Fabian said nervously wiping the sweat from his face. "I took it when nobody was there. But if anyone finds out that I..."

He couldn't continue. Angela put a finger on his lips. Besides asking him to stop talking, she felt an uncontrollable desire to kiss him.

"Thanks..." she whispered. She only had to lean a bit more to reach his mouth. Their first contact was tentative, as if they were seeking permission from the other to go on.

Angela put her arms around his neck and, to overcome fainting from sheer desire, held onto his strong body. She felt Fabian's arms on her back. As their kissing intensified, the space around them liquefied like fresh watercolors leaving them floating in a brand new place, created just for them.

But reality resurfaced and so did Almahue, the house, and the kitchen when Rosa entered with a tray full of freshly baked bread. Fabian backed up like a panther and Angela pretended she was looking for something on the table. Rosa passed by them and, without saying a word, put her steamy cargo into a little basket.

"Did you have breakfast?" she asked grabbing two cups.

"We were just leaving," Angela answered signaling Fabian to cover Egon's computer.

"So soon?"

"We have a lot to do," Angela said as she walked to the door. "We'll see you later."

Discretely, Angela took a sharp knife and hid it in her coat. Fabian looked at her puzzled but she signaled for him to keep quiet. There would be time to explain. They said goodbye to Rosa.

"Do not lose the knife! It is one of my favorites," Rosa said as they left the kitchen.

Angela left feeling that there were too many things happening under that roof and behind every single one was the landlady. No sooner had Angela set foot on the street than she felt Azabache move between her legs.

"You're not going anywhere, little one," Angela said lifting the cat from the ground to bring it back inside the house.

The cat resisted for a few seconds meowing and trying to escape. Finally, Angela was able to leave it in the hallway and slip out to the street.

"Now we are ready," Fabian said. "What a cat!"

The cold morning air disheartened Angela. Although the feeble rays of the sun shed enough light to create long shadows, they couldn't warm anything. She trotted three steps behind Fabian, who kept Egon's computer wrapped in the blanket and close to his chest. Worried, he turned to her.

"Where are we going?"

"You told me there's a public phone by the wharf," she answered.

"Yes, but it doesn't work."

"It doesn't matter! Let's go!" Indeed, the telephone that hung on a wooden post half eaten by years of rain and snow didn't look promising. The metal casing that housed the coin slot, the little change tray and the rotary dial was faded and dented. The horseshoe-shaped fisherman's wharf was a few feet away. There were only a few colorful wooden boats docked. A strong smell of salt saturated the air. A distant thunderstorm was the backdrop for the loud cries of hysterical seagulls mobbing the nets looking for food or fighting to get the fish guts lying on the beach. The dense, gray clouds transformed the sky into a scattering of gunpowder about to explode into a devastating storm.

"What are you going to do with the computer?" Fabian asked.

"If Patricia wants me to find out about Karl Wilhelm, I need access to the Internet. You don't have a library here, my iPhone is broken and Carlos Ule is not around," Angela answered. "I have no other choice. She didn't write the name of Rayen's father for nothing. She wants me to find something of his!"

She motioned Fabian to hand her the computer. Increasingly nervous, he passed it to her, fearing that someone would see them. But Angela was oblivious and totally focused on her idea. She took the knife and began unscrewing the case of the laptop.

Terrified, Fabian tried to stop her, but it was too late. She confidently removed the keyboard, exposing the electronic guts of the computer. She took the handset of the telephone and frowned. All she needed was a weak signal, and a little luck. The coin slot was clogged with red clay and leaves. She unscrewed the mouthpiece and yanked out the microphone.

"Oops! Now it's really broken!" she said tongue in cheek.

Using the knife, she scraped off the insulation and the remains of the solder from the tips of the wires connected to the microphone. She asked Fabian to hold Egon's disemboweled computer, as he looked on, utterly impressed by her skill. When she connected the wires to the circuits there were a couple of sparks. Fabian smiled.

"Good!" Angela thought, "It's transmitting data."

She was relieved there was still a signal in the damaged artifact. She searched her pockets and pulled out a piece of gum that she handed to Fabian.

"No, thanks," he said.

"I need you to chew it a little bit, please!" she said as she stuck the gum in his mouth.

Perplexed, Fabian chewed until the gum was soft. He was going to say something but the sudden appearance of the shadow of a bird on the ground stopped him. He looked up. Angela did the same. It was not a seagull. It was the enormous white heron they had seen flying over Almahue a few days ago. The same one that scared her and that now watched her with its big black eyes. The bird turned around and glided on the wind, steering with imperceptible movements of its wings. It grazed their heads and then climbed, becoming one with the white clouds.

"That bird is looking at me as if it knew me," Angela confessed and immediately felt embarrassed for the absurdity of her comment.

But Fabian wasn't listening. He urged her to finish. Angela turned her eyes back to the laptop and asked him to give her the chewing gum. He spat it shyly in his hand and gave it to her.

Angela mashed the gum to the wires of the microphone connected to the circuits. She replaced the keyboard and the back cover, crossed her fingers and pressed the Power button. She heard the system booting up. She smiled with satisfaction when the desktop appeared with all its icons, files, and folders. A window popped up announcing the dial-up option. It was working! She clicked "Connect" and the modem began dialing a telephone number. "Connecting" appeared on the screen. The speakers cackled and they heard a series of beeps, some longer than others, that took her back ten years.

"This computer couldn't be older!" she said as she realized that she had forgotten how slow and difficult modems used to be.

A new window popped up: "Connected: 9600 bps." A version of Netscape that was as obsolete as the operating system opened. The page took an eternity to download because of the weak and unstable connection. Angela knew it could be lost at any moment and she would have to begin all over again, delaying the return of the computer. The thought that Egon could come home and notice that something was missing from his desk made her very anxious. Who were they going to blame without giving it a second thought? They were going to blame Fabian, of course, the cook's son who wasn't even allowed to enter the house through the main door.

They heard a couple of shouts to their right. Scared, they tried to hide the broken handset and the computer by bringing their bodies together. They held their breath. Angela remembered that Walter Schmied had promised her that he would search for Patricia. She imagined him approaching them and limping furiously as he saw his son's laptop practically destroyed. How could she explain what she was doing?

For a few seconds neither of them dared to turn around. Then Fabian decided to face whatever it was. He was relieved to see a couple of fishermen who were loading a boat calling to each other out loud in order to speed up the task.

Angela knew that the clock was ticking. She also knew that her family was worried by her absence. They had probably called her several times and the fact that she couldn't answer only made things worse. She imagined her mother sleepless, trying to contact her, thinking of all sorts of possible accidents, tragedies, and mishaps. That was why, although it wasn't part of the original plan, she logged in to Gmail. Anguished, she saw that she had almost fifty unread emails. Several were from her mother, her brother and her friends from school. There were three from her research advisor. There would be time to reply later. She clicked "Compose".

"Hurry up, hurry up!" she mumbled with her eyes fixed on the screen.

As soon as she was able to start, she wrote a very brief message to her mother explaining her that she was still in the mountains with Patricia's parents; that she had lost her cell phone; that there was no easy way to contact her but she need not worry at all. Everything was going just fine and soon she would be back in Concepción and she would call then. She frowned as she reread her lies. She hit "Send" before she could change her mind. Nonetheless, she was relieved. At least she had solved one of her problems.

Now she had to take care of something slightly more complicated... and dangerous.

When Google finally opened, she searched for "Karl Wilhelm." The progress bar indicated that the search was in progress but the connection was not steady.

She looked at her cautious companion. He was silent, alert, and ready to escape with the laptop if anyone found them.

"Where did you learn to do that?" Fabian asked, intrigued.

"My brother Mauricio is an expert in assembling and disassembling anything he gets his hands on," she explained. "He is a geek. He taught me a couple of tricks I haven't forgotten."

Angela paused her story when a long list of links appeared on the screen. According to Google, there were almost two million results under Karl Wilhelm.

"Two million pages? Was Rayen's father that famous?" Fabian asked awestruck by the amount of information on the mysterious botanist.

Angela didn't answer. She was focused on carefully moving the cursor towards the first link. She clicked to open the Wikipedia page.

A shout behind them froze the blood in their veins. It was the voice of a woman. Angela clenched her jaws so hard she gave herself a headache. She prepared to receive the order not to move until the police arrived to take care of them. She silently prayed that it wasn't Silvia Poblete. That would really complicate things. Having the Schmieds as enemies was worse than having the whole village of Almahue against her.

Out of the corner of her eye, Angela was relieved to see a couple of women, wearing ponchos that looked like they had been soaked and dried a thousand times, carrying baskets full of fish and hawking their goods as they walked away. Fortunately, the women were in a hurry because the rain was fast approaching. They paid no attention to Angela and Fabian.

Angela felt a flush of blood in her head, a mixture of anger and frustration. "I need my iPhone now!" she complained, biting her lips. "I feel trapped in another century!"

"Please, hurry up," Fabian pleaded in anguish. "It's almost lunch time and..."

"It's not my fault that this thing is so slow!" she blurted, almost losing her patience because of the connection. "Besides, I don't think Egon will dare to say anything if he finds out... You and I could report him to the authorities as the main suspect in Patricia's disappearance!"

Fabian knew that Angela had found something because her skin paled and her eyes widened as she looked at the screen. She put her hand to her mouth in order to stifle any sound that the fishermen might hear. Fabian leaned in to see what had caused her reaction. He could only read the first paragraph, diagrammed next to an old photograph of a bearded man with thinning, combed-back hair. "Karl Wilhelm von Nägeli: Kilchberg 1817-Munich 1891, famous Swiss botanist whose major achievement was the discovery of chromosomes. His scientific research focused mainly on the microscopic study of plants..."

"He died in 1891? That can't be," Fabian stopped reading and looked at Angela. "Rayen's father died in 1939.

Angela clicked on a link that took her to a virtual European library where she confirmed that the information published in Wikipedia was correct. "Karl Wilhelm von Nägeli was born on March 27, 1817 in Kilchberg (Switzerland). He began studying Philosophy but switched to Botany. He taught at Freiburg, Zurich and Munich. He described with unparalleled precision the process of cell division, in which he characterized transitory cytoblasts that were actually chromosomes. He also characterized and described several unicellular algae and studied their process of osmosis. He died in Munich on May 10, 1891."

Angela was flabbergasted. "What could this mean?" she asked.

The third link simply confirmed what the remaining two million links most likely stated. Karl Wilhelm was a Swiss scientist who lived and died in the nineteenth century and, of course, never set foot in Almahue. In fact, he had been buried in Germany for more than forty years by the time he and his daughter allegedly arrived in the village.

Angela pulled the telephone wires off the circuits and put the computer back together.

"So Rayen's father was an impostor who used the name of a dead scientist?" Fabian asked when he put one and one together.

"How should I know?" Angela exclaimed as she nodded her head. "I don't understand anything anymore!"

Nevertheless, her instinct told her that Rayen's father was a liar, capable of deceiving the whole village in order to execute a mysterious plan. His true identity could be either an unscrupulous lunatic or a misunderstood genius.

They had so many more questions than answers. Who was chasing her friend? Who was Rayen's father and did he attempt to hide his true identity? Was there a connection between Egon and the botanist who died in the fire in 1939?

"I don't know what to do next..."

"I'll tell you what we are going to do as soon as we return this thing," Fabian said with a frown as a thunderclap broke the silence of the landscape. "We are going to follow Patricia's map step by step. Before we go to the police, who certainly answer to the Schmied's, we will follow Patricia's lead."

14 UNEXPECTED ENCOUNTERS

Everything looked the same. After Angela snuck back into Egon Schmied's bedroom with Fabian, and saw that it was exactly as she had left it, she knew one of two things was true: either Walter's son was an obsessive man incapable of creating any disorder or Silvia Poblete was the perfect housekeeper.

She was surprised by the highly polished woodwork, the straight, ironed corners of the comforter on the bed and the exact opening of the curtains on each side of the window. In contrast, she remembered her own bedroom, always full of papers with clothes strewn about the floor, and a closet that was on the verge of exploding. She smiled faintly. She certainly preferred her lifestyle. So much discipline and order made her suspicious. She imagined a disturbed mind behind this façade of neatness and perfection.

Fabian touched her arm, rousing her from her reflection and urging her to return the laptop to the desk. She moved it around slightly, plugged it in, and backed up a step to check her work. Perfect. No one could tell that the obsolete IBM had spent the entire morning with its guts exposed.

"Great, let's go," Fabian begged grabbing her by the hand to take her towards the door.

They were stopped dead in their tracks by Egon Schmied appearing at the threshold. He opened his eyes wide upon finding the intruders in his room.

"What are you doing in here?" he questioned when the initial shock had worn off.

"We were waiting for you," replied Angela, approaching him, remembering that the best defense is a strong offense.

"Here?"

"Yes, here. Does that bother you? Or do you have something you are trying to hide?" she said, staring at him accusingly.

Egon walked into the room and saw that everything was in its place. The drawers were closed and the sliding closet door was completely shut. Relieved to sense that his belongings had not been perturbed, he turned towards Fabian with a raised eyebrow.

"You, out! No one gave you permission to be in this part of the house," he declared imperiously. But Fabian didn't move. "Didn't you hear me? Get out of here!" "I am not going to leave her alone with you," was Fabian's challenging response.

"Fabian doesn't leave my side. I asked him to accompany me," Angela intervened in his defense.

"I don't wish to appear rude but you do not seem to understand. I don't intrude in his space, do I?"

"I have proof that you did know Patricia," Angela interrupted with a sarcastic smile. "Don't deny it."

A heavy silence hung in the air. Egon Schmied Poblete didn't know what to say. He passed his hand through his slicked-back hair, trying to buy time.

Angela looked at Fabian and winked at him. With her opponent on the mat, she continued to fight.

"I found her cell phone in this very room, inside this closet," she said. "Patricia took photos of you. They're all there, in her telephone. Are you going to continue denying it? Are you going to keep lying?"

"Look, I only saw her a couple of times," Egon sputtered as he unfolded a handkerchief.

"It only takes a second to make someone disappear," Angela said.

Egon seemed to be losing control. His face blanched as he covered it with his hands to hide his anguish. Where had this girl who dared to challenge him under his own roof come from? What had he done wrong? Why had that damn cell phone ended up in the wrong hands?

He had to think quickly but his mind kept going around in circles. "Get out of here!" was the only thing he managed to blurt out. But Angela didn't move an inch. Things had already gone too far and she wasn't going to be intimidated by Egon's bombast. She was going to strike again but Fabian beat her to it. "Either you tell us where Patricia is or I'm going to the police," he threatened.

"Get out of here!" Egon bellowed, as he moved to shove Angela out of the doorway.

Fabian came between them and raised his arms, impeding Egon's advance like a wall of steel.

"Watch out," he warned, "she's not alone."

The two looked at each other in silence; one panting and feeling like his world was falling apart; the other emboldened and ready to defend Angela at all costs. Egon's overwhelming cologne enveloped them all.

"You have three seconds to get out of here or I won't be responsible for what happens," Egon whispered.

"Where is Patricia?" asked Angela.

But Egon was done talking. He went into the hallway, finding Silvia Poblete who had just climbed the stairs, drawn in by the shouting.

"What's going on here? And you... What are you doing here?" she asked Angela.

"Nothing! They were just leaving!" Egon said, trying to discretely wipe the sweat on his forehead.

"How did you get in here? Who gave you permission to come upstairs? Elvira! Elvira!" Silvia exclaimed leaning over the balustrade.

"I would like to speak with you ma'am," was all that Angela was able to say before Fabian took her by the arm towards the steps.

"Nobody moves from here until you explain what you were doing in Egon's room!"

No one paid any attention to her command.

Fabian took Angela full-speed, passing Elvira, who hurried out of the kitchen when she heard Silvia Poblete's shouts. She was startled when she saw her son going in the direction of the front door as though he were a fugitive.

"What did you do?" she muttered, fear written on her face.

Before rushing outside, still holding his friend's hand, Fabian only had time to gesture with his hand as if to say: "Calm down, nothing happened." The cook, however, didn't believe him and anxiously turned to the stairs only to discover Silvia's enraged face.

"Since when is your son invited upstairs, to the bedrooms no less? Where is Walter? Why isn't my husband around when he's needed?"

Despite the commotion and threats, Elvira's blood ran cold when she saw Egon on the second floor landing.

She had never seen such an expression of hate and rancor. Egon's fists were grasping the handrail and his clenched jaw betrayed the fury he tried to control. For a moment, the cook didn't recognize him. And she was immediately afraid for Fabian's future. They'd never been fond of each other, even in childhood, but now Fabian had an enemy that would be very difficult to evade.

15 THE BREATH OF THE FOREST

Neither said a word until they were far enough from the Schmied's house. Angela stopped, leaned on a millenary *coihue*, and took a deep breath trying to calm her galloping heart. Fabian didn't show any sign of fatigue.

"Thanks for defending me."

"You don't have to thank me for anything," Fabian answered tenderly, looking at her.

"Egon is way off base if he thinks he'll get away with this. If he's hurt Patricia, I swear I'll...!" she exclaimed, her eyes full of tears.

She couldn't keep talking. She had reached her limit. For the first time since her arrival in Almahue she felt she couldn't cope with the situation. She was overwhelmed by a sense of claustrophobia, of moving in circles. All she could do was cry out of frustration. Fabian put his arms around her. She held on to him with all her strength. She felt his slightly awkward yet loving hand touching her hair, trying to calm her down.

"It's okay. Your friend is going to be fine," he whispered in her ear.

"You promise?"

"I promise." Angela believed him. There was something about his voice that made her trust him. She felt as if she had been listening to it all her life, and that made her immensely happy. She held him tightly, filling her senses with his fragrance of wood and freshly washed clothes.

"Did you bring Patricia's map?" he asked after a few seconds. "She nodded and pulled it out of one of her pockets. She unfolded it and they looked at the shaky drawing that showed the way to a cave in the middle of the forest. Fabian frowned as he examined the location. A cross marked the beginning of the path. From there, a straight line going north ended in another cross, marked "Forest."

"We have no choice but to start walking," he said stretching his hand to her. "Did you bring your flashlight?" she asked and smiled as her partner nodded. Angela wished she had her iPhone so she could keep track of the time. It wasn't smart to wander into the untamed vegetation with the possibility of finding themselves in the middle of nowhere after dark. But the idea of spending the rest of the day with Fabian seemed a very sensible thing to do.

They began walking along a narrow dirt path and soon began the climb into the hills surrounding Almahue. The huge *tepa* trees formed a sheltering canopy. As they walked deeper into the forest, the sweet and humid breath of the foliage became more intense: a smell of mud mixed with decomposing leaves and decayed wood. Angela breathed through her mouth to block out the smell.

Fabian looked at the map against the landscape in front of him.

"Very well. We're at the first mark. From here we'll have to walk east as your friend indicates."

"But I don't have a compass. My iPhone had an application..." Angela began to say.

"Who needs a compass when we have the sun?" Fabian interrupted her with a smile and started walking again.

They walked with their arms stretched forward because, little by little, the path they were on disappeared and it became necessary to clear a way through the shrubs, roots and long bindweeds. The forest was bathed in an aqueous light that gave it a dreamy appearance.

Angela felt trapped in a delicate bubble that was about to burst. The incessant buzz of wings along with the frantic sounds of the animals stunned her at times. She had to shake her head and rub her ears in order to muffle the noise.

Fabian stopped in front of the cross-shaped tree that Patricia had drawn on the map.

"We're doing alright," he encouraged her. "How do you feel?"

Angela tried to nod but she was too befuddled to move her head up and down. She never imagined that entering the heart of the forest could be so strenuous. The lack of light, the sticky air, the mosquito bites and the muddy, slippery ground discouraged her to the point of wanting to throw in the towel.

She gathered her pride and did the best she could. She cracked a smile that looked more like the sardonic grin of someone sitting on death row, and moved ahead.

The constant buzz of the insects was like a purr of sorts that increased by the minute until it became an ear-splitting noise that suffocated her. Mosquitoes stuck to her skin, attracted by the acidic smell of her sweat. She wanted to scream but nothing came out.

The booming sound of distant thunder, muffled by the vegetation, portended the beginning of the storm. Almost immediately, a heavy curtain of rain fell through the tree branches, soaking the ground and weighing her down. She barely had the chance to raise her hood, which of course wasn't enough to keep her from getting soaked to the skin. Angela couldn't tell if her eyes were open or shut. She couldn't tell where she was either. She could only guess by what her hands touched: coarse, stiff bodies, gooey ridges that ran through her fingers, hairy roots and tentacles that wrapped around her ankles.

Fabian? Where was Fabian? The last time she saw him, he was just a few steps ahead of her, clearing the way.

She opened her mouth to call to him but a bug flew in, practically down her throat, making her cough and gag. As she brought her head closer to the ground she could clearly hear the sound of the larvae crawling on the leaves, the endless chirp of the crickets and the unflagging march of the roaches over her shoes. She felt as if she were going mad.

Then she heard laughter, a raucous feminine laughter. "Fabian, did you hear that?" Angela screamed. The cackle mixed with the hooting of an owl flying over her. She tried to turn around but the branches, intertwined in an unbreakable net around her body, wouldn't let her. Although she couldn't see them, she felt a pair of strange eyes staring at her. She heard breathing that wasn't hers.

"Fabian! Help me!"

She tried to free her arms from the grip of the sharp, jagged leaves. Darkness receded to reveal her organic cage. How did she get there? Had the same thing happened to Patricia?

"Rayen! Rayen, where are you? Rayen!"

A young man ran past her. He was tall with luxuriant blonde hair and a child's face. He was elegantly dressed although his clothes were outdated. He wore fine boots.

"Oh, I see... you want to play... Very well then, we'll play. You want me to find you? Here I come!"

It can't be. It can't be! Young Ernesto Schmied ran by her without even looking at her. The feminine laughter went on.

"I want us to marry under these trees, on this bed of leaves, surrounded by nature!"

Where is she? I want to see her. Angela tried to move her head but a mane of roots climbed up to her temples paralyzing her and covering her eyes.

"I want to live forever among these trees, Ernesto. This is the place where I want to grow old, where I want to die!"

"Fabian, please, help me!"

The rain fell furiously, splashing her face. A hand covered her mouth. The face of a man came into view above her.

"Are you ever going to wear shoes?"

"Never! I love to feel the clay, the moss, even the stones on my feet! It makes me feel alive!"

Angela saw her reflection in a pair of glasses suspended on the tip of a stranger's nose. He was wearing a white apron. When she saw the yellow-eyed owl perched on his left shoulder, the Coo, the omen of misfortune and death, she wanted to scream a warning but she couldn't.

"It's the Coo!" But she could only manage a ragged whisper.

Defeated by the forest and overtaken by hallucinations, she collapsed in a frothy cream of insects, leaves and worms that silently and solemnly covered her.

16 FINDINGS

Fabian found Angela lying on the floor with her eyes closed, muttering incoherently. She was saying something about Rayen, the witch who hid in the vegetation. She also complained about an owl perched on the shoulder of an unknown man who was looking at her through round glasses. She was delirious. Her red hair contrasted vividly with the green blanket upon which she laid, defeated by fatigue and effort.

Fabian knew that the unexpected, blinding rain would dissipate as quickly as it had appeared. Deluges from punishing storms that flooded the valley and left a dense fog were common in Almahue. There were terrible years in which the village was submerged up to the rafters after sudden storms, and many of the carts of its inhabitants were stranded like barges in the center of the square. "Fortunately, nothing like that happened this time," Fabian thought, leaning over Angela.

He gently caressed the curve of her cheek, briefly touching her freckles that he found so attractive. She was the prettiest girl he had ever seen: fragile and independent at the same time. She never accepted the first answer and, despite her obvious fears and inexperience, was capable of jumping into the most dangerous adventure. He admired her courage and tenacity in the face of adversity. Yet, going into the heart of the forest was something else. Angela didn't have the survival skills to confront and conquer the untamed vegetation that lay before them.

Dazed, Angela opened her eyes and realized where she was. She was scared. She sat up and tried to hide her queasiness from Fabian, who was looking at her with a smile on his lips. His clothes were stuck to his body. He was soaking wet from head to toe.

"What happened to me?"

"You fainted. I got a little bit ahead so that I could clear the way and when I saw that you weren't behind me, I came back to look for you."

Angela tried to stand, but he kept her from getting up.

"Stay here a little bit longer, until you feel better. You're not used to this climate," he advised.

"But I've never felt better!" she lied, trying to sound convincing.

In spite of her eagerness to appear strong and brave, she decided to stay down on the ground for a few more minutes until her head stopped spinning.

She could barely talk. The thick air made it difficult for her to breathe. There was a loud hum in her ears that wouldn't go away. Angela remembered Patricia's video. Her friend's hair was tangled and full of leaves and dry branches. Could she have followed this same path before drawing the map? For the time being, the storm had ended but the forest floor was transformed into a swamp.

Suddenly, a bush shook violently and a cat emerged from the branches. It stared directly at Angela from a distance, arching its shiny back.

"Azabache?" she exclaimed, incredulous. Not a sound. The cat jumped and disappeared in the dense forest. Angela stood up, feeling the strength returning to her legs. What was Rosa's cat doing here? Had it followed her? Maybe it wasn't Azabache, but another animal that looked like it. "All cats look the same in the dark," she thought. But there was something in its glance that convinced her she was not mistaken. She shuddered. Maybe the cat was trying to tell her something.

"We are very close to where your friend wrote "Rayen" on the map," Fabian said looking at the paper. "Although I still don't know what we are looking for."

"We're looking for a cave," Angela answered with certainty.

She took the map from his hands and turned it around. On the back, she read "Karl Wilhelm. Cave."

"How can you be so sure?"

"I don't know. I just know that's how it is," she answered walking away. The last leg of the walk was much less scary than she expected. The muddy path gave way to firm and rocky ground that was easier to cross in their boots.

The trees were impossibly high. Their canopies practically touched the low-hanging clouds. It was dark and the branches acted like an impenetrable roof, blocking the sunlight. Angela couldn't estimate what time it was or how long she had been in the forest. She had lost all notion of time. Her world had been reduced to an intense green mass that unfolded before her eyes.

Their path tended abruptly at what appeared to be a very high wall, covered with moss the steep slope of a mountain. The absence of light and the excessive vegetation that surrounded it made it difficult to determine its actual size.

"Well," Fabian said, "I guess we're going to have to climb."

"No," Angela contradicted him, repeating what a voice inside her head was whispering. "We're here."

Perplexed by her response, Fabian frowned.

Angela began to separate the leaves that covered the hill looking for something that she alone appeared to know. Fabian followed her lead. "It has to be around here! It has to be around here!" she repeated. Angela yanked the roots and branches to expose bare earth. If her inexplicable feeling was correct, then what they were looking for was right in front of them, hidden in the thicket. They worked for several more minutes, Angela's muscles burning from the effort.

At last, she found a vine that, as if it were a thread, wove a net above the hillside. When she pulled it, she discovered that along with the net, plants with enormous leaves fell down. It was at that point that she saw it: a thin crack that opened up a cleft in the rock, an opening into the mountain.

"Fabian!" she shouted triumphantly.

He ran to join her. His eyes widened when he saw what Angela showed him with her bruised hand. "I give you the entrance to Rayen's cave," Angela said solemnly. "Shall ..."

She had not finished asking her question when a flapping of wings made her jump back. A furious owl flew out of the cave, shrieking, extending its claws, ready to defend its territory. It attacked Angela, who barely had time to cover her face before the claws scratched her skin.

The bird rose a bit, turned around and prepared to assault her again. Fabian looked for a branch to scare it away to no avail. The bird dove at Angela, who had to run for cover. It seemed like the entire forest was defending the cave's secret. The owl clung to Angela's hair. Then a sharp screech and it released her hair.

Angela looked up to see a majestic white heron rise, holding the Coo in its beak. The bird did a couple of pirouettes close to the tree canopy, its prisoner in the throes of death, and flew away flapping its wings as stealthily and discretely as it had arrived.

This was no coincidence. There were two groups in Almahue: those who helped Angela and those who wished to destroy her. The heron was one of her allies.

Feeling overwhelmed, and safer, she entered the cave.

17 THE CAVE

The beam of light from the lantern illuminated the narrow gallery that stretched several feet and ended in a dark cavity. The sound of their footsteps bounced off the stone walls. They were holding hands, enduring the fetid smell of humidity and putrefaction. The air made them cough because of the fine dust that stuck in their noses and throats. Their eyes itched; their sight was blurred. Fabian pointed the light to the ground. They could see the footprints that lead to the end of the gallery.

"Someone has been here," he whispered.

"Of course. Lots of people. From Rayen to Patricia," Angela answered and took the lantern to lead the way.

She walked to the end. It became so narrow that they had to squat. Fabian pushed her gently, protectively to the side leaving no doubt as to who was going in first. He kneeled and began to crawl though the opening in the wall.

Angela followed him, lighting up a tunnel. For a brief moment she felt as if she were buried alive. She could feel the pressure of the ceiling on her back and shoulders, and the pebbles lacerating her legs. The gallery opened and they found themselves in a very large cavern. They were relieved to be able to stand up again. They could hear the echo of constant dripping. The lantern wasn't powerful enough to illuminate the whole space. It only produced a small circle of yellow light. Angela moved closer to Fabian. His presence made her feel safe. She continued shining the light on the walls, covered with mold and mildew.

"Wait a moment!"

Fabian took the lantern and shined it on the wall. The light revealed a set of symbols that were drawn in red ink.

"What is that?" Angela mumbled.

She took a few steps forward and swore, angry that she didn't have her iPhone to photograph the symbols. When Fabian put the light to them she was better able to see them:

Angela was momentarily paralyzed. She had a strong sense of déjà vu. Where and when had she seen these drawings? She was sure she had seen them recently... perhaps in an exhibition or in the pages of a book of Anthropology? They looked neither Christian nor Native, yet there was something familiar about their style. The memory of those circles, crosses and triangles was so fresh in her mind that it couldn't have been long since she'd last laid eyes on them. Where had she seen them? When?

She tried to move closer but her feet stumbled on something quite large lying on the floor. She lost her balance and fell over it. As she tried to get back on her feet, her hands touched fabric of some sort, leather? Why would there be leather in cave?

"Fabian!" she screamed so he could orient himself in the dark and shine the light in her direction.

The light found Angela's face and then moved to one side revealing a skull that looked at them with hollow eyes and a frozen smile. Angela screamed, causing a sprinkle of fine dust to fall on their heads. As she crawled back, she inadvertently scattered some bones that poked through the rags and what had clearly been a leather jacket.

Terrified, Angela ran to Fabian who held her with one arm as he continued shining the light on the corpse with the other. Next to the ribs, fibulas, and femurs there was a leather bag that seemed to hold something.

"It's a dead body!" she screamed rubbing her hands against her clothes, trying to clean whatever was left on them from the corpse.

She suddenly hushed, even more terrified. The idea that it could be

Patricia's body made her weak in the knees. She thought she was going to faint but her scientific knowledge brought her back to her senses. In only two weeks, a body would not be in such an advanced state of decomposition. Whomever that skeleton belonged to had been resting inside that mountain for a long time.

Fabian slowly came closer. With the tip of his boot he brought the bag closer to him. The metallic buckles jingled. When he finally dragged it away from the bones, he bent down and picked it up. He handed the lantern to Angela and looked inside the bag. He found a rusty metallic pen, a magnifying glass, a wooden pipe, and a little bag of a greenish, foul-smelling mass that he supposed had been tobacco. He pulled out a notebook, the pages of which were almost transparent because of the humidity. Nonetheless, on the cover they could clearly read the name of its owner: Benedicto Mohr.

"It's the body of the explorer!" Fabian said as he dropped the bag.

"Mohr had lived in Almahue for some time while he was writing a book about Rayen. Shortly after he finished it, he disappeared mysteriously." Don Ernesto's words came back to her ears like a speeding bullet. There was the answer to his enigmatic disappearance. The European explorer died in that cave, in the heart of the forest, a silent witness to the symbols drawn on the wall. Or maybe someone had taken him there after he died.

A muffled sound followed by a shaking of the earth alerted them. The ground under their feet shook and a groan coming from the rock announced the earthquake. Parts of the ceiling began to fall on Mohr's bones. The stone where the symbols were drawn cracked and crumbled to the ground. The walls of the cave leaned towards the center threatening to fall at any moment. The shaking of the ground intensified and their air was filled with the asphyxiating stench of death.

As he was trying to feel his way to the opening that led outside, Fabian pushed Angela forward. A rock fell on her back, knocking her on her face. She closed her eyes, just like she did whenever she was overwhelmed with fear and there seemed to be no possible solution to her problems. The darkness inside the darkness made her hearing more acute. She could clearly hear the stone walls cracking and the earth convulsing as it sunk.

Someone was dragging her through the narrow tunnel through which they had entered. She dared to open her eyes and saw Fabian's bruised and dirty face. He moved forward with determination dodging the falling rocks and the rising cloud of dust. She put her arms around his neck and let him lead the way.

The blocks of granite that crashed against the ground buried their footprints. The gallery collapsed like a house of cards. Fabian intensified his effort. Just a few feet ahead, they could see an intense green. Fabian held Angela very tightly and ran. A crack in the ground stopped them dead in their tracks. It opened a deep, dark pit at their feet.

"Hold on!" Fabian yelled in anguish.

Knowing he had no other option, he backed up to get a running start. Angela guessed what he was about to do and shut her eyes so tightly that she could see sparks.

Fabian ran, trying to keep his balance despite the shaking ground and the collapsing ceiling. He vaulted over the crack in the earth, and his strong legs carried them through the air. Time stood still. They seemed frozen in mid-air, horrified by the destruction, their bodies struggling against the pull of the enormous, deadly mouth about to swallow them. They didn't even feel the pain when they fell on the other side, still holding each other. They quickly got back on their feet but the ground beneath them began to yield to the relentless hunger of the fissure that grew bigger and deeper. They ran without looking back, without saying a word, focusing on the opening that would finally lead them out of hell.

The way out. Close. Very close. A few more steps...

The fresh air hit their faces. They were back in the forest. They had emerged unharmed. Over Fabian's shoulder Angela saw how the crack on the side of the mountain opened until it collapsed with a visceral roar, forever blocking the way to Rayen's cave. The foliage immediately took over covering everything with leaves. In an instant, nature erased all human traces. The earthquake didn't seem to have impacted anything but Rayen's hiding place.

They both fell on the ground, panting and coughing out the dust that had stuck in their lungs. They were covered with a thick layer of mud and they had blood and bruises all over their bodies. But they were still breathing and they celebrated by hugging each other with great enthusiasm and emotion.

Angela caressed Fabian's face and kissed his cheeks and lips.

They were grateful for their good fortune and for Fabian's skills.

Nevertheless, she couldn't stop thinking that it had been in vain. Everything she was looking for was buried several feet underground. At least Patricia wasn't in there.

A whistle interrupted her thoughts.

The high pitch note made its way through the trunks and the huge leaves of the trees straight to her head. Angela thought it was a bird but soon realized that it was a human whistle, an obvious tune. Someone was walking near them.

She knew that Fabian was going to get up and meet the visitor. Her instincts took over. She held him tightly by the arm preventing him from moving. He looked at her perplexed. Angela begged him to keep quiet by putting a finger to his lips and shaking her head vigorously. Like an animal, she crawled backwards and hid in the foliage. Fabian followed her. They heard the rustle of branches crushed by footsteps. They saw a pair of men's shoes. The right leg limped while the left leg stretched forward and waited for its crippled partner.

The whistle grew closer. Walter Schmied walked by them as if he were strolling through his own backyard. He didn't seem to be in a hurry and he didn't hesitate along his path. He kept walking, his mouth straight, his nose red from the cold. He disappeared into the green that swallowed his body and muffled his tune until it could no longer be heard.

Only then did Angela and Fabian peek out of their hiding place. "What is he doing here?" Fabian asked suspiciously.

"Well, he said that he had organized a search party to look for Patricia. Maybe that's what he's doing," Angela replied, trying to offer a sensible answer.

"Really? So why is he by himself? Besides, he didn't seem to be looking for anyone. He seemed to just be walking around..." They remained silent. The sudden appearance of Silvia Poblete's spouse in the middle of the forest was an enigma, a mystery as unfathomable as that of Benedicto Mohr's body inside the cave; the symbols drawn in the rock, the Coo and the elusive heron that seemed to smile at Angela each time it flew over her head.

~

Later that night, after the long hike back to Almahue and Rosa's place, she silently bid Fabian farewell on the street with a tender and grateful kiss for having saved her life. She walked carefully through the hallway because she didn't want Rosa, who was probably in the kitchen or in her workshop, to hear her. The last thing she wanted was to explain what she had been doing or what she had seen. She only wanted to take a hot bath. Unfortunately, her mind insisted on playing over and over the gloomy image of the scientist's skeleton under the rags. She shook her head trying to erase the vision from her memory but it didn't work. The scattered bones and skull were fixed behind her eyelids.

Resigned, she decided that the best she could do after drying her hair and putting on her pajamas was to get in bed and read the last pages of Don Ernesto's notebook. She took off her coat and her boots. She massaged her feet, numbed by the cold and the fatigue.

Before going to the bathroom, she stopped and looked at her room. Everything was in its place, perfectly in place. The earthquake that she and Fabian survived was not felt in Almahue. Nonetheless, following her instincts, she frowned and leaned over the table. She moved it to the side and lifted the board that covered her hiding place. The black notebook and her friend's cellular phone were still there.

Relieved, she put the board back in its place and walked to the door. Although everything seemed to be in the same place she had left it, something didn't seem right. She went over the furniture, her luggage, her backpack that was on the chair, the closet, and the table. Everything was in its place.

Still, something was making her uncomfortable: an intangible presence, an uneasiness that wouldn't subside. She took a deep breath and realized that there was something different in the room: a smell, a signature scent. She shuddered with fear when she realized who had been rummaging through her stuff.

18 DECEMBER, 1939

*I*t's a white cross. Two perpendicularly joined pieces of wood mark the spot where the remains of Karl Wilhelm rest. On one of the pieces of wood, Ernesto Schmied wrote the botanist's name in black paint, in his best calligraphy. Even though he went through all of the papers and records that survived the fire, he could never find Karl Wilhelm's date of birth. He disappeared from the face of the earth as mysteriously as he had arrived.

According to some of the men who went into the house after the fire, his body was unidentifiable. All that remained was just a small smoldering mound. Some went so far as to swear that those remains were not human: that perhaps they belonged to an animal or one of those strange creatures that, according to town gossip, the scientist held captive in his lab.

The fact of the matter is that even the priest of the neighboring town, who came to Almahue once a week to bless the newborns and hear confession, refused to preside over a service in the foreigner's honor. To justify himself, he said that his beliefs prevented him from looking after the soul of a sinner who defied nature by turning the town tree into a demonic monstrosity that bore apples, oranges, and pears.

Without anyone's knowledge, young Ernesto paid for a coffin and hired a couple of fishermen to bury the casket under cover of darkness as far away as possible. He chose the peak of one of the surrounding mountains. From there, one could see the entire valley, the range of mountains around Almahue, and the small arm of the sea that insinuated itself into the continent, giving birth to a bright coastline that shone like the scales of a silver fish. The young man feels the weight of guilt on his heart. That simple and sad cross reminds him, with a silent, painful cry, that he was unable to avert a tragedy. And he will never forgive himself for failing to stop the blind and frenzied mob.

He crosses himself and stands up. It is his custom to go there at twilight and offer a prayer for the eternal rest of Karl Wilhelm. If he were completely honest with himself, however, he'd have to admit that he goes up that mountain every afternoon with the hopes of seeing her again. But she never shows up. The forest has swallowed her.

He sighs as he gets back on his horse. For a second, he remembers the image of her delicate body, unconscious on a blanket of dry leaves, her skin covered in mud, her messy hair tangled with twigs, her tattered clothes. He shakes his head. The memories of Rayen still cause him pain. A lot of pain. Every afternoon, as he spurs his horse into a gallop, he shudders because he has the feeling that someone is watching him from the thick greenery: someone whose eyes follow his every move; someone who neither moves nor breathes until horse and rider fade into a blurry mirage and disappear with the last glimmer of sunlight.

~

As soon as he enters his father's study, Ernesto Schmied knows that the die is cast. He realizes it when he comes face to face with his father's stern look, his fingers drumming on the mahogany desk. His father waits for him in silence, his eyes are fixed on him, on his nineteen-year-old son, who feels like a helpless kid whenever he enters that place. The fire crackles in the chimney and draws moving shadows on the walls and ceiling. The pendulum of a very tall grandfather clock swings back and forth, reminding Ernesto that time is an eternal fugitive and that, no matter how hard he tries to grasp it, it will always slip away like a fish.

"Come in, Ernesto. Close the door," his father orders and Ernesto obeys.

For a moment, the young man is distracted by the sight of the library that covers the entire wall. Hundreds of volumes, bound in fragrant leather, stand side by side in perfect order. It is clear that their owner, Otto Schmied, is an educated man.

"I was told, sir, that you were looking for me..." Ernesto mumbles, half hidden by the shadows.

The man nods as he points to a chair, ordering him to sit. Ernesto, as usual, obeys.

"I presume you are aware that your mother invited the Moras to dinner tonight."

"Yes, I know," he lies hiding his displeasure. *"And I assume you also know the purpose of their visit."* Ernesto doesn't have a response. However, he is not naïve. He guesses the agenda behind their visit. Three months have passed since the fire that killed Karl Wilhelm. Ninety painful days have passed since he last saw Rayen. Peace has already returned to Almahue, and its inhabitants seem to have forgotten that fateful day on which they all became accomplices to a murder. Not even the death of a scientist and the disappearance of his daughter are reason enough for Aurora and Otto Schmied to abandon their plans for their only son.

"What are your dreams, son?"

The question catches him off guard. He is not used to his father wanting to know the reasons behind his actions, or the ideas and dreams that live in his head. Perhaps it is true. Maybe his father is beginning to see him as a man. If that's the case, he must get used to the idea that their relationship is that of two men who share the same piece of the world and bear the burden of a family on their shoulders.

"I want to know. What are your dreams, Ernesto? What do you expect from life?"

"To be like you, sir. To follow your steps," he lies again, as the intimate nature of the conversation places him squarely in uncharted territory. Otto Schmied nods in satisfaction. That was exactly the answer he was looking for.

"And I suppose you'll want to start a family."

"I've always wanted to please you."

"And I also suppose when the time comes you will want to take care of my business and continue to increase our estate," he says in an authoritative tone. How could he tell his father that he doesn't care about the two thousand head of cattle he was destined to inherit? And that Clara Mora, the woman they chose for him, doesn't possess any of the qualities he values in a woman? That she is small minded and seems too comfortable with the idea of other

people defining her destiny. He cannot even bring himself to think about the day of Rayen's disappearance, and the mob, and what part Clara played in it.

Rayen. Where is Rayen?

Given his son's silence, Otto Schmied stands up. Steadily, he walks towards an elaborate desk covered with a green blotter. He takes out a sheaf of papers tied with a ribbon and tosses it to Ernesto.

"The situation at the cattle ranch is getting worse by the day," he sadly confesses. "These are the financial statements."

"Does my mother know?" the young man asks as he skims the documents.

"Your mother is a woman and that prevents her from understanding the gravity of the situation we are facing!" Otto exclaims returning to his chair. "Our financial outlook is bleak. I'm afraid we may lose everything I've built."

Earlier, when he entered his father's study, he had sensed that his fate was sealed. Now he had the evidence in his hands to prove it. Those dismal reports showed a growing debt, one that swelled like the tide of the fjord during winter.

"The duty of a first-born son is not only to continue the work started by his forefathers," the elder Schmied proclaims, "but it is also to sacrifice himself for the well-being of his future offspring and all the members of his family."

Otto Schmied pauses. The pendulum counts each second of uncomfortable silence. "The Moras are, along with us, one of best families in town. They are educated, honorable and resourceful. And Clara is a good girl. You are going to be happy with her. You are going to have a good life, son."

"Some day I'll inherit my father's fortune and I want to offer it to you. I promise that you will have a good life with me, my love..." He had said these words to Rayen in the forest where they secretly met and where they planned to live together forever. Words almost identical to the ones he now hears his father say, though referring to Clara Mora. How could he have raised Rayen's hopes if he wasn't free to choose the woman he wanted marry! He will never forgive himself for having betrayed her.

"Clara will be a good mother to your children. And, thanks to that marriage, we will be able to keep our cattle and build a shipyard," Otto Schmied adds as he takes the papers away from his son. "Now, I want you to go change your clothes and, as soon as the Moras arrive, go to the dining room knowing that the future belongs to you."

Ernesto, not yet twenty, is capable of imagining the rest of his life: a flat line with no peaks or surprises; an endless path without detours to explore. He knows that every day will go by just like the previous one. His life will be a useless succession of hours, years, and decades. He wishes he could gallop into oblivion. Yet he stands up and goes to the door. When he grabs the doorknob, he shivers upon touching the metal. It is frozen, but he cannot tell whether the cold comes from outside or inside his body.

"The Schmieds have always made the best decisions, son. Don't ever forget that," his father solemnly utters. Ernesto tries to say something but can't think of anything. Upset, he leaves the studio, crosses the hall and runs upstairs. As he enters his bedroom, he feels the urge to jump out the window, shattering the glass with his body, and letting the long fall take care of his problems. But he is a coward and he knows it. Instead, he walks to his bed and lies down. He drops on the mattress and buries his face in his hands.

The door opens. His mother's perfume tickles his nose with its unmistakable scent of lavender and jasmine. He feels like a condemned man being led to his execution.

"The Moras have arrived, my dear. Clara is very happy about seeing you again. Don't dawdle," Aurora instructs from the doorway. Ernesto has no choice but to surrender to the inexorable destiny that has turned his life into a nightmare before his dreams could take flight.

~

The bells spread joy all over town. Their jubilant peal summons everyone to the ceremony. The church is packed with guests and onlookers for the most important wedding in the short history of Almahue. Filomena and Aurora, the proud mothers of the bride and groom, had white flowers sent from Chiloé to decorate the altar and the aisle. They had regalia and gowns shipped from Europe, and organized a banquet worthy of royalty. Otto Schmied ordered a monumental feast following the ceremony, and he personally oversaw the delivery of the cases of champagne and red wine that his associates sent from the capital.

The priest begins the ceremony.

"My brethren, we are gathered here today in the sight of God and in the face of this congregation to bear witness to the loving union of Clara Mora and Ernesto Schmied."

Clara cannot contain her emotion. She can barely breathe, her rib cage crushed by a corset, the fastening of which required the help of three people earlier that morning. Her dress is silk, a beautiful white like eternal snows, and its long train is carried by a group of children carefully chosen by Filomena. Next to her, Ernesto's eyes are fixed on the enormous cross crowning the altar. He is wearing a black bow tie and an elegant tuxedo that contrasts sharply with the modest church and the untamed landscape that surrounds it.

"Clara, do you take Ernesto Schmied as your wedded husband? To have and to hold, from this day forward, for better, for worse, for richer, for poorer, in sickness or in health, to love and to cherish 'till death do you part?"

Through the windows, some guests notice black clouds moving towards Almahue. They form an immense dark stain, a menacing shadow that warns of a storm. The wind increases, shaking the branches of the trees and forming whirlwinds of leaves.

"I do," Clara replies, holding back tears of joy.

Filomena, her mother, puffs out her rosy cheeks before blowing her nose. She is all laughter and joy as she sees her daughter marrying the Schmied's only son. She winks knowingly across the aisle to Aurora, holding onto Otto's arm and watching the ceremony with a taciturn expression.

In the distance, thunder rumbles, prompting some murmurs. The weather can no longer be trusted. Sunday had dawned unusually sunny and they had not set up tents. Otto Schmied frowns, trying picturing the open-air feast that will be ready when the ceremony ends. Filomena Mora imagines her exquisite daughter exiting the church in the middle of a rainstorm and a surge of anxiety gets the better of her. She turns towards the cross and silently prays to prevent such an important day for the town from being ruined by a whim of nature.

"Ernesto, do you take Clara Mora as your wedded wife? To have and to hold, from this day forward, for better, for worse, for richer, for poorer, in sickness or in health, to love and to cherish 'till death do you part?"

His prolonged silence is interrupted by another clap of thunder over the roof of the church. Some women are startled and others cross themselves. Even the priest, unable to disregard what is going on, looks up at the oil lamp trembling with the vibrations from the disturbed sky. He then remembers that the groom still hasn't declared his consent. The priest opens his eyes wide at Ernesto.

"Ernesto, do you accept Clara Mora as your wife?" he insists.

Ernesto opens his mouth to answer but the words get caught in his throat. He misses Rayen so much that he can almost smell her, as if she was the one standing next to him and not the young woman whom he barely knows and who, in a few minutes, will be his companion for life.

Rayen. His Rayen.

Filomena places one hand on her chest grabbing her pearl necklace. The silence is now unbearable and leads to stares and a few whispers among the guests.

"Answer him!" Filomena says, to everyone's surprise. Ernesto seems to wake up from a trance. He blinks a few times and calmly turns to Clara who's also been expectantly watching him.

"I do."

"What God has joined, men must not divide. Amen," the priest declares and triumphantly adds, "You are now husband and wife." At that moment, the heavy, wooden doors of the church open as if struck by an enraged fist. A gust of wind billows down the aisle, stripping petals off flowers, lifting skirts and sending up a cloud of dust that makes everyone sneeze.

A violent bolt of lightning crosses the sky, cutting a slash of light in the vault of the church. The gust blows out the candles and topples the colorful banners at each side of the altar. Through the windows and the open door, the townspeople bear witness to the torrential rain that blurs the landscape, transforming it into a gloomy smudge.

A new clap of thunder shakes the building from its foundations, shattering a stained glass window. Filomena screams and holds onto her husband. Everyone gathered in the church bears witness to nature unleashing its wrath. The chandelier swings violently and the priest yells that it's time to leave the church, that they are probably safer outside than in. But nobody moves, even as the ceiling beams creak with every gust of wind. No one dares to even breathe.

A silhouette is cast against the curtain of water visible through the door. It's a thin and delicate figure with snakelike hair. Her clothes are in shreds and she is covered with wilted leaves. Her fiery eyes light up a face that used to smile and now only terrorizes.

"Rayen," mumbles Ernesto Schmied, trying to walk towards her. But Clara holds fast to his arm, preventing him from leaving her side.

Rayen raises one arm. Raindrops start to spiral around her. Her body seems submerged in a column of water that envelops her as she walks down the aisle to the altar.

Women cry from the pews but no one dares move.

The sky howls with fury, the electric blast of dark clouds shaking the earth. Ernesto cannot take his eyes off Rayen. He watches as she comes near, walking barefoot down the aisle in her short dress and with a hellish fire in her eyes.

Rain pours into the church through the broken windows and the open door. The floor has flooded and water drips from the walls and even from the ceiling beams.

Rayen stops. She raises her arm and points at Ernesto's impeccable figure.

"I curse you, Ernesto Schmied," she mumbles and her voice sounds like rocks colliding, like bats screeching in the night, like a volcano spewing molten lava.

The oil lamp shakes, causing the chain that holds it to rattle.

"I curse you, Ernesto Schmied! I curse you and all your descendants!" Rayen howls as the raindrops that surround her disperse.

Another window explodes into a thousand pieces, launching bits of colored glass like projectiles. Chaos takes over.

Amidst the commotion and destruction, Rayen's voice can be clearly heard.

"I curse all the people of Almahue, their children, and the children of their children, to Malamor! No one in this town will ever be able to love!" the witch yells. "And anyone who dares to defy me will die!"

A crack opens in the ceiling, and more rain and wind rush in. The chandelier plummets to the altar breaking the crucifix in two and injuring a few people.

Clara Mora throws herself in Ernesto's arms while others push their way to the door. But an even stronger blast of wind throws people to the ground and slams them against the walls.

Rayen seems to rise above the water on her way to the door. Ernesto lets go of his wife, who cries and whimpers like a little girl, to run after Rayen. Outside, his body doubles under the weight of the storm that lashes at him and obscures his vision.

"No one can hurt me anymore!" he hears from the distance.

When he finally looks up, he finds her taking refuge in the foliage of the giant tree in the square, the same tree that Karl Wilhelm grafted. He is not sure, perhaps it's the fury of nature that prevents him from seeing things clearly, but Rayen's feet no longer seem to touch the ground. And her arms have extended like thin branches that shake in the wind and point at him.

"And so you remember how much I hate all of you, the day that this tree dies, the whole town shall disappear! Swallowed by the earth and swept away by the wind!"

Her words echo off of every stone and shrub. Along with a deep cry that floods Almahue, an ear-splitting thunderclap is heard. A bolt of lightning unleashed from above violently strikes Rayen's body, her arms still raised. A flash of light blinds everyone for an instant. Ernesto closes his eyes, protecting his face with one arm. When he dares to open them, the rain and the wind have stopped. Rayen is gone. In her place, there's only the scorched imprint of the lightening strike that puts an end to the storm and marks the beginning of a dreadful legend.

19 WRITING A SUMMARY

Daybreak found Angela awake but groggy, victim of an invincible insomnia. The intensity of the events of the previous day was stronger than fatigue and, as much as she tried, she couldn't forget the haunting series of images. She relived her journey into the forest, the moment she fainted, her visions, discovering Rayen's cave, Benedicto Mohr's body, the strange symbols drawn on the rock and the earthquake that put a violent end to the search.

She pulled her iPod out of her backpack. A little bit of music would help her shift her focus. She slid her finger over the screen until she found the song *Hoy ya me voy* by Kany García. The singer's voice whispered in her ear: *"I'm leaving today, my love, and I fare you well... and I won't cry..."* She stopped for a moment and remained still, realizing that soon she would have to leave Almahue and go back to Santiago, to her life, her home, her school. What about Fabian? Could he come with her? Would *Malamor* follow him? "It hurts me to leave you with the sorrow and the pain..."

This wasn't the moment to think about that. She had to concentrate. There would be time to think about it later. She pulled a notebook out of her backpack, opened it to a blank page, and started writing in capital letters.

SUMMARY

Pensive, she began to write quickly so she wouldn't forget anything important.

1. Egon met Patricia. He hid her cellular phone and is now very scared.

2. SP is Egon Schmied Poblete's last two initials.

3. Patricia feared for her safety.

That is why she hid the message inside the scarecrow.

4. Rayen's father was not who he said he was. He stole a dead man's identity. Who was he?

5. Benedicto Mohr died in the cave inhabited by Rayen.

6. What was Walter Schmied doing in the forest by himself yesterday?

7. What did the symbols in Rayen's cave mean?

Angela tried to reproduce the glyphs drawn on the wall of the cave but even though they were so familiar, she wasn't able to remember them exactly.

She knew there were four. There was a circle and a triangle with a cross on the top. She also remembered they were connected by arrows, like an equation of sorts. She couldn't remember the rest. If only she had been able to snap a picture! In an effort to avoid forgetting them completely, she drew what she could remember.

She put her notebook aside and went back to her unmade bed to get Don Ernesto Schmied's notebook. She was able to finish reading it during her long sleepless hours. She had much to thank Egon's grandfather for. His prose was clear and precise and the amount of detail he gave allowed her to feel as if she had lived the terrible events of 1939. It wasn't hard to evoke Rayen's apparition and she was able to imagine the indelible destruction caused by the fury of the botanist's daughter. The botanist, of course, was another matter. No one knew Karl Wilhelm was an impostor. She could swear that she had seen him appear just before she fainted in the middle of the storm, the memory of the round glasses caused her to shudder. His eyes, dangerous as burning embers, seemed as real as Fabian making way in front of her.

Angela rubbed her face, bewildered, but determined not to think about him anymore. She went to return Don Ernesto's notebook to its place under the floorboards, but stopped short. She sat on the bed and opened the notebook on the paragraph that mentioned the fire in the laboratory and the man's fate after he died in the flames.

... his body was unidentifiable. All that remained was just a small smoldering mound. Some went as far as to swear that those remains were not human: that perhaps they belonged to an animal or one of those strange creatures that, according to town gossip, the scientist held captive in his lab.

If what Don Ernesto wrote in those pages was true, no one could be sure that the body that was buried on the top of the hill was the body of Rayen's father. Could he have escaped the flames?

Maybe, while he was carrying out his comprehensive research on the witch's curse, Benedicto Mohr found out that the impostor was not dead. Maybe that had cost him his life. Maybe Patricia had come to the same conclusion after two weeks in the village and she left Angela a message with Karl Wilhelm's name so she could discover that he was an impostor.

Two perpendicularly joined pieces of wood mark the spot where the remains of Karl Wilhelm rest.

"Very well," Angela said to herself closing the notebook with determination. If that cross was still standing, she would find it. And, once there, she would dig until she found out what was buried underground.

∀ → ○ → ♂

PART III

...for the world, as we know it, as we have seen it, yields but one ending: death...
Joseph Campbell, *The Hero with a Thousand Faces*

1 DARK EYES

Fabian walked in the kitchen freshly bathed and dssed to find Silvia Poblete and Elvira Caicheo. When they saw him at the door, they stopped their conversation, which, judging by the tense silence that remained, wasn't at all friendly. Silvia Poblete took a deep breath and finished what she was doing. Apparently, the confrontation with Egon was still a sore spot.

"I hope today you can serve lunch at two o'clock when my son returns from the shipyard," she told the cook harshly as she walked out the door.

Before leaving, Silvia stared at Fabian for a few seconds. Her eyes were like two little pieces of coal on her pale face. She didn't say a word but Fabian could read her thin-lipped expression and her arched brows, reminding him of his place in the household hierarchy. He was already barred from entering the house through the main door. And now, given what had happened in Egon's room the day before, he guessed he would not be allowed to go upstairs either. Testing his hunch, Fabian looked at his mother and said, "I'm going to say hello to Don Ernesto and see if he needs anything."

"That won't be necessary," Silvia stopped him, staring at him with contempt. "My father-in-law is doing just fine. He doesn't need any help from you."

Fabian bit his tongue. He wouldn't be allowed to see his only friend in that house. He would have liked to confront, once and for all, that woman who took such pleasure in looking down on him. Her fancying herself a fine lady was pathetic and anachronistic. "This is a village with a population of a few hundred people," he thought, "why pretend she is something that she isn't? Everybody knows where she comes from." But out of respect for his mother, who was already in enough trouble, he kept his mouth shut and counted to ten while staring at his worn shoes. He might still be able to speak with Don Ernesto when Silvia wasn't home.

"The poor old man gets all flustered when you go to his room. So I order you to leave him alone. At his age, the last thing he needs is to be upset. Have I made myself clear?" she added imperatively, leaving no room for discussion.

Since Fabian didn't reply, Silvia repeated her question in a louder voice. "Have I made myself clear?"

"Yes," Fabian mumbled without looking at her. Satisfied with the answer, she nodded and fixed a lock of hair that had fallen out of her chignon. She quickly looked at her watch and, pretending she was late for something, turned on her heels and left the kitchen.

When they were alone, Elvira turned to Fabian with her hands on her hips.

"What are you up to?" she asked him. "Do you want me to lose my job and get us kicked out of our home? Mrs. Silvia is furious because you went into Egon's room yesterday!"

"Mother, please, listen to me," he implored. "A lot of strange things are happening in this house. Angela thinks Egon is responsible for..."

"I don't care what that girl thinks!" she interrupted him. "Ever since she arrived in Almahue you haven't been yourself. What does she want? To ruin your life? To leave you for dead?"

"No, she only wants to find her friend," Fabian answered categorically.

"Then tell her to look for her somewhere else, not in my boss' house." Elvira walked to the huge stove, abruptly ending the conversation. Fabian knew it was time to leave. Elvira's mood had changed completely and when she frowned like that it was better to stay as far away from her as possible. He put on his old coat and left without saying goodbye.

~

The temperature outside had dropped considerably. Fabian could see his breath as he walked along the dirt road that led to the square. Angrily, he kicked a couple of stones on the way. Maybe it was time to get started with his plans, the projects he didn't dare tell anyone about but had hatched during sleepless nights. He dreamed about leaving the village, going to Puerto Montt or Chiloé and finding a job in a shipyard. He was very skilled, he could get a job repairing ships. Fabian was sure that he could build a better future for himself far away from the Schmied's household. And now there was Angela... He thought about her luminous smile, the audacious blaze of her hair, so unlike anyone else's, her eyes both daring and shy.

He had no doubt. His heart belonged to Angela Galvez. As he thought about her he felt a spasm in his chest. He stopped cold. It was a spasm, not an emotional reaction. Apparently, the effects of Rosa's potions were beginning to wear off. The idea of suffering acute pain for loving her made his hands sweat.

"Fabian!"

It was Angela's unmistakable voice. No one said his name like she did. When he turned his head he saw her approaching him, all bundled up in a heavy coat and a cap that topped her flaming red hair. "I need you to take me to Don Ernesto," she asked him after greeting him with a kiss.

"I don't recommend that you go in the house," he warned her. "Everyone is in a bad mood... and Mrs. Silvia has forbidden me to go upstairs."

"She can't do that!"

"Of course she can. It's her house." Angela remained silent for a moment as she considered her options. Fabian took her hand, interlacing their fingers. A sudden jolt of electricity ran through his backbone out to his fingertips. The symptoms were returning, not as intensely as the first time but painfully enough to concern him.

"I need to find where Rayen's father is buried," Angela said with frustration. "Don Ernesto is the only person who knows where his grave is." Before Fabian could interrupt her, she added: "And you're going to help me open it. I need to find out what's inside."

Fabian fell silent for an instant. He could have never imagined Angela asking him to do something like that. To desecrate a grave! She told him what she had been thinking: if the botanist pretended he was Karl Wilhelm, he must have had a reason. Maybe he was hiding a bigger and more dangerous secret. No one was sure he had died in the fire. According to Don Ernesto's notebook, it was impossible to identify his body after the tragedy. Some even ventured to say that the remains they found belonged to an animal. What if the botanist had fooled the entire village? What if he had survived the fire in his laboratory?

"Our only option is to open his grave. Last night, I read that it's at the top of one of the mountains surrounding Almahue. A white cross marks the exact place.

"Do you know how many mountains surround the village? It could take us a year to find it!"

"That's why I need to talk to Don Ernesto! He's the only one who can tell me where..."

Angela didn't finish her sentence. Instinctively she put her hands to her head when out of the corner of her eye saw something flying in her direction. The white heron was gliding close to the ground and staring at her.

"It's that bird again!" she said, taken aback.

The bird flew quietly in circles over them. Its sleek body cut the air like a sharp knife. It looked like a white weather vane indicating the four cardinal points every time it turned.

The bird descended. This time, Angela didn't look away or cover herself. She stood there ready to face whatever came her way, and the heron didn't scare her, on the contrary, she was happy to see it. The bird croaked hoarsely and spread its wings like a dancer about to perform the most sublime movement.

"Watch out!" Fabian cried when he noticed that the bird was not going to change its course.

But Angela didn't move. She remained motionless, facing the wind from the flapping of its wings as she looked straight into its dark eyes, so perplexingly human, so vivacious and smart that they didn't seem to belong to the body they were attached to. When the heron was about to touch her face, it bent its long neck and turned around with scrupulous precision, barely grazing Angela's face like a gentle caress. Then it spiraled up in the air.

"It's trying to tell us something," Angela mumbled in awe. "Fabian, it wants us to follow it!"

"How do you know?"

"I saw it in its eyes. Can you get a shovel?"

"Yes, there's one in the workshop."

"Then go get it. And come back soon," she begged. When she looked up, Angela could swear that the dark eyed bird gave her a knowing smile.

2 SIX FEET UNDER

The bird's shadow was their constant companion along the way. Angela and Fabian hiked long stretches that were covered in mud and *calafate* bushes. It was as if the cold had turned the wind to glass that had to be broken in order to keep going. Angela didn't complain. Not once. Her sight was fixed on the winged creature that was showing them the way. Fabian led with a walking stick in one hand, clearing *nalca* leaves and ferns with the other so that they could pass more easily.

When they began to climb a steep slope, Angela asked herself for the first time if it hadn't been an irresponsible decision to allow a heron to determine their fate. She took a deep breath and grabbed a bamboo stalk to push herself along the way.

They walked in silence. The only thing Angela heard was Fabian's rhythmic breathing. He was as used to this climb as the heron that flew above them was. When they were on the verge of the summit, Angela stopped for a few moments to catch her breath. She looked around and got chills from the overwhelming beauty of the place. From there, she could see the entire valley, the mountains that surrounded Almahue, the ocean that penetrated the continent and the colorful vessels heading out to sea.

"Angela..."

It was the first time he had called her by her name. Although she had heard those three syllables thousands of times before, they had never sounded sweeter. "Angela." Even in the midst of so much uncertainty, and even danger, she was grateful for having followed her instincts to travel to the end of the world to find Patricia. If she hadn't, she would have never met Fabian. When she turned around to look at him, he was pointing upwards. His mouth hung open. She traced the line he was indicating and saw that, at the highest point, there was a rickety wooden cross. There, the heron rested.

Angela ran to the apex and fell to her knees next to the bird and next to the grave they had been searching. There were still flecks of the white paint that had, at one time, covered the cross. If one looked closely, "Karl Wilhelm" could still be seen, written in Don Ernesto Schmied's perfect calligraphy.

"We found it!" Angela shouted. The bird spread its wings in what seemed like a bow and rose to the sky, disappearing in the clouds.

~

Fabian dug his shovel into the dirt while Angela removed the stones that surrounded the cross. Neither spoke. They were interrupting the eternal rest of a dead man. They supposed there would be consequences even though there might not be a body. In any case, they would carry out their task with the utmost respect.

For what seemed like an eternity, the only thing they heard was the monotonous sound of the metal burying itself in the earth and the passing of a raucous flock of parrots flapping their yellow-green wings.

Noon erased the shadows. By this time, the hole was quite deep. Fabian was in his shirtsleeves, the muscles in his arms visible under the fabric, bulging each time he dug the shovel into the pebbles. He was sweating despite the cold and the wind. Even though they were expecting it, they were still startled by the unexpected sound of the shovel hitting something.

Fabian looked at Angela, who stood up to get into the hole.

"Did you get to the coffin?" she asked anxiously. Fabian didn't answer. He used the shovel to clean surface, revealing wood.

He hit it a couple of times. The planks, rotted from the years and the humidity, cracked before yielding a little bit. Fabian gave the tool to Angela and kneeled to continue with his hands. He put his fingers in a small opening and pressed a bit to the side. A groan alerted them that the lid of the coffin was about to break and reveal its contents.

"Do you want to see what's inside?" Fabian asked, lifting his head and seeing that Angela was pale with fright.

Angela shook her head and took a step backward. She didn't feel like she was capable of looking into a coffin that had been buried for almost seventy years.

She thought for a moment. Whatever was in there couldn't be worse than having stumbled upon the remains of Benedicto Mohr in Rayen's cave. Or, maybe that's not what scared her. Maybe it wasn't the presence of a decomposing body that was causing her fear. It was something else: precisely the opposite. She reproached herself for always taking things to the limit only to waver at the climax. She still had a long, long way to go before she could consider herself a brave person.

When she heard Fabian trying to remove a few more planks to enlarge the hole, she knew that it was time to close her eyes. A whiff of foul air hit her in the face. She closed her eyes even tighter. Fabian had opened the coffin.

"You've got to see this," was the only thing he said.

No. She wasn't going to see anything. She didn't need to see anything to understand what was happening. That's why she backed up even further, shaking from head to toe. She shook her head to dispel the dread that was growing in her heart. As much as she tried, she couldn't forget the tracks in the mud that she had found outside her window, and the unexplainable disappearance of the Rayen book. Everything made sense now. The mysterious author of these misdeeds finally had a name.

"It's empty! There's no one here! They buried a coffin full of rocks!" she heard Fabian shout.

Of course, she already knew that. Deep down, she had always known. The heron had brought her here to once and for all confirm her suspicions. There was no doubt. Rayen's father, Karl Wilhelm, or whatever the unfortunate botanist was named, had kidnapped Patricia and was now after her.

He was as alive as anyone in Almahue. And that was what scared her the most.

3 WARP AND WOOF

By the time Angela entered Rosa's house, night had arrived much earlier than usual. At two o'clock in the afternoon the sky was covered by a canopy of clouds and had become totally dark. "It's The Gloom," Fabian had told her as he shoveled the dirt back into the empty grave of the presumed Karl Wilhelm. He had looked up to the sky and frowned. Bad news. And he was right because they had to feel their way back to the village through the shadows, guided only by the humming of the insects and Fabian's innate sense of direction.

In order to keep Angela distracted on their way down, and to avoid her being scared by the sudden darkness, Fabian told her that The Gloom rarely occurred, and that it was caused by variations in the weather. He explained that whenever this happened, the temperature dropped and a thick, solid layer of clouds resembling a frozen shield of water vapor blocked the sunlight. On the ground, the confused animals lay down to sleep, birds flew back to their nests, foxes ran back to their foxholes, cattle closed their eyes, and hens stopped laying eggs waiting for daybreak. Pessimists said that if it lasted too long, there would be considerable damage to agriculture and livestock. But this had never happened. In Almahue there were no records of The Gloom having lasted more than one afternoon.

Nonetheless, the excessively pious attributed The Gloom to divine wrath or to the imminent end of the world. Fabian laughed when he remembered an anecdote: many years ago, on one of those gloomy days, Mrs. Hortense, a most sanctimonious woman, stood on a bench in the square and alerted the village to the clear signs of the impeding apocalypse.

"One of the biblical plagues is universal darkness! The time for crying has come! Get on your knees and repent for your sins before it's too late!" she cried.

Fortunately, no one listened to her, and shortly after her speech, the clouds dissolved in the rain. Birds flew from their nests, foxes left their foxholes, the cattle chewed their cud, and the hens went back to laying eggs.

Despite Fabian's best attempts to calm her down, Angela was able to read his concern between the lines. She didn't like the idea of an endless night, of being forever deprived of sunlight.

When they parted in front of Rosa's door, they couldn't even see their own hands, although it was only five o'clock. Don't worry. This will be over sooner than you know," Fabian told her and gave her a quick kiss.

The moment his lips touched hers, he felt another spasm, the strongest he had felt so far. Angela backed off immediately feeling the violent shudder in Fabian.

"Are you alright?" she asked.

"It's *Malamor* again," he muttered as he looked for something to lean on due to the sudden weakness in his limbs.

"We need to ask Rosa for more of the antidote."

"Don't worry. I'm fine, I only need to rest for a while." Despite Angela's pleas, Fabian didn't go in the house with her to ask Rosa for a new potion. She watched as he disappeared into the thick darkness. Angela entered the house and groped in the dark of the long, silent hallway.

"Rosa!" she cried but heard only the sound of her own voice bouncing off each wall.

She passed by the kitchen door. The kitchen was deserted and silent. "Rosa must be in her workshop," she concluded.

She went to the back of the house. "Come in," Rosa said, as Angela was just about to knock on the door. When she entered the room, she saw Rosa sitting in front of the loom, intertwining threads of wool, her delicate hands dancing rhythmically. Angela was just about to tell Rosa about the adventure on the hilltop, and ask her if she could brew another dose of the potion that vanquished *Malamor*, when her gaze fell on a rug that hung on one of the walls. She had seen it the first time she entered the workshop. It was woven with three colors of thread: brown, red and black. In the center it had a circle out of which circles and triangles of different sizes sprang. Some had crosses and arrows on the top.

The blood froze in her veins.

These were the same symbols she had seen in Rayen's cave, the same symbols that had been drawn in red ink on the wall next to where they found Benedicto Mohr's bones. That explained the feeling of déjà vu when she saw them under the light of the lantern!

There they were. Finally. Clearly drawn into the warp and woof of the rug.

"What do the symbols mean on the rug that's hanging on the wall? Where do they come from?" she asked holding Rosa by the arm and forcing her to stop her work.

Rosa's face hardened. For the first time, a scowl crossed her face transmitting her annoyance at Angela's questions. "Please, it's very important," Angela begged.

"I dreamed them." was all Rosa answered, in a tone that suggested no further information would be forthcoming. Azabache's unexpected and heartrending meow took them both aback. The cat stumbled into the room, bumping into the chair where Rosa was sitting. It collapsed on the floor as if totally befuddled or dying.

"The Gloom... Yes, Azabache, this time it's really bad... really bad!" Rosa lamented as she jumped on her feet and left Angela alone in the room.

Paralyzed, Angela stared at the symbols on the rug until she memorized them forever. "What do they mean? What do they mean?" If only she could connect to the Internet and look it up, or if Carlos Ule were near, it would be easier for her to find the answer to her questions. Carlos seemed to know everything. And what he didn't know, he could find in his Bookmobile. The problem was locating him. She could go to the Schmied shipyard and try to call Puerto Chacabuco on the old radio. Perhaps if someone heard her, they could give him her urgent message.

"As soon as the sun comes out I will get to it," she decided.

But the sun was not coming out. At least not for her.

4 TRANSMUTATION

Curled up on her side of the bed, Silvia was snoring softly when Walter sat up next to her and checked that she was still asleep. He quietly got up, walked to the window and opened the curtain, gazing outside at the darkest night he could ever recall. No signs of daybreak. How would he know if she was looking for him? He hadn't been in the forest for two days to calm her down. Ever since the news that the tree in the square had sprouted, she was anxious, upset. For the first time in almost seventy years *something* had subdued the power of *Malamor*. And that *something* had to do with the stranger. He couldn't allow things to change. The situation was far more dangerous than he had thought. The fate of that damned tree was to die and drag Almahue to its destruction. That was the punishment for the atrocity they committed against them.

He had to stop Angela Galvez…

Walter put on his heavy coat, took his scarf, and quietly left the room. The truth was that he didn't know why he took so much care not to wake his wife. She never opened her eyes. After taking a sleeping pill and putting her head on the pillow there was no human power that could bring her back from her dreams. "That has been very convenient," Walter thought as he went downstairs.

When he opened the door the cold air slapped him in the face. He had to slow down. But it was not the cold that kept him from walking as fast as he wished, nor was it the muddy roads. The darkness that had taken over Almahue was the worst he could recall. She must be really angry to call The Gloom.

He imagined her in the forest vibrating with the rhythm of the foliage in the trees that sheltered her. She had probably raised her arms, her enormous and infinite arms, to summon the western clouds to stop the rays of the sun from reaching the ground. She had growled at them, urging them to block any light that could give warmth or life to the wretched people that ruined her. Walter knew that The Gloom would last longer than it normally did. "Of course," he said to himself, "things had never gotten this far. No one has been so close to finding out her secret."

He had to stop Angela Galvez.

The echo of his uneven steps followed him. His limp didn't allow him to move faster. He looked around but couldn't see beyond the end of his nose. He was safe. Darkness was his ally.

He groped about in the dark to the middle of street looking for the space he needed. He closed his eyes and sank in a dark well. He took a deep breath, filling his lungs with the cool air. The smell of damp earth unsettled the cells in his body and rushed the blood through his veins. His pulse became a thunderous drum. His temples pounded so hard that his entire head creaked.

To speed up the process, he began to exhale a warm breath that turned into vapor when it hit the cold night air. His feet sank in the mud and his fingers became rigid. He waited for the seizure to begin the process. He felt it growing in his lower back. First it was a like a small tickling. Then it turned into an avalanche of lava that climbed up his spine to his neck. An infernal heat ran through his arms and legs. He bit his lip so that he wouldn't scream from the unbearable burning that melted his ligaments.

He was about to cross the threshold.

He squeezed his eyes shut, anticipating the intense vertigo that would follow. His body began to vibrate. It moved forward and backwards as if he were walking on the deck of a boat, rocking in the waves. The swell soon became worse. Though planted on the ground, Walter Schmied twisted in ways that defied the laws of gravity. The rocking movement intensified. His forehead almost touched the ground. Then his body was pushed back until the back of his head almost touched it again. The rotation transformed his body into a blur, a flash of light generating wind like a propeller.

There he was, turning into an explosion, a Big Bang that would soon put a new order in the chaos. He could feel his muscles melt as he floated in the air for an instant, waiting to regenerate into a new form. The next step was to disappear, like paint that is washed away with a solvent until no trace of it is left. But before everything vanished away, the acceleration slowly decreased and what seemed like a shapeless mass began to take form. Instead of Walter Schmied, from the center of the vortex emerged another person: a bald, curved man with a prominent belly.

Convinced that no one had witnessed his transmutation, he walked up the street with renewed strength. Angela had only seen him twice in this form: one night on board of the ferry, *Evangelistas*, and briefly in front of the tree in the square.

Then, knowing that the intruder was running out of time, he directed his steps to the forest where his daughter was surely waiting for him with open arms.

5 DARKNESS

After ten hours of uninterrupted sleep, Angela opened her eyes feeling much better than she had in days. The walk to the top of the mountain where Karl Wilhelm's mortal remains were supposedly buried had left her completely exhausted, but her body had not just been suffering the consequences of spending an entire day walking. The empty grave only proved that something very serious was happening, and she was befuddled by it. She never imagined that a legend that was passed on by a group of gullible and superstitious people could be as real as the fact that her life was in danger. And not only her life but also Patricia's and Fabian's, who was again suffering the effects of *Malamor* and whose heart had become a time bomb.

A big yawn brought Angela's sleep to an end. She jumped out of the bed, went to the window, and vigorously opened the curtain. Angela hoped that the sunlight would fill her with renewed energy, but even with the curtains opened wide, her bedroom remained as dark. Outside, the garden was a large black spot, so dense and impenetrable that she couldn't make out the slightest detail. Even the ever-present scarecrow had disappeared into the gullet of the hungry Gloom.

For an instant, Angela was disoriented and thought that perhaps she had woken up in the middle of the night, her body clock mixed up because of the overwhelming events of the past twenty-four hours. But, when she opened the bedroom door and heard Rosa in the kitchen, she knew that it was daytime, that she was hungry for breakfast, and that Almahue was still under the effects of the sinister and strange climatological phenomenon. How long would the darkness last?

She found Rosa wrapping freshly baked bread in white cloths. The fragrant contents of the teapot were slowly steeping on the fire. Unlike other mornings, Rosa didn't speak a word when Angela sat at the table and began fixing herself a sandwich. Rosa ignored Angela, who was taken aback by her sudden change of attitude.

"Good morning," she said cautiously, when it was evident that Rosa was not going to say anything.

Rosa nodded and walked to the stove. She took the teapot and poured some tea for herself.

"Is there anything wrong?" Angela asked, eager to put an end to the awkwardness that had begun the night before.

Rosa put the steaming cup aside, took a deep breath and walked towards Angela. She took her by the elbow, forcing her to stand up. Angela tried to break loose but Rosa was holding her so firmly that she couldn't move.

"Pack your bags... get out of Almahue," she commanded. "Now!"

Shocked by Rosa's hostility and rudeness, Angela tried to defend herself but couldn't. Rosa dragged Angela out of the kitchen down the hallway and shoved into her room making her stumble over her bags.

"Don't you understand?" Rosa yelled. "You have to leave today. As soon as possible!"

"No! I won't leave until I find Patricia," Angela answered, still in shock.

"Fabian will die if you stay. Don't you care about him?"

"Not if you fix him one of your antidotes."

"It won't work twice, Angela. I'm sorry but a lot of people are in danger because of you. The whole village will suffer the consequences of your...!" But Rosa couldn't finish her sentence. The bedroom had suddenly tipped to one side, as if the foundations of the house had sunk. The armoire doors opened and the contents tumbled out. The heavy bronze bed jumped and skated to the end of the room, pushing Angela against the wall. A crack split the ceiling in two, causing dangerous short circuits in the cables that began sparking.

The second shock was even stronger. The windows shattered. Outside, the terrorized neighbors ran into the dark streets screaming. Angela heard Azabache's heartrending meow. Big chunks of plaster fell from the ceiling filling the air with a fine, white dust. Angela shut her eyes, trying to concentrate in order to find her way out of what seemed like the imminent destruction of Almahue's oldest house. The noise was deafening.

After a raging roar that came from the depths of the earth and splintered the parquet floor, an unexpected calm took over. Angela waited several seconds to open her eyes. She was scared of what she would find. When she finally did, she saw that everything had been destroyed. The wall that divided the bedroom from the hallway had a huge hole. The armoire had fallen forward and was broken in two. Parts of the ceiling had fallen on the bed and the little lamp on the night table was shattered. The floor had opened in several places swallowing the chair and the table where she used to read. A black bundle peeped out.

Azabache shook the splinters and the dirt off of its fur. The cat jumped in Angela's arms and she had no choice but to hold it tightly against her chest.

Where was Rosa?

Looking for her meant that Angela had to get out of the place where she was trapped, and that would take some time. She tried to move a big piece of wood blocking her way out when she heard a noise coming from the other side of the window. When she turned around, she saw a fluttering of white wings that took off from the garden and disappeared into the darkness. Her heron?

A sudden flash turned the sky red before all the lights in the village went off. Angela felt as if she were floating in the middle of the room, incapable of knowing the way out.

"The high voltage tower fell!" she heard someone crying from the street.

The whole village was now in total darkness. With The Gloom blocking the sunlight and without electricity, the people of Almahue were condemned to virtual blindness. There was nowhere to run in such unrelenting darkness. She held Azabache closely and groped her way through the rubble. She bumped into a bundle on the floor. Her backpack! She opened one of the external pockets, pulled out her iPod and turned it on. Fortunately she had charged the battery the last time she listened to music. It should last for a couple of hours. Angela shined the bright screen ahead of her, as if it were a flashlight, and made her way to the door.

On her way to the hallway, something caught her attention. On top of what was left of the armoire, she saw a long, beautiful, white feather. Azabache climbed up to her neck and curled around her like a scarf. Anxious, Angela took the feather knowing that the explanation for its presence was far more amazing than she was willing to admit. When she pointed the iPod to the floor, she saw another feather at her feet and then another by the curtain. Three feathers marked the path from where Rosa had been to the window. Angela went into the hallway, searching for her host, but she was nowhere. Rejecting the crazy explanation she had for Rosa's sudden disappearance, Angela assumed she'd gotten out.

Angela took to the street that was crowded with terrorized people improvising encampments and lighting candles to overcome The Gloom. They were so busy dealing with the earthquake that no one noticed her frantic race to the shipyard. She was so entirely focused on the road, her arms extended to the front, to warn her of any obstacles in the way, that she didn't notice someone was closely following the reddish trace of her hair.

Nothing was going to stop her from accomplishing the mission she had set for herself the night before asking Carlos Ule to help her decipher the symbols she saw in the cave and on the rug. And this time, she would do it alone to protect Fabian. If Rosa was right and her potions couldn't help him overcome the curse of *Malamor*, then her mere presence could hurt him.

"Come, Azabache. You'll be my partner now."

6 THE ENCOUNTER

"Please, come with me. Let's get out of here," Egon urged Don Ernesto, who was standing in the middle of the mess the earthquake left behind.

The bronze lamp was still swinging from the rafters when the young man, concerned for his grandfather's well-being, rushed into the attic. He had found him clinging to one of the columns that supported the ceiling, illuminated only by the wood stove. Egon cast a glance about the room. Fortunately, the damage was relatively minor. The beveled mirror and the decorations were broken and the books were all over the floor, but there were no cracks on the walls, no windows were askew, and the round window was intact. Just like in the past, the house had resisted the earthquake.

"Let's go downstairs. There may be an aftershock. Let me help you," Egon suggested as he slicked his hair back.

Don Ernesto didn't answer. He was not going to join Walter and Silvia, whom he could still hear frantically screaming on the first floor. He nodded and walked to the round window, sorting through the chaos.

"Grandfather, are you going to stay here? Alone?" Egon asked surprised. Walter staggered into the room. He was short of breath, probably due to the effort of climbing upstairs with his bad leg. "What's going on?" Walter asked without looking at his father.

"He won't come down," Egon replied. Don Ernesto Schmied stared at Walter. His wrinkled face showed both bewilderment and repulsion.

"This is quite a surprise. What are you doing here?" the old man confronted Walter. "When was the last time you came to see me?"

"If he doesn't want to come down, it's his problem," Walter told Egon, totally ignoring Don Ernesto's words. "This place isn't safe. Let's go!"

"You are not my son!" Don Ernesto cried, pointing a trembling yet defiant finger at Walter.

Walter turned to his son with a look of exhaustion on his face, letting him know that the confrontation was about to begin. Egon nodded and quietly went down into the hallway. He didn't want to witness another quarrel.

"Go with him," the old man shouted at him. "You have no business here."

"Listen to yourself! Listen to yourself, father! You're demented."

"Don't call me father again. I don't know who you are, but I'm sure you're not my son, the one I watched grow up, the son who disappeared in the forest..." Walter clenched his fists and bit his lower lip. He felt the blood rushing to his head like a wave. A weak buzz filled his ears, a prelude to a fight that could end badly. He had to control himself and avoid any error in front of them. That could be his end. And *hers.*

"And who am I supposed to be?" he asked and took a very deep breath to get rid of the buzzing in his ears.

"Who knows? An impostor. Someone who knew how to take his place," Don Ernesto said raising his voice to confront Walter. "Did you think I wouldn't notice? Where is my real son? Tell me! What did you do to him?"

Silvia's husband thought it was time to leave.

The decrepit old man had turned out to be smarter, and closer to his son, than he thought. As hard as he tried to imitate the real Walter there had always been details that he couldn't master. Nonetheless, transmuting himself into the son of the Schmieds had been quite successful. He had been able to enter the family that had so hurt him and his daughter. The day he found Walter in the forest he had fallen down the mountainside and was dying. His right ankle had an open fracture and he had a dislocated hip and a deep cut on his head. He couldn't walk. He may have sped up the dying process a little bit, which was inevitable during the process of taking Walter's form anyway. He hid in the cave to add a dramatic touch to the whole matter and justify whatever doubt should arise from his new behavior. If he couldn't master a perfect Walter, he could say that the nightmare he had lived in the forest changed him, inside and out. That's what he did. Silvia had always been a distant wife anyway. She never noticed anything. And she didn't ask any questions when he spent long periods of time in the forest to be in touch with nature, his life, his strength.

"You're a poor old man, a fool, an idiot. No one will believe you," he answered with a different voice, an ancient voice that Don Ernesto had heard seventy years earlier.

"You can't offend me. I know what I'm saying."

"To be ignorant like the simplest creatures is the greatest offense that you can commit. Don't forget that, *father*," he exaggerated the last word, and smiling, left the room.

Don Ernest Schmied closed his eyes. He was bewildered. He felt that he had opened a door to the past, a door through which Karl Wilhelm had entered his room. He collapsed on the bed, his bones and his soul shaking uncontrollably. Could it be possible?

7 A CLOSED DOOR

Unlike the first time she went to the shipyard, this time there were no employees or seagulls to greet Angela. On the contrary, the place seemed like a solitary and decrepit warehouse, and every corner smelled like salt air and varnish. Despite the darkness, from the moment she opened the door, Angela could tell that the earthquake had caused serious damage to the Schmied's business. What was once the monumental frame of a ship now looked like a broken skeleton whose bones had been scattered all over the place. Part of the ceiling had collapsed and cold drafts of air blew in through the cracks freezing the already foul air. Angela rushed to the back, lighting her way with the screen of her iPod, Rosa's cat still curled around her neck.

She was on her way to Egon's private office when she stopped dead in her tracks. She heard footsteps behind her. The blood froze in her veins. If anyone found her there they could accuse her of trespassing on private property or of looting in the midst of the chaos and devastation.

"Did you hear that too, Azabache?" she whispered to the cat that rubbed its head against her ear.

Persuaded that the noise was in her mind or was produced by the Patagonian wind, she opened the door and entered Egon's office. A quick scan with her improvised flashlight allowed her to see that the photos of yachts, cruise ships, catamarans and other types of vessels were no longer hanging on the walls but scattered across the floor. She found the old radio on the side table, under a few folders and papers that had fallen from the shelves, surrounded by the collection of ships in bottles, few of which were intact.

The cat jumped to the floor and stayed by the desk. Angela flipped the radio's power switch and a green light turned on. She had never been so grateful for batteries in her life. She turned the knob that looked like it was for "Volume" and a series of indistinct squeals came out of the speaker. Not paying attention to the static that made its small antenna vibrate, she took the microphone and pressed the side button just as she had seen the captain of the *Evangelistas* ferry do on her way to Almahue.

"Hello? Hello? I'm Angela Galvez and I'm calling from Almahue. Can anybody hear me?"

She waited in silence.

The only sound she heard was Azabache's claws scratching a surface. She found the cat by one of the legs of the desk, scratching a board on the floor. She snapped her fingers but it went on, focusing on its task and totally disregarding Angela's efforts to stop it.

"I'm Angela Galvez and I'm calling from the shipyard in Almahue. I need to speak to Carlos Ule in Puerto Chacabuco. Can anybody hear me?" she repeated in a higher voice.

Suddenly the metallic buzz turned into a series of sharp, rhythmic beeps. And, underneath the squealing, Angela could hear a faint voice.

"Attention. Puerto Chacabuco to Almahue. Over."

Angela repeated, her voice breaking from the emotion, that she urgently needed to reach Carlos Ule, the teacher with the Bookmobile. If anyone knew him or could get a message to him, she pleaded that they ask him to get to Almahue as soon as possible because there were matters of life and death that required his presence. She also told the person on the other end that an earthquake had hit the village, causing damage and toppling a high-voltage tower.

"Copy. Thank you. Over and out."

As quickly as it had appeared, the metallic voice disappeared into the static. Angela was quiet for a few moments, unsuccessfully waiting for confirmation that her message about Carlos Ule had arrived loud and clear at its destination. The only thing she heard was Azabache frantically scratching at the floorboards next to Egon's desk.

"What's wrong?" she asked approaching the cat, shining the light at it.

She could see that the cat had cleared the way for her to see what looked like a deep fissure between the boards. Unlike the damage caused by the earthquake, this wasn't a crack with jagged edges. It was perfectly straight. Angela brought her hand close and touching it, felt a faint draft escape from the cleft. Azabache kept rubbing its paw energetically against a metal ring that was screwed into the floor. Angela had a flashback. *"That's the entrance to an old cellar. I'm constantly twisting my ankle when I step on it,"* was Egon's explanation when she tripped over it.

"Do you want me to open it? Is that it?" she suggested, receiving an immediate meow as an answer.

Angela pushed the desk to the side, revealing the hatch that led to what she supposed was a subterranean warehouse. She grasped the metal ring, the only means by which to raise it, and pulled with all her strength. It didn't budge. Securing her feet against the floor, she breathed deeply and pulled on the ring with both hands. It was futile. It appeared to be a door condemned to disuse during years. Salt air, corrosion and rust had blocked it forever.

"I'm sorry, I can't open it," she apologized to Azabache who arched its back in protest. "Let's go, please."

Just as she began to walk out of the office, a man grabbed her by her arms. She was ready to defend herself against the intruder, but she smelled the aroma of smoked wood, of the forest after the rain, of the sky covered by clouds and her heart instantly calmed down.

"Fabian!" she exclaimed scarcely able to believe her eyes. "What are you doing here?" he asked, his voice charged with worry.

"The question is what are you doing here?"

"I followed you from Rosa's house. I thought you might need some help and so I..." Fabian stopped in the middle of his answer. He doubled over with a convulsion, grabbing his abdomen. Frightened, Angela stepped back knowing that she was responsible for the terrible pain that afflicted him.

"Please go! I don't want to hurt you. Rosa told me that she can't prepare another antidote for *Malamor*."

Fabian straightened up as soon as he could, clenching his jaw to manage the pain. He wasn't going to let a curse that had nothing to do with him force him to put an end to the strongest and most beautiful feeling he had ever experienced. He was prepared to put up a fight. Even if his body succumbed to the seizures and the cramps, Angela was worth the sacrifice.

"Please, leave me alone! We're talking about your life and..."

This time Angela wasn't able to finish her sentence. A surprising kiss erased everything around them and united their worlds. They kissed as never before, trying to hide inside each other, measuring the strength of their love with their tongues and lips. Their hearts were beating so strongly that even Azabache could hear them.

They separated after several seconds. Thanks to the feeble light of the iPod, Angela saw Fabian smile like a little boy who had done something he shouldn't but didn't feel guilty about it.

"Now let's get out of here," he said decisively although his head was spinning and he had an overpowering buzz in his ears.

Despite his intentions, he wasn't able to make it to the office door. He had to lean on something to keep his knees from giving out from under as the pain that was took over his insides.

"Let's wait a bit," he suggested. "Until I feel better."

"Let me go for help," Angela implored.

"I'm fine. Take it easy. I'll be ready to keep going in a minute."

Angela brought Egon's chair over. She took advantage of the time to see if she could find something to finally open up the hatch in the floor. When Fabian asked her why she was doing that, she explained how Azabache had insistently drawn her attention to what must be the access to the cellar. Fabian leaned over and took the ring in his hands.

"No, be careful. You're weak," Angela warned.

Moved by curiosity, Fabian began to pull at the ring for all he was worth. A thick vein stood out on his neck. The muscles in his arms flexed. The groan of the old hinges alerted Angela to the fact that Fabian had been successful. He gave it one final try, his red hands seizing the metal ring. The heavy hatch fell backwards, exposing an opening in the floor. The cat immediately jumped into it, disappearing in the middle of the darkness.

"Azabache, no!" Angela shouted.

Fabian took the iPod out of her hands and shined it into the hole. The light it produced, weakening by the minute, illuminated two steps of a makeshift wooden ladder that penetrated the darkness. A fetid odor of humidity, damp earth and rotting food burst from the depths. A distant meowing let them know that there was quite a distance between them and the cat. Far below them, they could see the eyes of the cat shining like twin stars in deep space. Suddenly, without any warning at all, two other eyes could be seen blinking briefly and then disappearing.

"There's someone down there!" Fabian exclaimed.

Angela tried to hold him back by his clothes, determined to keep him from descending into the darkness, but couldn't. She saw him leap into the void and then heard his footsteps penetrating the darkness. The light from the iPod was getting farther and farther away, flickering like the tiny flame of a candle that was threatening to go out.

Angela knew that she didn't have any other option. She stretched out her foot and rested it on the first rung. She supported herself as well as she could on the edge of the hatch and began to descend. When her head was below the floor, it was even darker. She brushed her hand against a rough wall that helped steady her, but the rungs were getting weaker and more slippery because of the humidity.

"Fabian?" she whispered, and the echo of her voice bounced a hundred times before evaporating in a vibration that sounded like a musical note.

"Here..."

At the bottom of the ladder she stood on an uneven surface covered with pebbles. Scared she might fall in a hole or lose her way back to the ladder, she didn't want to let go of the wall. She didn't move, thinking about what to do next, trying to orient herself in the midst of her open-eyed blindness.

"Fabian...?" she repeated, frightened by his prolonged silence.

Several yards ahead, the screen of her iPod caught her attention. Relieved, she took a breath. There was Fabian illuminating himself so that she could see him. Then he shined the light on another body, that of a woman whose wrist was chained to the wall, unable to move.

On the verge of fainting from the agony, Patricia looked up from the floor and her eyes shone with hope.

8 VIGIL

Although no one had actually suggested it, the activity around the tree in the square became a hub of constant hustle and bustle for all the villagers. Despite the fact that the clock had just struck eleven o'clock in the morning, the impenetrable darkness that reigned made the people behave as if it were midnight. Many had decided not to return to their homes, frightened that an aftershock could end up knocking down what was still standing. One by one they rested on their mattresses, chairs or even the tables they had managed to salvage. To ward off the cold, some had improvised tents. They tied a rope around the trunk of the tree and attached it to the post of the lone nearby streetlight that, like the rest of the village, was dark. From the rope they suspended blankets, bedspreads, and even ponchos to act as temporary shelters. Others lit fires to warm their lunches that, given the circumstances, seemed more like dinners. And others brought votive candles they had taken from the chapel, and placed them at strategic points to light what they imagined would be a long vigil.

Silvia Poblete commandeered one of the four benches in the square and no human force was capable of moving her from there. The earth hadn't even stopped shaking when she stumbled down the stairs shouting that everyone should abandon the house. She ran into the street without putting on a coat and from there saw her house quake from top to bottom like a box of matches that someone was shaking to see if there was anything inside. She anxiously looked at the crown of the tree, praying to heaven that sap still ran through at least one of the green leaves on the branches.

"And so you remember how much I hate all of you, the day that this tree dies, the whole town shall disappear! Swallowed by the earth and swept away by the wind!" Rayen's words had been passed down from generation to generation so that nobody could forget the mortal threat hanging over their heads. "For now we should be calm," Silvia thought upon seeing that the only two healthy branches were still intact. She made herself comfortable on the bench as Elvira came outside carrying a heavy woolen shawl that she draped around Silvia's shoulders.

"What about Egon? And Walter? Where are they?" she exclaimed, exaggerating the vibrato of her anguish so that no one within earshot would have any doubt that she was worried for her family.

"I think they went up to see Don Ernesto, ma'am," Elvira replied.

"No! They must come down. It could be dangerous," she lamented. "And Fabian? Where is he? I don't see him."

Elvira was sick at heart. She didn't know where her son was but she knew whom he was with. They hadn't spoken since their argument in the kitchen. And the outsider was to blame. If only that girl had listened when Elvira begged her to return to the capital. Elvira's problems with Fabian were Angela's fault!

"Egon, never leave me alone again!" Silvia shouted opening her arms as if she were on stage and not in the middle of the street when she saw her son emerge from their house.

Egon crossed the square just in time to hold his mother who broke into tears and lamentations. By doing this, the villagers would realize that not only was she sensitive but also an exemplary mother who had brought up her only son to watch out for her and her well-being.

"There, there, mother. The worst is over."

"And your father?"

"He's with grandfather, who doesn't want to come down." He looked up at the apex of the façade where the faintly illuminated round window could be seen.

"That's impossible! If my father-in-law wants to keep playing hermit, that's his business. But Walter! Walter!" she shrieked to no avail. "Egon, go look for him and bring him even if he doesn't want to come! Is that clear?"

Egon nodded and went back into the house. Everything was dark. He stood on the first step of the stairway and yelled up to the second floor.

"Father!" He heard a door close behind him. "Father, is that you?" No one answered. He crossed the hall, where the tick-tock of the grandfather clock and the creak of his feet on the parquet were the only things to be heard. He went into the kitchen. The aroma of the stew that Elvira had left behind when she ran out during the earthquake hit him full in the face, reminding him how hungry he was.

"Father?"

A shadow, outlined by the outside darkness, crossed in front of a window. Someone was on the servants' patio. Egon rushed outside, prepared to confront whoever it was. It was probably someone who had broken into the house to rob it, taking advantage of the prevailing darkness.

"Who's there?" he shouted without getting a response.

He waited a few moments. He listened hard but didn't hear anything. Maybe it had just been his imagination. Things were so agitated in the village and inside his head that it wouldn't be strange to see something that wasn't there. Shrugging his shoulders, he went back into the kitchen.

Outside, hiding motionless behind the wooden fence, Walter Schmied let out a deep sigh. He had to hurry if he wanted to get back before Silvia and his son began to worry about his absence. It wouldn't take much time to go to the shipyard, do what needed to be done and get back. On his way, he could come up with an excuse that explained his disappearance. As he figured it, Patricia must be dead. And if she wasn't dead by now he was going make sure that she soon would be. He felt the revolver hidden in his waist. "Everything is under control," he said.

It wouldn't be difficult to carry out his plan. He had done it so many times before. When Patricia died, he could transform into her and go far away from Almahue without raising suspicions that he was hiding inside the adolescent coed. He had been so delighted to find her in his son's office. And he was tired of having to be Walter. Ernesto Schmied's son led a very boring life. Gray. Useless. He looked forward to this new chapter in his life!

Unable to contain a broad smile of victory for future, he made his way to the shipyard.

9 FACE TO FACE

It was like embracing a skeleton, and Angela couldn't hold back her tears. No sooner had she wrapped her arms around Patricia than she erupted in sobs of relief and horror simultaneously. Fabian backed up a couple of steps in order to give them a bit of privacy. The battery of the iPod was almost exhausted. They had to get out of there.

"What happened? Why are you here? Who did this to you?" Angela bombarded Patricia with questions, scarcely able to get over the unexpected find.

"Water..." Patricia mumbled.

"Fabian! Come over here and help me get her out of here!" she cried full of anguish.

Fabian gave her the iPod and tried to detach the ring that held the chain to the wall. Although he tried with all of his strength, it didn't budge. He rolled up the chain in one hand, planted a foot on the wall and flexing his entire body, tried to weaken the bolts. Impossible. He would have to leave to find a tool to continue working.

"Stay with her," Angela firmly said. "I'm going up to look for something to weaken the chain."

"I would rather do it," he said.

"No, you're weak. If you can, keep trying to free her. When we came in, I saw some boxes with hammers, pliers... I am going to bring everything I find."

"Hurry up. There isn't much battery left," he motioned as he showed her the weak light on the screen.

Angela wasn't able to say anything. A spasm of anguish tightened her throat and for a moment she couldn't breath. Responsibility bore down on her shoulders like a backpack full of rocks. She had to act quickly. She was still in shock by how emaciated Patricia had become. She had probably not eaten for weeks.

"Hurry up!" Fabian urged. Angela groped her way through the dark to find the first step. She heard the voice of her friend behind her. It sounded more like a death rattle than her friend. "You have to look for..."

Angela stopped. She saw Fabian shining the iPod towards Patricia's haggard and pale face. She was no longer able to open her eyes.

"The husband..." she made a great effort to mutter. What was she trying to say? Had she heard correctly? She suppressed the urge to return to her friend and ask her to finish her sentence. Who was responsible for this atrocity? Who did she intend to blame by saying that?

"Please, go quickly!" Fabian compelled, grabbing the chain again trying to loosen the ring.

Angela flew up the ladder. She almost lost her step a couple of times, tripping, desperate to reach the door of Egon's office. Her shoe slipped on a patch of what she thought was moss, or part of the step that had rotted, and she fell to her knees. She hit her elbow and her arm tingled all the way to her fingertips. She wanted to scream in frustration. It felt like she had spent her whole life living like a mole, moving blindly, her eyes useless in the insurmountable darkness. Angela got up as best as she could and continued climbing. The difference in temperature and darkness let her know that she had left the cellar. Before entering the office, she heard Fabian's heavy breathing, certainly as a result of trying to pull the chain that held Patricia captive.

Angela crossed the office as quickly as she could in the darkness. When she was about to open the door to the workshop, she unexpectedly heard a metallic voice, halfway hidden under a series of whistles and static interference.

"Attention Almahue. Attention Almahue. Puerto Chacabuco here. Over."

The radio. Carlos Ule and a response to her message. She hesitated to go to the microphone and speak.

"Attention Almahue. Do you read me? Over."

No, she couldn't. Fabian was below, urgently waiting for the tools and

Patricia needed water. She shook her head, denying the urge to take the microphone, and opened the door to the workshop.

The shipyard was completely quiet.

Where had she seen the toolbox? She walked along one of the walls. As much as she tried to concentrate in the dark, she couldn't keep thinking about who "the husband" could be, the person responsible for her captivity.

She stopped, bringing a hand to her chest.

"Angela, it's horrible! Horrible! You have to help me! Please! Please! Come save me, I beg you! You have to look for...!" Which husband? If this was the case, Egon Schmied Poblete wasn't to blame; he was still single. Patricia was a prisoner in the shipyard that belonged to the Schmied's. This meant that one of its members was probably responsible for the kidnapping. That was logical; they had access to the place. No one would find it strange to see them entering and leaving their own property. Who? Which husband? Was she referring to...?

A whistle interrupted her thoughts. The shrill note cut through the debris and the clutter, resonating in her head. Horrified, Angela understood everything. It wasn't difficult to imagine Walter tying up Patricia, dragging her under cover of night to the warehouse office. Why? What were his reasons? And, most of all, what was he doing there now?

Angela sought refuge behind a large panel of wood that had fallen from the ceiling and made the perfect hiding place. She poked her head out to the side. She could make out Walter Schmied's silhouette wearily advancing, betrayed by the limp in his right leg. He was alone. His hands hung at his sides. His neck was straight, defiant. Angela understood that she had no choice. If Silvia's husband was on his way to the office to descend into the cellar, she had to do something about it.

She looked for something to hit him with, or at least to slow him down while she warned Fabian. She urgently felt the area around her. There was just garbage, wires and some shelves.

The man's steps kept getting closer. She could hear them as they approached. She closed her eyes so tightly that an uncontrollable display of fireworks went off in her head. For a moment, she had a recurring fantasy: upon opening her eyes she would be safe at home, with her mother and Mauricio. And Patricia. The four would be laughing at some trivial thing. But, no. It didn't happen this time either. She was at the mercy of what she couldn't control.

The footsteps stopped.

Angela opened her eyes and looked out again from her hiding place. She saw Walter leaning over something she couldn't make out. He struck a match. The fire lit up a small area, an orange bubble that moved towards an oil lamp hanging from a hook on the wall.

Walter Schmied planned to go down to the cellar.

The workshop filled with shadows that danced to the rhythm of the wick. The brief light allowed her to spot a heavy hook several yards away. Fabian could use it for leverage and probably free the chain from the wall. "Perfect!" she thought. She just had to leave her hiding place, pick it up without making noise and run back to the office before Walter discovered her.

Could she do it? She didn't have a choice. She took another look at Walter's back as he concentrated on adjusting the lamp.

It was the moment to act.

Angela tried to control the surge of adrenaline that was clouding her sight and simultaneously making her brave. As quietly as possible, she left her hiding place. She grabbed the hook and lifted it up. So far, so good. Walter was still busy, oblivious to what was going on behind him. Holding onto the hook, she began to walk back to the door with the golden letters. Step by step. Angela sped up. Because she was looking forward, she hadn't noticed a roll of cable and she tripped over it. The hook made a loud noise when it bounced off the planks. Surprised, Walter turned around and saw Angela, who, from the floor, looked at him in terror.

"What are you doing here?" he exclaimed taking out the revolver concealed under his clothing.

The color drained from Angela's face when she saw the gun. Walter set the oil lamp he was holding on the floor and began walking towards Angela, who hadn't even tried to stand up. "What are you doing here?" he repeated in a voice that didn't sound anything like the friendly one she knew.

"Why did you do this? Why have you locked my friend in your cellar?" Angela shouted.

Walter's face froze in surprise. How could this stupid girl know what he had done? Had she been able to open the cellar door? He squeezed his fingers around the grip of the gun. The best thing to do would be to shoot her. They were alone. There weren't any witnesses. Everyone in Almahue was in the square, unaware of what was happening in the shipyard. He put his finger on the trigger. In fact, he could even take over the nosey girl's body instead of her friend's. It might be fun to be a redhead. He would dump her body with Patricia's, seal the door forever and that would be that.

She was terrified and defenseless, but Angela screamed at him through jaws clenched in anger. She was barely lit by the flickering glow of the oil lamp "I'm going to make sure that everyone knows who you are!"

Walter held back a guffaw. "Little girl, if you only knew who I really am," he said. "You made a big mistake coming here. You've dug your own grave."

He closed one eye to take aim.

As his index finger was about to pull the trigger, a hoarse croak distracted him. Puzzled, he turned around. A sharp beak punctured his cheek. Walter waved his arms around like the blades of a fan, trying to scare off whatever was attacking him. The enormous heron was positioning itself to attack him again. Walter got off a couple of blind shots. With the speed of a bullet, the bird flew straight at his body, wounding him in the neck. Angela took advantage of the confusion to stand up and grab the hook. She looked at the heron for a moment, impressed by its ability to navigate the columns of the workshop, rise up to the ceiling, and then drive right for Walter, stabbing him with its beak. Walter Schmied was screaming in pain.

"Thank you!" Angela shouted, receiving a short croak as a reply. Walter had no choice but to drop his gun and cover his face. Disoriented by the blows and the blood staining his hands, he didn't see the oil lamp and he kicked it as he tried to escape. The floor boards ignited. Angela's eyes opened wide. In a minute the workshop would be engulfed in flames. She desperately ran to Egon's office, went to the hatch in the floor and threw the hook inside.

"Fabian! Hurry up! The place is on fire!" she shrieked from above.

Fabian heard the tool fall but didn't know where. He turned on the iPod, praying that there was enough juice to find the hook. The screen blinked for an instant and displayed a message that read "Low Battery". He heard Angela shout from the office, "Did you find it?"

"No! I don't know where it fell!" he replied, feeling a growing discomfort taking over his body.

The terrible worry that Fabian felt for Angela was simply love, a love that was also punished by the witch's curse. Every time he imagined that she was in danger, a sharp jab pierced his body. When he heard that the shipyard was on fire, he felt like his lungs were bursting and he had to bite his lip to stifle a cry so as not to startle the two friends who were counting on him. His heart began to beat irregularly. It was an out of tune drum that wasn't pumping enough blood to his body. Cold sweat bathed his neck and he shivered. He knew he was going to collapse soon. He was about to lose the fight with *Malamor*.

Desperate, he fell to his knees and felt around on the ground for the tool. Suddenly his fingers grazed the cold metal of the hook. "Please hurry!" Angela implored from above. "Everything is filling with smoke!"

When he got up, Fabian shined the weak light of the iPod on the wall supporting the ladder. He could see some drawings etched into the stone:

They were the same symbols they had seen before on the walls of the cave where they had found Benedicto Mohr.

What the hell was going on?

"Walter Schmied is here with a gun and he is trying to kill me!" Angela screamed, sticking her head through the opening. "He is the one! Please free Patricia!"

Fabian ran to the ring. Using the hook for leverage, he began to force it. He closed his eyes and pressed his lips together in concentration, trying to summon the last bit of energy in his body. The orange glow flickering on the roof outlined the hatch. The flames were getting closer. He kept trying to separate the ring from the wall using the hook for leverage. He could hear the bolts beginning to yield.

Angela thought about going into the cellar to help Fabian. But she turned toward the door in horror and saw smoke filtering in through the frame. "Attention Almahue. Puerto Chacabuco here. Over," she heard through the speaker of the short wave, and she had new hope.

She ran over to the radio. She cleared away the glass from Egon's shattered bottle collection, grabbed the microphone, pushed the button on its side and exclaimed to whoever was listening: "Almahue here! The shipyard is on fire! People are trapped! We need help!"

Suddenly she felt a man's hand on her shoulder. For an instant she thought that it was Fabian who, having finally freed Patricia, was back in the office. But it wasn't his smell, or the warmth of his hand.

"You made a big mistake coming here," she heard a menacing whisper. Walter Schmied grabbed her by the neck, pinning her. He brought his bloody face near hers. "You've ruined everything," he muttered. "She's angry. Very angry."

Walter tightened his grip on Angela's throat. And the heron? Where was her friend to defend her? Was this the end? Is this how everything would finish? A strange lethargy was taking over her limbs and her muscles were beginning to tingle. From the distance, she could hear Fabian below.

"I did it! I broke the chain!"

Surprised, Walter made a hoarse sound and was momentarily distracted. Angela took advantage of the moment to stretch out her arm and grab one of the few bottles that were intact. She hit her assailant on the head with all the strength she could muster. She felt the crash, and the pressure on her throat immediately stopped.

She ran to the office door. When she opened it, the fiery tongues of the blaze paralyzed her. Most of the workshop was on fire. Ceiling beams were threatening to collapse at any moment. Smoke and soot filled the air.

She heard an urgent meow. "Azabache? Is that you?" she asked. She turned her head in the direction of the cat's sound and found it with its back arched in alarm. Next to the cat, in a pile of rubble from the earthquake, she saw it, dangerously close to the flames. The heron was wounded and Azabache was alerting her. She ran to the bird and cradled it in her arms. It had a red stain just under its wing. The wound was from a gunshot. The bird arched its long neck. Its intense black eyes were fixed on Angela's. There was no need for words. Everything was said when their eyes met.

"Easy does it, Rosa. I'm going to get you out of here," she soothed, stroking its feathers. "And you too, Azabache!"

Rapid steps behind her alerted Angela to the danger. Walter emerged from the flames, huffing like an animal in the throes of death. He went back into the office to retrieve the gun. Taking it in his hands, he turned around and pointed it at her. His vision was clouded by hatred; his face was splattered with blood. Behind him the flames luridly licked the walls, turning everything into a whirlwind of yellows and reds.

"You're going to die, you nosy little bitch."

"Father?" a voice cried out above the flames. Egon ran in, cutting through the smoke and protecting his head with his arms. Horrified, he looked at Walter pointing a gun at Angela. "What are you doing?" he exclaimed, scarcely able to believe his eyes. Walter turned to his son and without a word, shot at him. Egon felt the bullet whiz past his ear and strike one of the columns a few yards behind him. Had his father gone mad? Walter had missed his target by only a couple of inches! It was a miracle Egon was still alive! Walter raised his arms. His fists were clenched and he leaned his head backwards. A huge and pulsating vein stood out underneath his skin, dividing his face in two.

"I'm not your father!" he yelled in a voice that was definitely not his. Walter closed his eyes and breathed deeply, filling his lungs with smoke. His heartbeats became erratic. He breathed in the air that was getting hotter by the minute, more frenzied by the minute, stoked by the fire.

"What's going on?" Egon groaned, unable to understand what was unfolding in front of him.

Angela protected the heron against her chest and let Azabache hide behind her legs.

Dumbstruck, she saw Walter's body convulsing as if he were having an epileptic fit. He began to vibrate as well. He moved back and forth, anchored by his feet, bending in ways that completely defied the laws of gravity. His inclination and speed increased until he became a blur of wind and movement. From the middle of the tornado, a new image began to materialize: a dark, counterfeit anatomy, with long arms that looked more like tree branches than human limbs.

Where his head had been was now a shapeless mass, crisscrossed by fissures and veins, with two cruel and bloodthirsty eyes in the middle of its face. It made a creaking sound and unfolded upon itself, quivering, lifting what looked like a root, smelling the air in search of food and minerals.

Angela screamed in terror, unable to accept what she was seeing through the smoke and the embers flying through the air. She heard Fabian throw open the office door; he had an unconscious Patricia in his arms. He stopped short when he saw the repulsive and threatening nightmare in the middle of the workshop.

With one of its sinewy arms the creature struck Egon, who slumped over a pile of boxes. Then it turned to Angela, who quickly understood she was next. She tried to move but she was nailed to the spot by terror.

A violent crash stuck the front doors of the workshop, flinging them open.

Two powerful headlights blinded everyone for an instant. The roar of the engine swooped in at full speed opening a path in the flames in a risky and daring maneuver. Angela was able to read "Bookmobile" on the side of the body before the vehicle sped up towards what until moments before had been Walter Schmied.

Everyone heard the fatal sound of the collision. The creature was thrown into the fire. It immediately began to burn, crackling like dry wood. A viscous and flammable liquid gushed out of its skeleton forming an enormous stain on the floor. A pained lament reached the walls, the roof and the entire area when the blaze consumed the hellish figure. Then there was silence.

"Everyone in the van!" Carlos Ule yelled from behind the steering wheel. "The building is coming down at any minute!"

Angela, bewildered and devastated, immediately obeyed.

∀ → O → �***̇*** → �{V}

EPILOGUE

Who looks outside, dreams.
Who looks inside, awakens.
Carl Jung

1 THE REASON AND THE MOTIVES

Her mother smiled from the window. She was very happy to see her again. She raised her hand and motioned to her to cross the street and come inside. Angela only had a few steps to go to be with her, to leave the horrors of the recent past behind. But she couldn't get there. Although she walked without stopping, the street kept getting wider; the sidewalks separated from each other like opposing mirrors that multiplied their dimensions to infinity. The image of her mother smiling at her, urging her to come, receded without her being able to reach her. "Hurry up, dear. Come. I'm waiting for you," Angela could hear her mother calling from afar. Then she began to run. But the street changed into an enormous plain of asphalt, into a universe of cement crossed by a yellow crosswalk. "Mom! Mom! Mom!" Angela yelled in a silent scream.

When Angela awoke, it took her several seconds to realize where she was.

Disoriented, she looked at the ceiling and the bare walls. When she saw the round window, she knew she was in Don Ernesto's room. She was scared, very scared. She was going to get out of bed when a hand stopped her very gently and obliged her to remain in bed.

"Take it easy," Fabian requested sweetly. "There's no hurry. No hurry at all." He was seated next to her, smiling. Angela sat up, confused. What was she doing there? She squinted from the light that shined through the window and bounced around the attic. "What happened to The Gloom?"

"Don't you remember?" Fabian asked, waiting for her reply.

The first thing Angela dredged from her memory was the intense smell of smoke, of burning wood. Toxic air. Her ears filled once more with the intense crackling of the fire. There they were in the burning workshop again; Carlos Ule's miraculous van and Walter Schmied's body, or whatever it had become, screaming in pain, engulfed by the fire, and consumed by it.

Then she remembered her race to the Bookmobile, skillfully dodging the danger, the wounded heron clutched to her chest. Fabian made it quickly to her side and rested Patricia in the front seat. Her friend's eyes were closed. Her body had used its last ounce of strength. Fabian then went back to help Egon get out from the boxes after the man he had thought was his father pushed him.

As soon as they were in the vehicle, Carlos Ule stepped on the gas, making the tires squeal. He thanked the heavens that he had answered his mobile phone when they called him from Puerto Chacabuco with an urgent message from a girl named Angela Galvez in Almahue, who desperately needed his help.

Through the windshield, they saw the workshop begin to collapse, becoming an inferno that they had to break through. They heard the crash of the beams against the roof of the vehicle, like explosions that made the windows shake. Carlos seized the steering wheel and held a scream when he saw the door vanish, consumed by the blaze. They had no option but to cross the threshold and pass over the rubble that blocked their way.

"Hold on!" he shouted before pushing the accelerator to the floor.

From Don Ernesto Schmied's bed, Angela relived the panic she felt when her view was blinded by a burning tongue that enveloped the van and licked the windows. The heat shot up in a second. The wheels climbed up the debris and catapulted the vehicle into space.

For a moment, a very brief moment, they had the sensation of floating in the air. Light. The embers scratched the belly of the van that landed with a racket. All of the books jumped from their shelves, burying Fabian and Egon who were in the rear. The frame of the van creaked like it would break in half while the tires skidded on the wet ground. Carlos stepped on the brakes a few yards before they would have fallen into the ocean, leaving a long skid mark in the mud. From there, they could see the workshop collapse in on its foundation, illuminating the darkness with its flames.

Suddenly, an intense glow lit up the coastline and the interior of the van was filled with watery reflections. Angela looked at the sky and witnessed a small yellow opening that appeared in a black vault. A perfect circle was growing like a dilating pupil, projecting a beam of light that immediately warmed the world.

The shadows fled to their hideouts, frightened by the incandescent tide that overpowered them. Defeated, The Gloom was forced to draw back its curtain of night.

Daylight had returned.

"How long have I been asleep?" Angela asked, making herself more comfortable in the bed.

"Almost a day. We didn't want to wake you up," Fabian said as he stroked her cheek. "You were very brave. Thanks to you, Patricia is safe."

"Where is she?"

"Downstairs, with Don Ernesto and Carlos. Don't worry," he calmed her. "My mother is feeding her. She's going to be fine."

Angela threw back the fluffy down comforter. She walked to the roll-top desk, full of little drawers and shelves that she opened without pause until she had found what she was looking for. Armed with paper and pencil, she sat down and began to draw lines on the sheet that was adorned with the Schmied family's monogram.

Curious, Fabian came over to look over her shoulder. "What are you doing?" "I'm drawing the symbols that we saw in the cave. I need to show them to Carlos," she responded, concentrating. "I also saw them in the cellar where Patricia was. Someone had painted them on the wall." When Angela was going to add that they were also part of one of Rosa's rugs, her heart skipped a beat. "Rosa!" she thought and immediately turned to Fabian. As if he could read her mind, he said: "Rosa is at home. She's fine. It seems that she hurt her shoulder in the earthquake, but it's only a scratch."

"And the bird?"

"What bird?"

"The heron. The heron I had in my arms when I got into Carlos's van." Fabian frowned, concerned.

"I don't remember a heron. Are you sure you had a *bird*?"

Angela didn't allow him to continue speaking. She put her finger to his lips. She wasn't sure about anything anymore, although she didn't need to close her eyes to see the heron flying through the air to attack Walter Schmied. Her white body left a track in the smoke. If Angela was alive, it was because of the white-feathered heron. There would be time to reward and thank her for saving her life.

They found Patricia wrapped up in a heavy woolen shawl and with a bowl of lentils in her hand. Egon was next to her, making sure she was eating everything. Don Ernesto and Carlos were talking by the window, still affected by what had happened.

"Sleeping beauty has woken up!" said the elderly man when he saw Angela enter.

After accepting a bowl of Elvira's lentils even though she wasn't hungry, Angela sat down next to Patricia and leaned her head on her friend's shoulder.

"Where's your mom?" Angela asked Egon.

"She's sedated. She's... well, imagine. She thinks that my... that he... died in the fire. I haven't explained anything. I don't think I will, either... she'd go crazy."

"I always said he was not my son," Don Ernesto added. "My real son died years ago in an accident in the forest. Whoever was living with us... it was not Walter."

"But then who was it?" Patricia left her bowl on the table as everyone looked at her. "When he tied me up to take me to the workshop, he looked very... human," she added ironically.

Contritely, Egon looked at Patricia. Before he spoke, he passed his fingers through his tussled hair. It was clear that he hadn't put any gel in it.

"Just to be clear, I never did anything to your friend," he confessed.

"Egon? No! Never! He never laid a finger on me," Patricia explained.

"But, what about the cell phone we found in the room?" Fabian asked.

"I found the phone in my office at the shipyard. I recognized it and it made me very nervous because Patricia had disappeared. I was afraid they'd blame me, so I hid it."

"That man took it away from me after I sent you the message," Patricia continued.

"I'm here thanks to him," she smiled at her friend. The two hugged. It seemed incredible that the anguish was finally over. "Can anyone tell me who Walter Schmied was?" Fabian asked.

"I think the key to understanding that is here," Angela said and she got up to give Carlos the drawing she had made in the attic. "I need to know what these symbols mean."

The teacher took the paper and silently studied it for several moments. "Where did you get this from?" Angela and Fabian told him about the three times they had seen these strokes: the first, in the cave with Benedicto Mohr's body; the second, in the rug in Rosa's studio; and the third, on the wall in the cellar where Walter had imprisoned Patricia. Without saying a word, Carlos ran outside. Through the window, they could see him duck into the rear of the van, poking around in the mess they could make out through its open door.

He returned to the house with a thick book in his hand. He sat down, moistened his fingertip with his tongue and began to quickly search through the pages.

"What are you looking for?" Angela managed to say before the teacher gestured to her to be silent.

Suddenly he showed a picture in the book with his index finger. "I knew it! Here it is!" he exclaimed. Everyone leaned toward the book that Carlos had on his knees. They read in large capital letters: "TRANSMUTATION." And, below this title, they all recognized the drawing.

"I don't understand... I don't understand anything!" Angela lamented.

"Transmutation is how one thing becomes something else?" Patricia guessed.

"Listen," Carlos said, and cleared his throat before continuing to read.

"Transmutation is the conversion of one chemical element into another by changing its nucleus, meaning a difference in the number of protons and neutrons."

A profound silence fell upon the room. The driver of the Bookmobile, knowing that the audience was hungry for more information, continued reading: "Transmutation is the physical transformation that the body of a living being experiences, accompanied not only by important physiological changes but also psychological changes and even changes in their aptitudes or capabilities."

Angela raised a hand to her mouth, stifling an exclamation. Carlos looked up and fixed his eyes on her and nodded.

"Yes. These drawings are a formula; an equation that allows one body to transmute into another."

"That's how he..." Egon stepped back, moving his head from side to side.

"Yes, that's how your father could transform himself in... into that which he became," Angela said without believing what her mouth was saying.

"Who was Walter Schmied?" Fabian intervened.

"Rayen's father," Don Ernesto answered with certainty. "I recognized his voice. It was the same that I heard seventy years ago. Who knows how long he and his daughter roamed the world before coming to Almahue?"

Trying to understand what he was hearing, Fabian's eyes opened wide and his mouth hung open. Finally, the pieces were falling into place in his head.

"So Rayen is alive?"

"Yes. It's very likely that she is," the old man answered. "Reincarnated in a different body."

Everyone spoke at once, but Carlos raised his hand asking for silence. He continued to read: "It's difficult to establish a clear difference between transmutation and metamorphosis, except for the fact that metamorphosis occurs in nature and transmutation doesn't," he said almost without pausing to breathe. He gulped some air and continued. "Metamorphosis occurs only once and is irreversible, while transmutation is, the opposite; it is repetitive and, perhaps reversible."

"Just a minute," Fabian said, raising his voice to be heard. "I understand that this formula was drawn in the cave where we found the explorer's body, because Rayen lived there. It's also clear that we saw it on the wall of the cellar because that was Walter's refuge. But why would Rosa use these symbols in a rug? How did she know them?"

No one could provide an answer; the only person who could, remained silent. Angela decided that this would be her secret with Rosa, a fair trade in exchange for having saved her life.

2 SECRETS REVEALED

In contrast to the rest of the house, the kitchen was intact after the earthquake. Enveloped in the fragrant smells that rose from the wood stove, the pots displayed their healthy leaves, stems and flowers. There was a large basket filled with potatoes of different sizes and colors in the middle of the kitchen. Despite the injury to her shoulder, Rosa moved around the space with her usual efficiency and confidence. She opened the doors of the cabinets, took out glasses, plates and cutlery, and set the table for lunch. Angela and Fabian helped her warm the bread in the oven and squeezed lemons to prepare a beverage.

"You don't have to worry," she reassured them as she handed them three linen napkins so they could sit down. "It doesn't hurt. It was just a scratch. I didn't see when part of the ceiling fell on me," she added with a smile.

Angela took her hands and stared at her. The landlady's cloudy pupils shined for an instant, filled with complicity. They understood each other without saying anything.

"Thank you."

"No, thank *you*."

"Don't worry, your secret is safe with me." They quietly smiled as they intertwined their fingers.

"You don't know how happy it makes me that your friend has turned up safe and sound," Rosa resumed the conversation. "Could you save your clothes from the rubble?"

"A little bit. Almost nothing, but it doesn't matter. And you, what are you going to do with this house. Are you going to go somewhere else?"

"Of course not. Many years ago this house was in ruins. I only have to rebuild the walls and the roof. It's fine. I have time."

Angela didn't want to delve any further. She couldn't imagine the slight Rosa hammering and lifting beams, but for some reason that she didn't care to explore, she knew that her hostess was serious.

"And you, Fabian. How do you feel?"

"Better than ever. I'm not in pain anymore," he said enthusiastically. "And I can hug, kiss and touch Angela without feeling like I'm going to die."

"I suppose that love did its job. That's why it exists, to defeat hatred," was her only response.

Having said this, she went to the stove. She opened the door and the caramelized aroma of the potato pie wafted into the kitchen.

"Lunch is ready."

"I'll go collect my things and leave them by the door so I'll be ready in case Carlos gets here with Patricia to take us to Puerto Chacabuco," Angela said sadly. "That way, I can save some time."

She left the kitchen with tears welling in her eyes.

The pain she was feeling had nothing to do with *Malamor*. It was a deep bitterness she had been trying to avoid, but was incapable of stopping. The time had come to say goodbye to Fabian, and the idea of having to get into the van that would take her far away from Almahue broke her heart.

She walked into what had been her room. In the full light of day, the damage was even more devastating. She found her backpack in a corner, together with the remains of the armoire. She was going to take it when a man's hand beat her to it and curtly snatched the knapsack.

When she turned around she discovered Fabian looking at her with shining eyes, holding back his tears.

"Stay," he entreated with a whisper. "I beg you, stay."

Angela remained quiet, trying to understand her own heart and mind. She saw her mother and her brother Mauricio waiting anxiously at home. She remembered the long and somber hallway at school where she wanted to return and tell her story, her bedroom, the posters of her favorite films, and her DVD collection under the television. That was her life. Santiago was her world. What would she do in Almahue? How could she continue her studies?

Fabian opened his mouth, but this time it wasn't to continue speaking.

He put his arms around her waist and hugged her with a tender force. He kissed her slowly, deeply: a kiss of true love, of immortal love, the kind that unites souls forever.

When he stepped back, he saw that Angela still had her eyes closed. "Stay," he repeated hopefully. "Let me make you happy." Angela opened her eyes and faced Fabian. She could hear the horn of Carlos Ule's van in the distance. He had arrived to pick her up. Time was up.

She breathed deeply, as deeply as she could, filling her lungs with air and her body with courage. She clenched her fists, knowing that she was taking a leap of faith without a safety net. And knowing that she might regret it for the rest of her life, she leaned on Fabian's shoulder and whispered her answer.

3 RETURN TO ALMAHUE

Her tears mix with the rain that beats down on the heart of the forest. Water pours down the trunks and the branches of the trees around her. A quagmire changes the humus into an angry tide that swallows everything in its path.

But it doesn't matter to her. She is blind. She can't hear. She can only sense the pain that racks her body. She screams to the heavens and thunderclap disrupts the currents in the sea. She screams again and lightning bolts crash over her head. She is suffering.

She is declaring that it's not over yet. Her father is at her feet, a pile of carbonized remains that she has rescued from the ashes of the shipyard belonging to the family that she hates with all her being. Another fire. But this time, he wasn't able to escape the flames like he did so many years ago. She stretches out an arm. She strokes what remains of the man who had taken care of her for centuries. And she screams again to unleash the heavy wind that makes the trees in the forest flutter like flags in a hurricane.

Dressed in fog and moisture, her body shakes. It vibrates with the intensity of an erupting volcano. It grows, reaching the canopies of her guardian friends. She opens her arms to gather all of their energy.

She has made up her mind. "This isn't over."

She closes her eyes. The sap that runs in her veins begins its frenetic race, nurturing the branches, arms, trunks, legs, toes, and roots. Her pores open like howling mouths, her body roars and scares the raindrops away from her.

Her fury has no limits.

Her skin, which over the years has hardened and cracked like a century-old tree, begins to soften. The furrows fill. The wrinkles disappear. The elasticity returns to her aged face. A series of circles, triangles and arrows appears behind her eyelids. The foliage of her head curls and becomes the tangled hair that falls over her shoulders. The entire forest witnesses the years that she sheds: four, five, seven decades.

A youthful laughter peals like a church bell on Sunday. It's her. She's back. Barefoot and indomitable.

Her scant and coarse dress slides up and shows her shapely thighs. Rayen smiles. It's time to visit Ernesto Schmied, the only person still alive that actually knew her all those years ago. She needs to look into the eyes of the insolent stranger who dared to challenge her. She wants to punish the cook's son who defeated her spell. It's time to get to work. She doesn't forget. She never will. The pain of a broken heart is immortal.

She bids farewell to her father with a kiss to the wind.

The puddles reflect her adolescent face. The rocks along the way celebrate her return. The forest says goodbye.

Rayen, the woman who cursed everyone with *Malamor*, stands up tall, purses her lips and, knowing that she's doing what she must, begins her return to Almahue.